THE MERSEY ANGELS

SHEILA RILEY

Boldwood

First published in Great Britain in 2021 by Boldwood Books Ltd.

Copyright © Sheila Riley, 2021

Cover Design by The Brewster Project

Cover Photography: Shutterstock, Alamy and Colin Thomas

A CIP catalogue record for this book is available from the British Library.

Paperback ISBN 978-1-80048-583-9

Large Print ISBN 978-1-80048-582-2

Hardback ISBN 978-1-80280-206-1

Ebook ISBN 978-1-80048-584-6

Kindle ISBN 978-1-80048-585-3

Audio CD ISBN 978-1-80048-577-8

MP3 CD ISBN 978-1-80048-578-5

Digital audio download ISBN 978-1-80048-581-5

Boldwood Books Ltd
23 Bowerdean Street
London SW6 3TN
www.boldwoodbooks.com

To the brave men and women who willingly gave their future for our tomorrows

PART I

PROLOGUE

MAY 1915

Jerky Woods sauntered along the dock road towards Great Homer Street, heading for Saint Martin's dance hall near the open-air marketplace. Unlike many Liverpool people who were in the doldrums about the sinking of RMS Lusitania, affectionately known by the people of Liverpool as 'The Lusy' because so many of her sons were serving on board, Jerky was in the mood for a good time.

RMS Lusitania had been sunk by an imperial German Navy U-boat off the south-west coast of Ireland, killing one thousand one hundred and ninety-eight civilians travelling from New York to Liverpool. The headlines in the local newspaper caused outrage. Not only in Liverpool, but elsewhere in Britain, but there was a strong maritime community in this part of Liverpool who were directly affected, when their son or husband had been caught up in the tragedy and killed.

What's the use of worrying? He whistled the tune of the popular new song knowing the words had never been more appropriate. He had no intentions of worrying about anything. Why should he? Nobody had ever worried about him.

Unless he counted Lottie Blythe, who was so clingy since her mother died, and no mistake. She didn't give him a minute to himself. Always wanting to go for *nice long walks.* Hands in pockets, he could think of nothing more depressing than wasting valuable alehouse drinking time to walk hand in hand with a soppy, doe-eyed girl who wittered endlessly about mundane things like weddings and how many kids she would like, her only interest was getting him down the aisle. She had even started coming to his lodgings to 'tidy up'. Telling him he needed a woman about the place. But she was scandalised when he asked her to move in with him. And why she kept insisting on calling him *Jerry,* he would never know.

Not without a ring on my finger, Jerry, she said. Well, he was having none of that marriage lark, they had been courting for just over a year, on and off, and she was always wanting to know where he was going and who with? What's it got to do with her? Jerky Woods knew if he wed her, he would be responsible for her upkeep. And he didn't like the sound of that. Paying good ale money for her food and board? Not likely!

Lottie even had the cheek to hint that he might want to take the King's shilling and join the khaki glory-hunters at the Front. No fear of that happening either, he thought. Look what happened to those poor innocent blighters on The Lusy.

The war had been raging for nine months, even though it was supposed to be over by last Christmas. Jerky Woods believed men had been conned into fighting a war for a country they had no interest in, and the thought chunnered away in his head. He had no beef with the Germans. Furthermore, if he fancied a bit of fisticuffs, he didn't need to join the army or navy to have a fight.

He intended to get what he could out of this war, though, by fair means or foul, and had no intention of becoming a name on the Town Hall List, like those poor buggers on the ship.

Twenty minutes. That was all it took to sink that fine liner. Twenty minutes.

You wouldn't credit such a thing was possible on a balmy night like this, he thought, as scarcely a ripple of a breeze was strong enough to cause the chip paper he had just discarded to stir from its resting place in the gutter. He was restless, on the lookout for a nice bit of skirt who wanted a good time and no ties. Even in these prim-and-proper times, being so close to the docks a man could still find a good-time girl for a quick canoodle in the moonlight. He would tell the unsuspecting female he was serving on board a warship, or awaiting orders to set off for Flanders battlefields, and the girls went weak in his arms. Easy-peasy after that.

Walking with a rolling gait, so familiar in this North Liverpool area of seamen, Jerky meandered past the market stalls that were closing for the night. He was more than ready to wet his lips with a pint or two. It was a good thing he had his eyes to business when he'd spied Lottie's rent money behind the clock on her mantlepiece. He could not stomach another night of her yapping and the money was quickly dispatched to his pocket.

A sudden outcry from the side street caught his attention, and before he managed to get to the dance, he could hear the heart-rending wail of women whose husbands had gone down with The Lusy.

It were a crying shame what the Hun did to that ship, he contradicted his earlier belief that the enemy had done nothing wrong to him or his community, and his footsteps slowed. She weren't even a warship, he thought. She was merchant class.

'You come out of there, Kruger, before we drag you out!' A rowdy crowd gathered outside the pork butcher shop and shouted up to the window above. Vicious threats were being directed against Germany, and anybody with a German name.

'It's a bleedin' shame it is,' Woods said to nobody in particular. 'I knew a few good lads on The Lusy,' he lied to a black-clad woman crying into her handkerchief who had just come out of Blackwall Street, where nearly every blind was drawn as a symbol of a death.

But when she threw her arms round him and sobbed into his freshly laundered jacket that only came out of pawn this morning, Jerky Woods stood like petrified stone, baffled. He did not know how to comfort the stricken woman. All he hoped was that her snotty tears didn't mark his clean lapel.

'Me son and me husband, both gone,' the woman sobbed. 'Most of the terraced houses round here were occupied by Irish coal-trimmers, firemen, and many of them were sailors who had been on the Lusitania...'

'Shame, that...' His words were superfluous, but she wouldn't notice. She was too lost in her grief. Although his blood rose when he noticed a gang congregating on the corner, and already drunk, they were fighting furious. Trouble was so thick in the air he could smell it. 'Never you mind, Ma, I'll make sure the Hun pay for what they've done to our boys.' It had been a long time since he had been involved in a good scramble. And as the adrenaline pumped through his veins, he was eager to be part of this one.

The dance was forgotten as he picked up his pace, impatient to be part of the action in any disturbance when he heard the loud crash coming from the pork butcher's shop near Great Howard Street, followed by a deafening shatter of glass and a volley of angry voices.

Hurrying up the road, he saw Kruger's butcher shop being ransacked. It didn't seem to matter to the baying crowd that the butcher was not a German immigrant, but Polish, when the front window had been knocked in with bricks and batons, and the pavement was littered with glistening shards of glass.

Jerky Woods saw a crowd of men and women demolishing the place, and he decided they needed his assistance when he picked up a discarded house brick and a wooden baton from a broken sash window. Joining in with much fervour, Woods was not satisfied until everything of foreign origin was smashed to smithereens, and as a finale he threw a lit rag into the devastated shop before stuffing his pockets with pork chops and sausages that had spilled out onto the street.

Women were filling their aprons with loins of pork, trotters and pigs' tails, obviously not too fastidious in nicking Mr Kruger's profits before heading home prior to the police vans turning up. But the night was yet young. When the police did arrive, Woods made sure he was nowhere to be seen.

Although, his luck had run out when he encountered a mob outside the jeweller's shop in Commutation Row, and as he filled his pockets full of sparklers, the bobbies snapped him in their own type of bracelet and bundled him into the back of a police van for an overnight stay in Cheapside before an early appointment with local magistrates the following morning.

1

The first thing Ruby Swift noticed was the clean front door, complete with gleaming brass furnishings polished to a high shine, and a spotless doorstep buffed white with a donkey stone. Izzy, on her knees, was scrubbing the doorstep until it was immaculately clean. The ground-floor windowsills had already received the same treatment, Ruby noticed. And through the sparkling front parlour window the pristine, heavy cotton lace, complemented the bright curtains.

'You look surprised, Mrs Swift,' Izzy Woods, on her knees, said in a more assured tone than the one she adopted five years earlier, when she cowed in the pawnshop doorway. Mother of Jerky Woods and her younger son Nipper, Izzy was married to the laziest drunk it had ever been Ruby's misfortune to encounter. And Izzy was no stranger to the pawnshop. She was on her uppers on that cold Christmas Eve back in 1910 when Ruby gave her a ten-shilling note to stave off the hunger and shame of having nothing for her family at Christmas. It changed her life. And she had never forgotten Ruby's kindness.

'Not surprised at all,' Ruby said, taking in the red, work-worn hands and short stubby nails that never had time to grow, and was not surprised by the untethered strands of prematurely silver-streaked hair that had escaped its turtleshell comb.

'Not everybody lives in a filthy hovel.' There was more than a hint of repressed anger in Izzy's tone when she sank her scrubbing brush into the white enamel pail of hot water, splashing the pavement and almost upending the bucket.

Ruby's eyes took in the front, lower-storey bricks and the pavement outside her front door which had been scrubbed to remove the sooty coal-fire coating and was drying in the bright spring morning sunshine, knowing that nothing she said would soothe Izzy's worries, especially when the Hun sent those destructive airships. The terrifying Zeppelin raids over Liverpool at the end of January had brought the war closer to home.

Ruby knew that these routines of propriety were not associated with class or place. They were almost exclusively the marker of a respectable position, which had not been attributed to Izzy Woods five years earlier, when her good-for-nothing husband stole the remainder of the money Ruby had donated and spent every penny on himself and his cronies in the dockside alehouses.

'Here, Freddy, wipe your nose,' Izzy said, taking a clean handkerchief from her rolled-up sleeve, offering it to a neighbour's child who was lolling against the bay-fronted bricks supporting the parlour window. 'Have you had your breakfast, yet?'

The child shook his head and, getting up from the step with the agility of a five-year-old, Izzy disappeared through the vestibule door and up the long thin lobby. Moments later, she returned with a hunk of freshly baked bread slathered with fruity home-made jam.

'Poor little sod, if he doesn't watch himself, Lord Kitchener will persuade him to rush headlong overseas too. Or Lord Derby might introduce him to a voluntary recruitment for infants.' Izzy sounded angry and who could blame her.

'I heard about Nipper joining up, and wondered if there was anything I could do to help?' Ruby knew Izzy's boy Nipper had signed up to fight only after he left her stables, telling Archie, Ruby's husband, he must do his bit.

'He isn't even old enough to get served in an alehouse,' Izzy said, her anxiety obvious in her galvanised delivery, 'yet they let him go to war.'

'Poor Nipper,' Ruby said to Izzy, watching the child scurry down the street devouring the morning feast. Ruby knew Izzy's kind-hearted nature was only allowed to come to the fore after her late, indolent, husband had toddled off his mortal coil after falling drunk into the River Mersey. 'I heard Jerky will be out soon,' Ruby said, knowing Izzy's oldest lad had caused her nothing but heartache.

'Aye, well... That's Jerky for you. I can't see prison changing him.' Izzy sighed, kneeling on an old newspaper to save her poor knees from the hard concrete. Leaning back on her heels, she rang out the floor cloth into the bucket of water. 'Always up to something, takes after his father, he does.' Her shame at the antics of her oldest lad was overshadowed by the pride she had in her youngest son. Young Nipper was serving his country while Jerky was incarcerated in Walton Gaol for ransacking the pork butcher's shop and attacking Mr Solomon's jewellery shop in Commutation Row. 'The authorities prolonged the sentence; he should have got out last December but he got another five months on top for fighting and it serves him right.'

Ruby agreed, although she did not voice her belief that Woods should have got far longer to serve behind bars.

'When your Archie gave me the job in the pawnshop, after

Jerky was locked up, I was ever so grateful,, the job gave me peace of mind.'

'Which you deserve,' said Ruby, knowing Izzy was a hard-working woman who tried to keep her head above water.

'My purse is safe from his sticky fingers, for now.' Izzy threw her head back and laughed; obviously, she had more to care about than her clean step, crisp lace curtains, and the most spotless laundry in the street. Yet, Ruby surmised keeping busy kept Izzy's mind from the worry of Nipper doing his bit for King and Country, even though he was not old enough to fight overseas.

'Any news from Nipper?' Ruby liked the young lad who was as different from his father and older brother as it was possible to be. She and Archie had not been surprised when Izzy's youngest lad came to Ashland Hall and told Archie he would not be working with him in the stables any more because he had joined the end of the line – took the King's shilling and was off to fight for his country.

Izzy looked thoughtful. '"*You've got to have one son to be proud of, Mam*", he said to me the day before I waved him off at Lime Street Station.' Izzy swallowed hard and it was obvious she still had not come to terms with the thought of possibly losing him forever. 'Like every other mother, I was proud to say my boy was doing his bit. But he wasn't the one who should have gone.'

'You must be worried sick, Izzy,' Ruby said when the mood took a sombre tone, knowing there was a young lad who wanted to do his bit, as the posters pasted on every wall and hoarding pushed home the message that Britain needed brave young men to fight for their country.

'Working in the pawnshop takes my mind off things for a while,' Izzy said. 'The security of a regular wage coming in is still a novelty and it helps to share a laugh or a tear with other mothers whose sons are away fighting and going through the same thing.'

'I'm sure you are right.' Ruby knew what it was like to be a mother who had no control over the well-being of her offspring. 'I admire your resilience, Izzy.'

'Thanks to you for giving me a chance when I most needed it,' Izzy said, getting up off her knees and picking up her bucket, beckoning Ruby to follow her inside with a sideways nod of her head. 'My luck changed for the better that time you gave me a ten-bob note.'

'I don't know what you mean,' Ruby said, knowing exactly what Izzy meant, recalling the time five years ago when she saw Izzy, destitute, outside the pawnshop waiting for it to open.

'I managed to pay my rent that Christmas Eve,' Izzy replied. 'So, *his nibs* didn't get all of it,' she said, referring to her lazy husband. 'And you could have knocked me over with a feather when the man from the Corporation told me I had this new house.' The three-up-three-down terraced house was further back from the confined spaces of disease and vermin ridden courts and had its own parlour, a privy in the yard and modern gas lighting.

'It's a credit to you,' Ruby said, looking round, admiring the clean cosy kitchen.

'Well, everybody knows you've got to be as close as God's sister to get an 'ouse round here,' Izzy said, watching Ruby closely. 'It was like stepping into a palace after my old place, in the court cellar.' She was quiet for a moment, searching for any signs of acknowledgment from Ruby. But there were none. 'You should play poker, Mrs Swift,' Izzy said, and her face broke into a smile as she placed the black-bottomed kettle onto the hob. 'I know you had a hand in getting me this house.'

'Be off with you,' Ruby scoffed, flicking her hand as if swatting a fly.

'When I moved in here with Nipper, the family reputation went before us, and the neighbours, no matter how poor they were, would not give me the time of day.'

'You deserved the chance of a better life, you and Nipper,' Ruby said, knowing Jerky and his father were the shrapnel Izzy had been forced to endure for years.

'Although, when my 'usband, Splinter – they called him that because of the surname – when he drowned in the dock, all the neighbours rallied round. Good as gold they were,' Izzy said. 'Splinter was well soused when they fished him out, which didn't surprise me. I didn't see him of course, but I was told you could smell him a mile off.'

'I'm sorry for your loss,' Ruby said, and Izzy shrugged her thin shoulders. Sitting at the kitchen table that was covered in a blue checked cotton tablecloth, Ruby was not shocked when Izzy said:

'Losing Splinter was the best thing that ever happened to me. That and Jerky being locked up gave me the peace of mind I didn't know I needed.' Izzy was silent for a moment and Ruby suspected the thought had only just occurred to her, especially when she added, 'I was like a caged bird set free.' She handed Ruby a cup of tea in a matching cup and saucer, and Ruby knew this was something that would have been unheard of in days gone by. 'Nothing could hold me back. And when your Archie offered me the job in the pawnshop, I thought I'd died and gone to heaven.'

'I'm glad the tide turned for you,' Ruby said, trying to fathom what kind of terrible life Izzy must have endured, to accept the death of her husband, the detention of her son and see a job in the pawnshop as a gift from the gods. 'You have a lovely home.' Ruby did not know what else to say and pounced on the first thing to enter her head as she took in the old but well-kept furniture, the polished wood, the pristine linoleum covered in bright, clean rag-rugs, the well-banked fire and the lingering smell of fresh-baked bread.

'"*They can take away all your money*", one wise old Mary-Ellen told me at Splinter's funeral.' Izzy leaned back in her chair, telling Ruby. 'Her wispy white hair was covered in the black mantilla she kept specially for the occasion, and she said...' Izzy lowered her voice in mock seriousness, '"*you might not have two farthings to rub together, Missus, but you can hold your head up, you've a spotless home*".' Izzy threw her head back and laughed again, something she did often these days, Ruby noted. 'How's that for getting your priorities, right?' Izzy gave a determined nod of her head. 'It doesn't matter that I didn't have a pot to piss in, excuse my language, and my husband got so drunk he landed hisself in Bramley-Moore dock – but as long as I had a nice clean house, I was respectable.'

Ruby laughed too. Izzy's impeccable standards of home-making were obvious everywhere she looked. Even the cheap pottery dogs on either side of the fireplace were gleaming and had not seen the inside of Archie's pawnshop since she started working there.

Respectability was the heavy burden some women relished. But Ruby pooh-poohed the idea, finding the notion suffocating and intolerable, therefore ignoring it completely. At her father's behest all those years ago, she had left his house and made him a promise, which Izzy would probably find scandalous. Ruby vowed to the great man, the master shipbuilder, Silas Ashland, that she would shame him in any way she could after what he had done. Ruby then struck out to live, work, and love in her own way. She vowed not to marry until her father was dead, knowing if she had married Archie before he died, she would be disowned, only marrying her beloved Archie to make them legally one after her father's death. She knew the shame of an illegitimate birth, and her living in sin with Archie for all those years would have been the biggest ignominy to be heaped on her father's shoulders, and that was why he had kept the secret hidden within the family for all those years.

'So, what can I do for you today, Mrs Swift?' Izzy said from the other side of the table.

'Two things,' Ruby said, placing her cup on the saucer, 'what would you say to a live-in position. Rent-free.'

Izzy felt her spirit's plummet knowing Ruby's home at Ashland Hall was a country estate set in hundreds of acres opposite the golden north-west shores overlooking the Mersey estuary. Nipper, at sixteen and the apple of her eye, had gone off with his head held high and shoulders back to shoot the Hun. When he came home a hero, she knew he would want to come back to the dockside. 'A live-in position?' she considered the request then said, 'I could not hold my son. So, I gave him wings and let him fly. But when he is ready to come back, his home is here on the dockside, with me.'

Everybody round here knew Ruby had inherited the grand house after her father drowned when the Titanic sank on its maiden voyage. Most were surprised she had come from such a grand family, but not Izzy. She knew Ruby had something about her that was much more refined than many people she had met.

'Rent-free?' Ruby's tone was full of persuasion and she waited.

Izzy loved living round the dockside. She knew these people. They were her people. But how could she possibly refuse such a wonderful position without causing offence? Especially after everything Ruby Swift had done for her in the past. 'You're asking me to move to Ashland Hall?'

'Not live at Ashland Hall,' Ruby answered, and Izzy did her

best not to look too relieved, 'I need someone to live over the shop, so to speak.'

'Over the shop, Mrs Swift?' Izzy looked puzzled. 'I don't understand...'

'It's like this,' Ruby said, outlining her thoughts with the tip of her finger on the tablecloth, 'Archie and I have moved to Ashland Hall on a permanent basis, as you know, but we don't want to give up the pawnshop or the Emporium completely.'

'I'm not surprised,' Izzy said, 'you love the Emporium. Not that I ever went in there, much, but I would cheer myself up by looking in the window. The Emporium weren't for the likes of me, not having two ha'pennies to rub together.'

'You would be surprised, Izzy,' Ruby replied, 'some of my best customers didn't have any money to begin with, either.'

'Well, you live and learn,' Izzy said, 'but what's all this got to do with me?'

'Archie and I feel we must do our bit for our brave boys like Nipper, so we met up with the Red Cross Society at the Town Hall and decided the Emporium would be better served as a charity shop to aid the war effort. Father's vessels have been commissioned as hospital ships for the duration. And, as Archie has volunteered for the police force, he cannot spare the time to run the pawnshop,' Ruby answered.

'Blimey,' Izzy's eyes widened, 'you lot don't do things by half, do you, Mrs Swift.'

Ruby smiled. She liked Izzy's forthright manner, and her inability to hide her true feelings. What you saw was what you got with Izzy. 'Lottie will run the charity shop with volunteers from the Red Cross, while Archie and I were hoping you would manage the pawnshop.'

'Me? A manageress? I never thought I'd see the day.' The relief caused Izzy to let out a little squeal of delight. 'I would like that, very much, and I'm thrilled you trust me. I won't let you down.'

'I know that,' Ruby said. Then she smiled and said in a mock threatening voice, 'I know where you live.'

Izzy threw her head back, laughing. The day just kept getting better, 'You said two things?'

'As a live-in caretaker, I will pay you, obviously.'

'You want me to move into your fine home?' Izzy could not believe her ears.

'Rent free,' Ruby hastened to add, 'but there is one condition... Lottie will be moving in too. She has been like an arm without a body since her mother died last year, and I know she has a soft spot for you.'

'For Jerky, more like.' Izzy knew Ruby would not entertain the idea of her son living over The Emporium, and nor would she. Jerky was the living embodiment of his father and was not to be trusted. If truth be told, she felt sorry for poor Lottie, who was as gullible as she herself had once been. 'Poor cow – he'd sell her the Liver Buildings and she would gladly pay.' She paused for a moment, obviously working something out before she said: 'It's best she lives with me, come to think of it. I can keep me eye on her, and there is less chance of her becoming prone to Jerky's persuasion.' Both women knew exactly what Izzy meant and, as women of the world, neither felt embarrassed by the implication. 'So, Mrs Swift, your offer suits me right down to the ground.' A responsible job and a respectable address. Izzy could think of nothing better. Except possibly, that her eldest lad may do something she could be proud of when he was released from prison. 'Will I lose my home if my circumstances change?' Izzy asked, suspecting her tenure over the pawnshop would end when her job did and was silenced when Ruby put up her hand.

'You have no need to worry on that score,' she said, 'you can stay in the flat for the rest of your days. There is no time limit.'

'Oh, Mrs Swift, I don't know what to say.' There were tears forming in Izzy's eyes. 'It's not right what some of them round here say.'

'What do they say, Izzy?' Not that she was worried, but Ruby liked to know where she stood in the parish. She saw Izzy's cheeks grow pink and realised she was not as old at close quarters as she initially reckoned.

'I don't listen to a word of it.' Izzy knew she had made a mistake voicing her thoughts and wondered how she was going to put it right without offending Mrs Swift. 'It's not right they say you are a hard woman.'

'But they are right, Izzy. I am a hard woman.' Ruby smiled. 'I do as I would be done by. And I take no prisoners. Especially with those who cross me.' Ruby stood up to leave. 'Life taught me to be strong in my beliefs. And I believe you are one of the most honest women round here. Otherwise, I would not have given you the time of day.'

Izzy studied the other woman for some moments, then she too smiled.

'I like it when I know where I stand,' Izzy said. Then she tilted her head to one side. 'I think we are opposite ends of the same stick, you and me.'

2

'What's the war got to do with us?' Jerky Woods was outraged when he was given a white feather by a passing suffragist. He'd had his sentence extended to the end of May due to fighting. 'I didn't think you'd come,' he said to Lottie as the gates of Walton prison slammed behind him and gave a two-fingered salute when he saw the posters of Lord Kitchener telling Britain's men that their country needed them. 'Let's get away from here,' he said, walking in the opposite direction of the recruiting office. The Military Service act, introduced in January, meant he would be required for subscription. All *single* men aged between eighteen and forty-one were obliged to be called up, but he had no intentions of fighting. Not after the year he'd just had. Having been incarcerated in Walton Gaol for incitement to violence during The Lusitania Riots, twelve months ago, Woods had no intentions of joining up, if he could avoid it, he would, especially when he saw the headlines on a local billboard outside the newsagent's shop about the mounting casualties. Brave men, one and all, said the headlines. Well, brave they might be, but he wasn't stupid enough to get called up. Married men were not being conscripted.

'I am so glad you are out of that awful place, Jerry.' Lottie did not believe her Jerry would do the wicked things he had been accused of. 'I can't understand why Ruby won't allow you to live with me and your mother over the Charity shop, there's plenty of room.'

'So, the Emporium is now the charity shop?' Jerky said. 'I see Lady Ruby didn't waste much time getting out of the dockside.'

'I've been put in charge,' said Lottie proudly. 'We send little comforts out to the troops fighting at the Front, cigarettes and sweets, that kind of thing.'

But Jerky was not impressed.

'Why should I risk my neck when the beak could do something so heartless as to side with a Hun pork butcher and a German jeweller against one of his own countrymen? It's a diabolical liberty. That's what it was.'

Hot-headed Jerky was incensed at the idea and Lottie could see he was building himself into a tizzy. She would have to try and calm him down, worried he might be tempted to smash some more windows.

'The authorities said the jeweller wasn't a German, he was Polish.' Nevertheless, she felt the power of his wrath in the glare he gave her, trying to ignore an old neighbour who called from across the cobbled road, 'They finally let him out then?'

Lottie straightened her back and put her nose in the air, trying to disregard the old wives of Queen Street tut-tutting and saying in a voice loud enough for both of them to hear that her mother would turn in her grave if she knew who her daughter had taken up with.

'Why does she want to trouble herself with the likes of him?'

Lottie heard the neighbour ask her companion. 'She's got that special place in the charity shop.'

'He'll drag her down, just you wait and see,' said another woman.

And although the comments were like needles in her flesh, Lottie chose to appear to pay no heed. She would show all of them how wrong they were about her dear Jerry. He had a good heart, and they didn't see the man she saw. They were prejudiced.

'What do they know, Jerry?' she said as dismissively as she could manage.

'Do you have to call me that?' he asked. 'I've answered to Jerky all me life.'

'I think Jerry suits you better,' Lottie said, with her head held high, linking her arm through his and passing the old Mary-Ellens dressed in their black shawls, singing loudly and proudly as more soldiers marched off to war. Lottie watched for a moment. She would have sung too but not while she was with Jerry.

'I don't see the point in going to war,' he said, as they ambled along the pavement, dodging young boys with sticks of wood pretending they were machine guns. 'Why should I fight for a country that won't even give me a job.'

'If you keep out of trouble long enough,' said a woman who was watching the long line of soldiers marching towards Lime Street station, 'then you would soon get a job.' Lottie regarded the well-meaning advice from women she had known all her life as an intrusion into her privacy.

'You didn't have to meet me,' he said as they neared The Tram Tavern, and his throat was dry for the want of a pint. 'I would have found my own way if you gave me the address of the lodgings.'

'I want you to see the place,' Lottie said, sure that Jerky would change and look after her when they were wed.

'So, where are these lodgings you managed to find then?' Woods asked, inhaling deeply as they ambled over the bridge to the sound of men's voices coming from the pub below, and the enticing smell of beery hops sailed up through the air and into his nostrils.

'Just round this corner, it's on the first floor,' Lottie's voice rose with excitement. 'I've given it a good clean, and bought new curtains and a bedspread, to brighten it up, and I've got a pan of ox-tail soup on the go.' She was sure that in the privacy of the lodgings, he would be much more agreeable, and the scowl he had worn since he came out of the prison gates would disappear.

Jerky Woods hardly noticed the nice little touches Lottie had brought to the room she had found him in the lodging house not far from the docks. Noisily sucking the gelatinous marrow from the core of an ox tail, his sly eyes took in Lottie's voluptuous curves and, now that his belly was full, he was aware of another desire, a pleasurable vibration that warmed his blood.

But he knew he would have to change his attitude if he was to get what he wanted. The beer could wait. For now. 'I don't care less what anybody thinks,' he said, knowing he had a willing supporter in Lottie. 'I've got what I want right here.' She might be a bit gullible, he thought, but she made an excellent soup, and she wasn't such a bad port in a storm. He stretched, showing off the muscles that his daily exercise had honed, aware of Lottie's appreciative gaze. 'It would be nice to have a bit of a lie-down after such a delicious meal. Maybe you'd like to keep me company,' he said, 'and show me some of that loving you spoke so much about in your letters.'

'Jerry!' Lottie's eyes widened in surprise. 'It is the middle of the afternoon.'

'What does the time have to do with anything?' Woods asked. 'We don't need no clock to tell us when we can be loving, do we?'

'No, Jerry, of course not,' Lottie replied. She had missed him so much but did not quite trust her loving feelings at that moment, knowing they could lead to somewhere very troubling.

The only sound in the room was the clock ticking on the mantlepiece and Lottie felt the need to fill the heavy silence.

'I was thinking of getting a job as a munitionette,' she said as she washed the soup bowls at the sink in the corner of the one-roomed flat. Ruby would never have allowed Jerry to live above the charity shop with her and his mother, Izzy. Nor would she be able to succumb to loving feelings if Izzy were hovering in the vicinity. Jerry was bad for business, Ruby had said when Lottie asked if he would be allowed to stay in the flat. 'The factory pay is much better than working in the charity shop,' Lottie added. 'We could be married in no time.'

She promised her mother she would keep herself pure until her wedding day. Nevertheless, watching Jerry rise from the table and head towards the bed, she did not feel strong enough to resist this particular temptation. It had been so long since he held her in his arms. Since he had kissed her and told her she meant the world to him. Maybe just lying next to him... Maybe just...

'I'm not allowing any wife of mine to work in munitions, Lottie, it's far too dangerous.' His voice was soft and inviting as he patted the mattress on the narrow iron bed, and Lottie could feel her temperature rise as a low quiver, like a light fingertip, traced her spine beneath her high-necked blouse.

'Your wife, Jerry?' she said breathlessly. How could she possibly refuse him when he wanted her to be his wife.

Jerky Woods grinned as Lottie, looking coy, lowered herself beside him on the narrow bed. He never was very keen on that marriage lark. But a man has needs. Lottie would never succumb without the promise of a ring at least. Although National Conscription introduced in January had called for single, not married men to fight, if he had been as clever as he thought he was, Woods would have realised that conscription for married men had followed shortly afterwards.

3

'Do you think any of these lot have actually seen action?' Anna asked Ellie, her best friend and fellow nurse, as they sat together at the lavish fundraising dinner hosted by Archie and Ruby, knowing the money raised would go towards enabling The Red Cross to equip Ashland Hall, which, it was hoped would become an auxiliary hospital for injured soldiers returning from overseas.

'I doubt some of them have seen their feet in years, never mind action,' said Ellie through unmoving lips, smiling and nodding to the upper echelon of society. People who did not need much encouragement to open their wallets to attend Aunt Ruby's popular fundraising dinner parties, the likes of which Ashland Hall and its staff had not seen in many a long year.

Anna laughed, her eyes skimming the length of the fifteen-foot banqueting table that hosted some of the top masterminds, and her thoughts turned, as always, to Ned. Her darling.

Engineer, first-class, Ned was a serving Chief Petty Officer in the Royal Navy and had shared so much of her formative twenty-two years. He too had come a long way since he was rescued by Ruby and Archie when his widowed father, a gypsy fist-fighter, was killed. Ned was the one man she loved with every beat of her heart. He and Anna had been friends from the moment they set eyes on each other back in Queen Street along Vauxhall road, before... before her home was burned down that Christmas Eve, six years ago, when she lost her mother and her three brothers. The two youngest died in the fire and Sam was shipped off to Canada by the church.

Anna had been taken in by Ruby and Archie and had worked in the Emporium. Ned worked for them too and both Anna and Ned regarded Ruby and Archie as their family.

* * *

Ruby gave a knowing smile, she had a good idea that both girls were not enjoying another sumptuous banquet after a full day's work at the Seaforth Military Hospital, which was full to bursting with injured soldiers who had been brought back from the Front.

Nevertheless, Ruby knew such functions were necessary to boost funds and hopefully, to enable them to open Ashland Hall as a fine voluntary nursing establishment. Being the best it could possibly be was the least she could do to help her brave boys to recover. All she had to do was persuade Archie that it was a good idea to turn their home into an auxiliary hospital, but she was a mistress of persuasion where her beloved husband was concerned. He would see things her way, she was sure.

Looking round the banqueting table, where honoured *paying* guests were enjoying the best food and drink that money could buy, Ruby knew the Reverend Giles Harrington, her abhorrent brother-in-law and mentor of her long-lasting heartache, would have given his eye-teeth to entertain some of this lot. And although Ruby had invited her despised in-law and her mild-mannered sister, May, to Ashland Hall many times, the answer was always the same resounding refusal.

Maybe Archie had been right after all, Ruby thought, maybe she *had* invited the vicar so she could rub his nose in her rightful inheritance of Ashland Hall, which the God-fearing cleric had planned to take for his own after she had disgraced her father. Ruby now realised; May would have had no say in any matters concerning Ashland Hall if Giles Harrington had got his grubby paws on their former home after their father was killed.

However, the reading of her father's Will proved she, formerly known as Lady Rowena Ashland, was the rightful owner of Ashland Hall, and almost everything else her father owned. Ruby suppressed a secret smile knowing she had never even heard some of the unholy words that came out of the reverend's mouth before he scuttled off back to Scarborough four years ago. Until her father died, Giles had not known where his sister-in-law, Rowena, was living or that as Ruby Swift she had run a successful business close by on the Liverpool dockside for twenty years.

Dabbing the corners of her mouth with a fine lawn napkin, Ruby allowed a satisfied smile. Revenge, she thought, truly was a tasty dish when served cold.

She would have been far happier if Harrington had not ordered her sister, May, to go back to Scarborough with him, however, May was his wife and as such he would expect her to do his bidding. She had been bequeathed the hunting lodge and Ruby knew her sister would have loved to put her own stamp on the self-sufficient, five-bedroomed lodge nestled in the vast grounds of Ashland Hall. But the toady reverend would not hear of her staying on here without him.

Ruby was aware May's desires had obviously counted for nothing, as far as Giles Harrington was concerned, and she was glad he was not here, brown-nosing some of the most powerful businessmen in the north-west, some of whom she had discreetly given a financial helping hand, in days when their bank balance needed it most, and were now returning the favour.

'Thank you, Hargreaves,' Ruby said as her plate was removed. She had reinstated her father's trusted staff, whom Giles Harrington had dismissed without so much as a *thank-you,* when he thought May, or rather he, would inherit Ashland Hall. The loyal staff had served the family well over the years, so when Ruby took her rightful place in the great mansion, she was determined to bring them back where they belonged. Those, that is, who had not already volunteered to fight for King and country. These were the people she trusted, and who trusted her.

The old guard, as her darling Archie called them, knew how to treat important people who enjoyed the cachet of banqueting at the same table as King Edward VII, who had weekended a couple of times a year in days gone by. Ruby intended to uphold Ashland Hall's quality reputation as an auxiliary hospital and made sure the dinners were a money-raising success.

'This house was legendary in its day,' Ruby said, regaling her guests, who loved to hear the royal stories they could then pass on. 'Ashland played host to royalty during the annual Waterloo Cup.' The Waterloo Cup, as everybody knew, was a three-day event held in February, when Great Altcar hosted the most important event in the hare-coursing year. 'My father plied his guests with ten-course dinners,' she told the gathered generals, officers and high-rolling contributors to the cause.

* * *

'The banquets were good for business in those days, so my father told me,' Ellie informed Anna. 'His Majesty came to Ashland Hall when he attended The Grand National steeplechase at Aintree, just a few miles up the road. Everybody who was anybody wanted an invitation.'

'Nothing has changed there,' Anna answered. 'The formal dinners obviously taught Ruby a valuable lesson she would never forget'

'No wonder this lot have no compunction about parting with their money when they have royalty to compete with,' Ellie whispered to Anna, pleased she had stayed on at Ashland Hall when her parents, May and Giles, went back to Scarborough. 'To say they dined at the same table as His Majesty is obviously enough to have them reaching for their wallets.'

'Ruby opening her previous account books, more like.' Anna gave a conspiratorial smile as, having no appetite, she moved her food round her plate. 'She is determined to do all she can to help her brave boys. She knows these successful men would dare not refuse after her helping hand earlier on in their own careers.' Anna's mind was temporarily taken off her worry of Ned serving on board ship in the middle of who-knows-where. If truth be told, Anna wanted to do more than just attend fundraising dinners. The only question was what could she do?

'You seem distracted,' Ellie said, seeing her friend's food hardly touched. 'Are you feeling out of sorts?'

Ned had been gone twenty months and his letters were becoming more sporadic. The last one she received from him had been read so many times the paper was beginning to grow thin round the edges. She had not heard anything from him for weeks, which made not seeing him even more unbearably raw. However, she was not going to burden Ellie with her worries about her beloved childhood sweetheart who grew to be so much more. 'I think I'm tired after the large intake of wounded servicemen which came in today,' Anna answered.

'Yes, we hardly stopped to draw breath. And we also had a talk from a member of The Royal Army Medical Corps who told us they carried out their first successful blood transfusion at the beginning of the year, using blood that had been stored and cooled. They are introducing it to military hospitals,' Ellie told Anna, who knew this medical practice would be a phenomenal turning point if it was made available to all.

'I've heard all the hospitals are running out of beds,' Anna said, wearily.

'I know,' Ellie answered, 'the Red Cross are clamouring for private houses to care for the wounded.'

'Ruby wants to turn Ashland Hall into a hospital,' Anna said, and Ellie nodded.

'Yes, of course, I expected Ruby to want to do such a thing to help the cause. Not to mention the government grant involved.' Ellie had a gleam in her eye as both girls tried to stifle a giggle. It was a well-known fact that Ruby had a heart of gold. But she also had a strong head for business.

'Who is catching your eye tonight,' Anna asked when she noticed Ellie's eyes were frequently drawn to the opposite side of the table, her dark eyelashes fluttering towards a handsome officer in the uniform of the King's Hussars. Her lingering looks told Anna she was obviously enjoying his attention. Uniforms, being a common sight these days, gave men an air of authority, sophistication and bravery that Ellie could not resist, and Anna knew she was keeping up morale by writing to a few officers who were serving overseas.

'Don't you think he's dashing?' Ellie said, again without moving her lips, but Anna, feeling particularly glum about missing Ned, was not really in the mood to watch another of Ellie's courting rituals.

She pushed her plate away, as her eyes took in the huge table groaning under the weight of sumptuous food and drink. Enough to feed a small town, she thought. She had heard the rumours of rationing. Food prices had more than doubled, and a lot of food was being sent to the Front to feed the soldiers. All the news she could glean was from the newspapers and newsreel footage at the cinema.

She knew the Royal Navy, in retaliation to the German's Zeppelin raids, were blockading German ports and hunting U-boats. The devastation had hit the innocents on both sides, who suffered as the battle raged on. Ships were being blown out of the water. Even the secretary of state for war, Lord Kitchener, along with hundreds of men, succumbed in June, when the ship on which he had been travelling to Russia, *H.M.S. Hampshire*, was sunk by a German mine off the Orkney Islands.

Ned, being part of the Grand Fleet and the biggest navy in the world, was on board a ship carrying soldiers and supplies to the Front, dodging attacks by German submarines. He must be going through a living hell to keep this country safe, she thought, and yet here she was, listening to men who spouted about what should be done when none of them had seen any action yet.

'I've heard that reports coming back from the Front will be censored,' said the owner of *The Corby Gazette*, a local newspaper that usually covered seaside outings and flower garden competitions, but now in a frenzy of patriotic fervour printed anything that even remotely hinted at news of the war, in a bid to sell as many papers as possible.

'Surely such a thing would not be allowed,' Archie said as his glass, half-tilted, stilled between the table and his lips. 'People have a right to know how their loved ones are faring overseas.'

'Apparently, there are too many gory reports,' said the editor from the *Gazette* with much authority, 'it is putting off young men from signing up. Now the initial excitement has worn off somewhat, young bucks are deciding that fighting overseas is something they have no wish to take part in.'

'I must say,' Ruby told a high-ranking businessman to her right, 'I don't think anybody expected the huge number of casualties that are coming back. So, I am not surprised to hear recruitment is on the wane.'

'I heard tell,' said Anna, joining in the conversation, 'the powers that be are accepting men who were previously rejected.'

'Yes,' Ellie agreed, 'those who were not accepted for service due to weak eyesight, defective teeth or other small physical shortcomings are now being asked to resubmit themselves for medical examination.'

'Do you think you may be called up, Archie?' Ruby sounded horrified, but Archie shook his head. He knew that his dwindling eyesight was a cause for some concern, and he would not be eligible to fight.

'Not while I am fulfilling my role as a police officer,' he said, knowing his explanation would pacify Ruby and prevent her asking any more questions.

'I saw a long line of sombre-looking recruits outside the drill hall in Park Street only this morning,' added Ellie, 'rumour had it that they had been given white feathers by suffragettes.' She paused. 'The hospitals are becoming overwhelmed,' Ellie informed the gathered company who were in the financial position of being able to offer much-needed charitable aid to the serving troops.

'I take it you have all heard the call for large houses to offer their service,' Ruby said.

'Here we go,' Ellie whispered to Anna, 'the sales pitch.'

'If anyone can get these men to part with their money, Ruby can,' Anna agreed.

'As you know, we at Ashland Hall were one of the first to offer our services for these poor wretched men being brought back on stretchers, and we are in talks about bringing in an army of able-bodied, dedicated nurses,' Ruby turned to Ellie and Anna and beamed a proud smile, 'led by our very own highly trained nursing angels.'

'Is she talking about us?' Anna was wide-eyed when she asked Ellie as Ruby went on to regale the local dignitaries with hopeful tales of medical care that bordered on the miraculous, in her bid to entice them to contribute to the coffers – and they did.

'Still no word from Ned?' Ellie asked only half-listening to Ruby's speech, and Anna shook her head.

'I secretly wished Ned would be injured.' Anna was shocked at the seriousness of her words and only realised how insensitive they sounded when she saw Ellie's shocked expression. 'Not much,' Anna hastened to assure her friend. 'Just enough for him to be sent back home, so I could look after him. Care for him. Keep him safe.' She lowered her gaze to the napkin resting on her lap as shame crept stealthily into her heart. *Didn't every girl think this way?* As soon as the enormity of the notion entered her head, she regretted having countenanced such a wicked thought. 'Of course, I don't want Ned to be injured,' she said, fighting back the urge to shed a tear. 'I just need to see him. He's been gone so long.'

Anna missed everything about him. His cheerful repartee, his enthusiasm, his energy. She missed his lips on hers, the manly, musky smell of him when he came in from the fields, the way his large hands gently but securely curled round hers and made her feel safe. They had been friends, then sweethearts. Part of each other's lives for such a long time. He was the other half of her. Her soul mate. Her one true love.

This situation felt odd, that he was no longer here to talk to, to have a laugh with, to ask questions and know his reply would be given with that pragmatic, logical opinion she had come to trust.

Anna sighed, it might feel strange, she thought, but times were strange these days. Nothing was the same any more. Life was challenging for everybody. Nobody was immune, it seemed. Even Lord Kitchener, what chance did poor Ned have?

'Rupert is good-looking in that dashing officer kind of way,' Ellie whispered, and Anna did her best to shake herself out of the doldrums. 'He has told me he is off to somewhere called The Somme, have you heard of it?'

Anna shook her head.

'But not before he takes me to tea at The Adelphi Hotel.'

'Ellie, you are incorrigible,' Anna raised her first smile of the evening. She really must try to be strong. For Ned's sake. The thought brought her back to the *here and now* and pushing her worries to the back of her mind, she said brightly, 'I wouldn't like to be behind some of this lot in a famine.' Her glance took in the cigar-smoking general, the wily politician – too old to fight but never too old to pontificate – and she knew she could not keep up the pretence.

'Excuse me,' Anna said, quickly knowing Ellie would not miss her too much when she had a dashing officer like Rupert to keep her company. 'I'm not feeling too well.' Her heart was too full of love and despair to entertain the gathered luminaries.

4

'The Lady Mayoress appealed for women to help with the care of the sick and wounded,' Ruby said, taking a seat opposite Archie, at the dinner table, 'I told her Ellie and Anna were capable nurses who will gladly offer their services.'

Archie said nothing, knowing Anna and Ellie had not given the slightest indication they wished to come back and work in Ashland Hall. But that would be of no consequence to Ruby. He knew his beloved wife assumed that if she had a good idea, then everybody would agree to it.

'There has been a positive and patriotic response to the call for requisites.' An ardent fundraiser for the suffragist movement, Ruby was now deeply involved with raising money and provisions for the war effort. 'When I saw neighbours donating hospital provisions, blankets, bandages, and the like, I decided I could donate beds, bedding, pyjamas, anything that might be of help.'

Archie could almost see Ruby's mind working overtime with schemes and good ideas. Usually more cautious than his headstrong wife, he could see the immediate need arising to accommodate wounded soldiers coming back from the Front. Ruby on the other hand saw everything in black and white. There were never any grey areas.

He knew his beloved wife was impulsive and usually right. If she had a notion to do something, then the idea had probably been hovering in the back of her mind for a while, as she got on with all the other busy things she had to do. Then when the concept elbowed its way to the front of her long list, she had already made up her mind to do it, no matter what he thought. Although he never felt the need to disagree with Ruby, knowing she always, even if only to a cursory degree, consulted him first.

'I knew you would be in favour of us doing our bit,' said Ruby.

'Would that have been around the time you decided to offer our home?'

'We must all do our bit for the cause, Archie. This house is wasted as a private residence,' Ruby's voice was full of excitement, as it always was when she got a new idea, Archie knew. Dressed in the uniform of volunteer sergeant of the local police force, he had witnessed this situation more than once and could see her enthusiasm far outweighed her common sense in this regard.

Ruby got up from the table, threw down her napkin and headed to the wide expanse of hallway, climbing the wide staircase to the extensive corridor that ran the length of the house and was followed by Archie. Ashland Hall was said to be one of the finest residences in England, situated on the golden north-west shore of the River Mersey.

'Anna and Ellie were right when they said you can offer so much. The War Office has considerably miscalculated the number of casualties,' Archie said.

'It was predicted that 50,000 hospital beds would be required and could be accommodated in existing military and voluntary hospitals. I agree that was a serious miscalculation, Archie,' Ruby said drily. 'This morning's paper said over 73,000 wounded men are already being brought back and it is clear that more beds will be urgently needed.'

'The chief constable was telling us that there has been a scramble for further hospital accommodation. Owners of country houses all over the country are volunteering their homes as convalescent establishments, while others are being requisitioned.' Archie knew that a local cottage hospital had been converted into a military hospital within hours.

'We will store the family heirlooms securely in the unused stables for safekeeping. Those pictures will be the first to be removed,' Ruby said, casting her eyes over the heavy, dark wooden framed pictures of her father's ships. Taking in the high walls, she did not fail to notice there was not one portrait of her, or May, nor even her mother. Yet, Silas Ashland's beloved ships took pride of place along the upper mezzanine walls. 'I must say, I will not be sorry to see the back of those ships. The staff will move to the attic rooms.' Her busy mind was working overtime now.

'Do I need to ask where we will go?' Archie's eyes crinkled into a smile that had for so many years held her fast and made Ruby's heart flip.

'We will move into the lodge, of course,' Ruby said. 'There is plenty of room.'

'But your father left the lodge to May,' Archie said, and Ruby answered with a wave of her hands.

'May is in Scarborough, I am sure she won't mind a bit. I will drop her a line explaining the circumstances, later today,' Ruby said. 'Obviously, she won't mind a bit when I tell her Ellie and Anna will also stay at the lodge with us.'

'It might be best to ask them if that is what they want to do, my love.' Archie remained straight-faced when he saw Ruby's astonished expression.

'Of course, they will wish to be here,' she said 'This is Ellie's natural home. Where else would she go?' Archie sighed. One day everything in this house would belong to their daughter, Ellie, who was stolen from them by the conniving Giles Harrington and Ruby's father, when she was only ten days old. 'We are only the custodians of Ellie's future, Archie, and glad to be so.'

'I know what you are thinking,' Archie said gently, knowing there was no use issuing suggestions when Ruby had made up her mind. But there was just one more thing he worried about. 'You want Ellie close as do I,' said Archie. 'It is understandable, given the years we had lost her.' His forehead pleated as if he was choosing his words very carefully so as not to upset Ruby, but she knew what he was going to say.

'She is home now, Archie, and believe me when I tell you, I will put up a bitter fight if the reverend wants to make something of it.'

'You will have to get behind me,' Archie said with a determination that brooked no argument, reminding Ruby of the time he scoured the north-west coast in his quest to find his daughter. 'She reminds me so much of you when you were her age.'

'I am so proud of the wonderful woman Ellie has become,' Ruby said, 'and I will admit I swelled with pride when she told me she would rather live here at Ashland Hall than go back to the rectory with that grasping cleric who browbeat my sister into subservience.'

'May has no say in any matter, I grant you,' Archie answered, 'she is a good wife. But she does not have the fortitude to fight Giles Harrington's emotional bullying.'

'If May had been more like me, she would...'

'She would never have given Giles Harrington the time of

day,' Archie smiled. 'And she would have been happy here, instead of on the East coast.'

While they both came back downstairs, Ruby thought about Archie's words for a little while and realised that what he said was right. But May had made her bed years ago and now she must lie in it – with the most odious, self-centred, greedy man it had ever been Ruby's misfortune to encounter. But she didn't want to talk about her sister and her despicable husband. Ruby had other things to think about now. Changing the subject quickly she said,

'We have raised sufficient funds to have electricity put into Ashland Hall, for when we open up as an auxiliary hospital,' Ruby told Archie, who raised an eyebrow. *Electricity?*

'For the benefit of injured servicemen who need our loving care and the best that fund-raised money can buy,' Ruby said, throwing open the doors. And Archie knew it had been a long-held ambition of Ruby's to have electricity installed in Ashland Hall, so what better time, he thought wryly; his wife had the perfect excuse and was obviously thinking of the long term. When the war was over, the electricity would still be here. Two birds, one stone. Trust Ruby.

The click of her busy heels echoing on the parquet floor covering the wide expanse of the front lobby. 'I can see it now,' she said dramatically, 'the ministering angels sitting beside the beds of injured servicemen. Their cool fingers soothing fevered brows.'

'Lady Corby does not recognise her own home any more,' Archie said, wondering if Ruby had bitten off more than she could chew this time, and for how long would he be able to see clearly enough to help her. 'She said it is full to bursting with military and medics.'

Ruby was oblivious to Archie's warning note. 'We must do our bit, Archie.'

'I'm sure you are right,' Archie agreed, knowing that to do otherwise was futile. Ruby would have her way no matter what. But if the reports in the newspaper were anything to go by, they would have to look lively. Injured soldiers were being brought home in droves. Some were so gravely wounded they were taken straight off the battlefield and placed onto the next hospital ship heading for home, still caked in the mud of the front line.

'Oh, and I have more news,' Ruby had a surprise up her sleeve. 'I have recruited a doctor.'

The new doctor was going to make an impression, thought Ruby. Of that she had no doubt.

5

'What about the library?' asked Archie as an army of volunteers came to help convert Ashland Hall into an auxiliary hospital and convalescent establishment. 'Will you close it?'

'I imagine recovering soldiers will relax more if they have something to read,' Ruby replied, ticking off items on her list of objects that were to be stored away. 'Reading will take their mind of their troubles, and give them something other than their wounds to concentrate on.'

'You are right, my dear. This will be a perfect spot,' Archie said, looking out of the window to the golden shore and the pewter waters beyond. He knew his wife had the biggest heart in the world, but she was also a shrewd businesswoman, and he had an inkling that offering Ashland Hall for the duration of the war called for something a bit more lucrative than a generous heart.

'As I said, Archie, this place will be so much more than the claustrophobic setting of unhappy memories.' Bought by her father before her mother died, this had been such a happy house. After her mother's sudden demise, she and May were reared by nursemaids and governesses, all but ignored by a father who could not let go of the grief in his heart to allow space for his daughters. 'Ashland Hall is crying out for life to be breathed back into it, by people who care. It needs to be opened and brightened up. The dusty drapes will be taken down and cleaned.' The whole place, decorated to her father's dark maritime taste, would be painted in clean bright pastel colours she said, and every conceivable space filled with pictures of the countryside and the beach nearby. As well as the paintings upstairs, the models of the frigates, the destroyers, the schooners her father had commissioned were to be cleared away and put into storage. 'He also thought more of those ships than he ever thought of me or May. What do you think, Archie?' Ruby asked.

He was quiet for a while and only the ticking of the grandfather clock in the lobby broke the silence.

'They are yours to do with as you see fit, Ruby.' Archie spoke slowly, carefully, each word bearing the weight of his conviction. 'If you wish to donate them to the war effort, then you will get no argument from me.'

'Oh Archie, you do say the nicest things.' Ruby's twinkling eyes danced when her husband's loving gaze rested on hers, and his handsome smile settled into soft deep lines that only added to his appealing allure and, as usual, their thoughts pooled.

'Will we ever tell Ellie the truth?' Archie asked, knowing she was, as she always had been, the most precious darling girl and never far from their thoughts. He asked the question in the same measured, thoughtful way, giving Ruby the impression that the decision was hers, and hers alone, and he would wholeheartedly stand by her decision.

'I don't know, Archie.' Now the time had come, Ruby was witness to the fine job May had done of bringing up their daughter. Her sister had doted on Ellie. That much was obvious. Ellie's heart and soul was full of the fire her mother once possessed, before Giles put it out. But right now, Ruby felt a haunting trepidation that bordered on fear. 'What if Ellie wants nothing more to do with us? When she finds out, I mean,' Ruby asked Archie, and he nodded, obviously thinking the same thing.

'I don't think there has ever been any love lost between Ellie and Giles.'

'I think she would garner more affection if she had four legs, a tail and ran the three-o'clock at Aintree.' Ruby's tone was brittle and betrayed the loathing she still felt for her underhanded brother-in-law. 'To think my daughter had to suffer that horrible little man for the past twenty years.'

'I think the suffering was all his.' There was the hint of a smile in Archie's answer, 'Every time he looked at Ellie, he would see you. Every time she spoke, he would hear your voice.'

'Of course, he would!' Ruby brightened. 'Believing all of this would be his to lord over me. Rubbing my nose in his greatest victory. Master of Ashland Hall.'

'Your father was many things, but he was not a fool.'

'You are right, Archie.' Ruby planted an ever-welcome kiss on his lips. 'What time are the girls coming home?' Ellie and Anna had agreed to come back to help set up Ashland Hall as an auxiliary hospital, and minister to wounded soldiers who would arrive sooner rather than later. They both agreed to live in the Lodge with Ruby and Archie, so they were always on hand to help out. Archie and Ruby could not have been happier.

'I will pick them up this evening from the station.'

'We must get in touch with the Red Cross. Arrange supplies.'

Ruby thought that Ashland Hall would be perfect with its vast grounds, tennis court, boating lake, and many bedrooms: ideal for convalescing servicemen.

'I remember the first day we came here,' she told Archie, recalling days when it was a common occurrence for her parents to play host to famous artists who took their easels down to the sprawling shoreline to capture the spectacular twilight sunsets. 'I used to hide in the sand dunes, waiting for unsuspecting May, who would scream with delight and hare off towards the water and I would chase her. We were quite wild, our legs cartwheeling down the great dunes.' It was not unusual to bump into members of the aristocracy and royalty, who came to stay, to benefit from the healthy seaside location and watch champion horses being exercised during Grand National week. 'It was such an exciting time when my parents opened the house for the three-day steeplechase.'

Looking out from Ashland's wide-ranging bay windows that allowed plenty of light into the capacious room and an exclusive panoramic view, Ruby remembered the crowds of sea-bathers who flocked to the coast in the summer months.

'Yet, after Mama died, my memories linger around autumn and winter. A melancholy sky hanging low to meet the far horizon in a spectacular show of Mother Nature's dominance.' She felt Archie's steadying hands on her shoulders, the gentle weight reassuring her, as he always did. 'On those days, it would be stark, even lonely, especially at high tide when the water came right over the tarry stones. I used to love navigating those large flat cobbles that lined the shore, but May would never dare venture further, fearing the strong undercurrents.'

'You still miss your sister, don't you?' Archie said, knowing Ruby had never got over, or even understood, her sister's heartbreaking betrayal when May broke her promise not to tell their father Ruby was having a child, Archie's child, out of wedlock.' However, conversing with Ellie over the last four years, gave Ruby a better insight as to her sister's true intentions.

'Of course, I miss her, Archie,' Ruby said quietly, her back toward him looking down the verdant expanse of lush green grass towards the sea beyond the far wall. 'We only had each other when we were young, after Mama died. But I don't know if I can forgive not being allowed to watch Ellie grow up.'

'I understand, my love.' Archie put his arm round her shoulder. 'When she was here, May told me she treasured every waking moment with Ellie.'

Ruby turned to face her husband, her eyes brimming with the tears no other person would ever see. 'I would have too – given the chance.'

'I know, my darling.' Archie took her in his arms and held her close, as he had done so many times before. 'But Ellie is coming home now. Things can never be undone, but we can make the most of what we have now.'

'You always say the right thing, Archie,' Ruby smiled and hugged his hand while she leaned her head on his shoulder, 'it is just one of the many reasons I love you so much.'

'You forgot to mention my devastating good looks and irresistible charm,' Archie said, and Ruby could hear the smile in his voice.

'Careful, Archie, or your head might swell so big you won't get it through the door.' Ruby smiled too, knowing she had made the right choice all those years ago when she decided she wanted to spend the rest of her life with this wonderful man. Class had nothing to do with affairs of the heart. The fact that he was considered by some to be in a lower class, being one of her father's staff, was neither here nor there. Archie would always be her equal and she, his.

Ruby knew having Ellie back in her rightful place was where she belonged. Instead of being suffocating in the dismal rectory her younger sister was forced to share in Scarborough with that odious little man to whom May was married. For a man of the cloth, Giles Harrington was the most greedy, dishonest and unholy person Ruby had ever met.

Since her father died, getting to know Ellie, who thought of her as an aunt rather than the mother who was forced to give her up, Ruby, paradoxically, felt it was the happiest and saddest time she had known. 'Ellie will not discover the truth from my lips unless it is an absolute necessity.' For, she could not bear to lose her daughter again. What if Ellie found the revelation too shocking to cope with?

'The shock could send her back to Scarborough with more questions than answers.'

'You're right, Archie, that's what I thought. She will have enough to contend with, nursing injured servicemen at the hospital, without having to deal with such a huge revelation.' Taking a deep breath, Ruby made up her mind. 'I think it will be better all-round if we let sleeping dogs lie.' Ruby felt that it was not the right time to enlighten their daughter as to her rightful parents. She had sacrificed so much in the past because her sister could not carry her own child, and Ruby was not married to Archie. After banishing her from Ashland Hall, her father and Giles Harrington agreed May would bring her daughter up, and being below the age of consent, Ruby had no say in the matter.

'She reminds me so much of you at that age,' Archie said. 'When she is outside the room and she laughs, I think it is you, and she is so full of fun and mischief sometimes that I do believe she has borrowed your soul. What a wonderful woman she has become.'

'In spite of, not because of, Giles Harrington,' Ruby countered and Archie agreed. 'How poor May has suffered, having him to contend with every day,' Ruby said, knowing that she and May had lost so much time. 'I would say she has definitely done her penance, don't you?'

'I would, my love,' said Archie.

'But one thing is for sure,' Ruby answered, 'one day this will all be Ellie's,' Ruby's hands encompassed the room, the grounds and even the sea beyond. 'That is not something we would ever have been sure of if the *unholy reverend* got his mitts on the place.'

'If he were going to contest the Will on May's behalf, he would have done it by now,' Archie said, and Ruby sighed with relief. She had a sneaking suspicion that his overwhelming gambling debts would spur him on to try and wrench the house and all its land from her. 'I'm glad Ellie and Anna get on so well,' Archie said, changing the subject. 'They are like sisters.'

'We have a ready-made family, Archie.' Ruby smiled, her eyes full of love for the man at her side, remembering the good times spent in this house before everything changed.

'They most certainly are our girls. Both of them,' Archie answered.

'And don't forget Ned,' Ruby said.

'How could I ever forget Ned.' Archie let out a low rumble of a laugh hiding the fact he knew Ned was in mortal danger.

6

'Hospitals are finding it so hard to cope with the number of casualties coming in, even the town hall has been converted into an auxiliary hospital,' Ellie told Ruby, and Anna nodded in agreement. 'The authorities are desperate for more accommodation.'

'That's what I wanted to talk to you about,' Ruby said, urging the two girls to sit in the spacious drawing room. 'I want to go over the details of Ashland Hall being turned over to the Red Cross as soon as the new doctor arrives.'

'I heard we will be known as Ashland Hall Auxiliary Hospital for the duration of the war.' Said Ellie.

'How exciting!' Anna said.

'Electricity has been installed in most rooms,' Ruby said proudly. And only the low rumble of engines stopped her from explaining the benefits of light at the flick of a switch.

'The medics are here,' Archie said as he came into the room, and in a flurry of excitement Ruby hurried towards the door. The two girls watched her eager exit with interest.

'Let's go and see.' Anna was first up, and Ellie quickly

followed. Every electric light had been turned on in readiness for the new doctor's arrival. Nothing Aunt Ruby did surprised them.

Outside, standing at the top of the semicircle of steps, they watched a fleet of motor vehicles being halted by a wiry-haired woman whose voice sounded much bigger than her diminutive stature.

'This way!' The woman's voice rang out across the vast acres of verdant lawns that surrounded Ashland Hall, while Ellie and Anna looked wide-eyed at each other, but said nothing, returning their gaze to the woman dressed in a military-style jacket and ankle-length skirt, her unruly rust-coloured hair appearing to fight to be freed from its captive fasteners. 'Stop!' Her booming instruction caused a flock of nesting birds to desert their post in the summer sunshine, and she held up the outstretched palm of her hand.

'Girls,' said Ruby, looking like she had just bagged the bargain of the age. 'I am thrilled to introduce you to Bea Tremaine. *Doctor* Bea Tremaine.'

'*Doctor* Tremaine?' Anna and Ellie chorused, knowing Ruby had kept that vital piece of information from them. They had heard about the female doctors who were now practising medicine, of course they had. But they had never actually met one of them.

'Aye, lassies,' Doctor Tremaine's brogue invited no further questioning when she asked, 'do we have any problems?'

Both nurses shook their heads and confirmed that they were quite happy with whatever had been arranged.

'I have handed over the Hall with immediate effect,' Ruby told the two girls, 'we will move into the lodge today.'

'We will be up and running as soon as we have everything in place,' Doctor Tremaine's springy red hair seemed to take on a life of its own as she talked, and after a hospitable cup of tea, the new lady doctor was eager to inspect each room for its suitability. 'I reckon we can take our key patients as soon as the Red Cross supplies start to arrive.'

'I also managed to obtain a whole new kitchen from Cunard,' Ruby said proudly. 'They were only too happy to donate.'

The two young nurses looked at each other, almost telepathically knowing that Ruby would never leave a fundraising empty-handed, especially when they saw supplies of bedding, towels, soap, cleaning requisites, buckets, mops, and many other cleaning accoutrements arriving, thanks to Ruby's many influential associates.

'I expect you girls are eager to get started immediately. And you will call me Doctor Bea,' Doctor Tremaine said expectantly.

'So soon?' Anna asked. 'We have not asked permission to leave Seaforth Military Hospital.'

'I have made all the arrangements,' said Doctor Bea, whose authority appeared to be matched by a fierce determination. 'Your things will be sent over. Matron is not expecting you back.'

Anna and Ellie accepted what was expected of them and enjoyed the hustle and bustle of the auxiliary hospital. They knew their services would obviously be needed here at Ashland Hall, and they were eager to get started in any capacity they could, to make sure the injured had a place to come home to.

In no time at all, the motor vehicles emptied, and the Hall was filled with volunteers who were clearing rooms and scrubbing floors, ready for hospital beds and other medical equipment.

'Isn't it exciting!' Ellie squeaked. 'I can't wait to see our first casualties.'

'Archie, come and meet Doctor Bea,' said Ruby, who turned to the doctor and said, 'you don't mind me calling you Doctor Bea?'

'I don't mind at all,' said Doctor Bea, who was suddenly more interested in Archie. Ruby bristled.

'Well now,' Doctor Bea stared into Archie's eyes, causing no end of consternation to Ruby. And after a moment of thought the doctor leaned forward and in hushed tones she said to Archie, 'I think we need a private word,'

Archie looked puzzled, and Ruby's deep-set frown told the two young nurses she was not happy with Doctor Bea's obvious attention to her husband.

* * *

The morning tore into the afternoon and Ashland Hall became a seething mass of bodies, busy in every room of the house. Men, women and even the local Boy Scouts and Girl Guides moved furniture, transported medication, lugged boxes of bandages, pills, and anything else that would be needed to supply a thirty-bed auxiliary hospital capable of receiving patients directly from ambulance trains.

People were rushing back and forth at breakneck speed, with barely a room finished before it was claimed by Doctor Bea and her upper-class band of Voluntary Aid Detachment nurses (or VADs as they were referred to) who, Ruby was reliably informed, had received three months training in The Royal Infirmary after attending twice a week for three hours at a time.

'At least they have had some training,' said Anna as wardrobes and beds were delivered, 'even if it is only the most rudimentary kind.'

Ellie nodded, directing volunteers.

'Where shall I put this?' Ruby asked, hugging a silver-crystal fruit bowl she had rescued from the Emporium.

'How about the table by the window, where it can be admired,' Anna suggested drily as she and Ellie manoeuvred a heavy wardrobe, walking it into the alcove in the drawing room.

'Of course,' said Ruby. 'It will catch the light there.' She ignored Anna's sardonic tone and, tilting her head to one side, stood back to admire her handiwork. 'Look how it sparkles... like a diamond...'

'Very nice,' Ellie managed. Wiping a trickle of perspiration from her brow, she was discouraged from saying something more unladylike by the timely interruption of a loud ran-tan on the front door.

'Who can it be, who has no respect for my door knocker?' Ruby asked. Her shapely bosom heaving with pride as she watched Archie leave the iron bed, which he was in the process of building, to go to answer the knock at the front door. Seeing that everybody was busy and being no observer of etiquette he did not mind answering his own front door. He looked very handsome dressed in his official police uniform, Ruby thought, knowing Archie had immediately volunteered to join the dwindling police force when the regulars went off to war.

'Right,' Mrs Hughes, the housekeeper called above the hubbub, 'it's about time everybody had a nice cup of tea.'

'Now, ladies,' Doctor Bea addressed the nurses gathered in the sunny room, knowing they all needed a short break. 'Let's all raise our cups and congratulate each other for all our hard work.' Then, more sombrely, she said, 'I have a feeling the hard work will continue for a long while yet.' Rallying, and not wanting the occasion to descend into gloom, she added, 'But we will meet it with strength and fortitude.'

'Strength and fortitude,' the volunteer nurses, suffragists before the war, all chorused, raising their cups high in the air. 'A toast to our heroes, marching through foreign fields, fighting for each and every one of us.'

As the room descended into unladylike whoops and cheers of encouragement, Anna's thought turned, as always, to Ned, who was held in that place she liked to ~~think of~~ as the harbour of tranquillity – her heart. A letter had arrived this morning, but she had not had time to read it yet, and it was burning a hole in her pale blue pocket. But her thoughts were not allowed to linger.

Ruby was pleased to see the front drawing room was ready for the first batch of casualties; gone was the fine furniture, which had been stored securely in the stables, the horses having been donated to the cause.

'So much work has been done to the house since you and Archie decided to turn it into an auxiliary hospital.' Anna smiled, knowing Aunt Ruby loved this huge room which looked out on to the shore, understanding the servicemen needed it far more than she did.

'The lodge on the other side of the lake has plenty of room for us,' Ruby said.

* * *

Ashland Hall was running efficiently under the blunt, plain-speaking and forthright Doctor Bea, who had worked mainly in the women's hospital and in paediatrics, given that, in her words, the backward-looking male doctors – even in this enlightened age – believed that women should sit still and behave themselves, not rampage into the Houses of Parliament and throw rotten tomatoes at ministers who refused to give women the vote.

However, she later told Ruby, all that had been put to one side while hostilities were the order of the day and she promised to concentrate on the patients under her care. Doctor Bea also made it clear she did not want any bad reports of hysterical girls spreading bloodcurdling rumours.

Anna knew that since the beginning of the war, there had

been stories of the enemy sneaking up the Mersey Estuary from the Irish Channel. Luckily, none had managed to get here yet.

'Will there be any answer, Sir?' asked the telegram girl who put the dreaded communication into Archie's capable hand. Archie looked at the telegram and invited the girl inside. His voice low and solemn when he asked her to wait a moment; unsure if there would be an answer. Walking back into the drawing room, he saw the two nurses engaged in making perfect envelope corners on a new hospital bed.

Dusting her hands, Anna was about to say something when she noticed the telegram in Archie's hand. And her heart flipped. A telegram was not a good sign in wartime.

Archie headed straight towards her and Anna resisted the urge to run from the room. She must be strong even though dreading the expected bad news to come, especially when the Navy were undergoing such heavy fighting to protect the Grand Fleet from U-boats.

Archie's face was grim as the words slipped from her lips in a whisper.

'Please, Lord. No.' Her darling, she could not bear the thought that she may never see him again... 'Not my Ned?'

'I'm afraid this is for you, Ellie,' Archie's words hung in the air as he handed her the telegram, while Anna remained still and silent, feeling a keen sense of shame that her first reaction to Ellie's news was relief.

Ellie's eyes went from one to the other in the room. Unasked questions and muddled thoughts took the place of good humour, which she and Anna had shared moments earlier.

As she took the dreaded telegram, her hands visibly shook as time seemed to stop still. Raw fear prickled Ellie's scalp, and needing to know what the message contained, yet dreading the news, she took a deep breath, gathering as much courage as she could before ripping open the telegram. A small, almost inaudible gasp escaped as her hands flew to her lips. Her eyes scanning the words, over and over again.

'German Zeppelins raided the East Coast,' she whispered. Looking up, her dark eyes, so like Ruby's, looked dazed, as if taking in nothing of what she saw. Her posture stiffened and she closed her eyes. 'My father has been killed in a Zeppelin raid.'

'Oh, my poor girl,' Ruby said, taking Ellie in her arms, her racing heart palpable. It was no secret to any of them that Ruby did not suffer Giles Harrington gladly. However, Ellie's feelings mattered a great deal. She could not bear to see her so upset. 'My poor, poor, girl.'

'Poor Mama,' said Ellie, her stoic eyes wide with unshed tears, 'she will be all alone. I must leave to be with her.'

'Archie,' Ruby said, taking immediate charge of the situation. Her usual level-headed pragmatism that saw her through so many testing times kicked in, and her dark eyes softened. 'When the funeral is over, May must come back home. Where she belongs.'

Archie gave a brief message to the telegram girl that would tell May they would be with her soon. When he closed the door, about to return to the front room, Archie was stopped by Doctor Bea. Again, she silently stared at him, making Archie feel extremely uncomfortable.

'How long have you suffered from decreased vision?' Her voice lowered and Archie looked round quickly to make sure Ruby was not in the vicinity to hear.

'I don't know what you mean,' Archie said, his body rigid as he squinted in the half-light of the hallway, trying to focus on the small doctor whose presence seemed to fill the house from the first time she entered Ashland Hall.

'The milky lens of your eyes tells me you have something called cataracts.' Doctor Bea did not rein in her words. 'And given the opaqueness, I would say they are ripe for removal.'

'You will do no such thing,' said Archie, 'I am not having anybody...'

'Let alone a woman...' Doctor Bea had heard the expression often.

'That is not what I was going to say,' Archie was no stranger to strong-minded women. 'I have it on good authority that I am losing my sight which is why I can't defend my country.'

'Whoever told you such a thing is a fool,' Doctor Bea sounded impatient and enraged. 'I know an excellent eye surgeon who has done brilliant work with men who have been injured in battle.'

'Surely, given these worrying times, his time will be taken up with more urgent matters.'

'I have successfully accompanied him in his many operations, I know what to do. If he is unavailable, I will remove them myself.'

'What if it goes wrong?' asked Archie. He was not worried for himself, although the procedure was not something he would willingly undergo if he had the choice, but he did worry about the effect his blindness would have on Ruby. 'I do not want my wife worried over this.'

'The worst thing is to do nothing,' she said, 'but you must inform your wife. There is no need for you to suffer. We will do it as soon as we have furnished the operating theatre,' said Doctor Bea, who had taken over the morning room because the light was better there. 'Or first thing tomorrow morning, whichever is soonest.'

'Will I be able to see straight away?' Archie asked.

'Your eyes will be covered to allow them to heal,' said the doctor. 'Then, after about six weeks or so, you will be able to do menial tasks until they are fully healed.'

'We have just learned of a death in the family,' Archie explained, 'I will be taking Ruby and my niece to Scarborough. Ellie's father was killed, and we will be bringing Ruby's sister back to the lodge.'

'In that case, we will perform the operation when you come back home. Help is at hand when you return.' Doctor Bea was sympathetic, but she sounded sterner when she said, 'A fully sighted policeman is of much more value than one half-blind. You will wear thick-lensed spectacles thereafter.'

'A small price to pay, don't you think?' said Archie, relieved that something could be done, knowing the hard part was telling his wife.

Doctor Bea nodded, setting in motion the confusion of springy curls.

7

JULY 1916

Anna and Ruby were at the Charity Shop by the docks, to drop off blankets which had been donated by the Corby Townswomen's Guild.

'I can't see any let-up,' Anna said. 'Not if the incoming casualties are anything to go by.' The war was getting worse.

'I doubt the war will be over by this time next year, either,' Lottie said. 'Who do they think they are kidding?'

'We will just have to wait and see,' Izzy answered. Glad her other son was now doing his duty, like his brother, instead of loitering round street corners with some of those other layabouts. Jerky had no choice when subscription was brought in, he had to take the King's shilling or go back to jail.

'The authorities are talking out of their backsides,' said Lottie, who had become embittered by her separation from her beloved *Jerry* and was in no mood to be placated. In fact, if she was honest, she wasn't in the mood for anything. She was so tired. The first thing she did each morning was throw her guts up in the lavatory, and the thought of a cup of tea made her feel worse.

'I heard tell the enemy was on its way over here.' Lottie said, trying to take her mind off her nervous stomach. She blamed everything on the war and the rumours that were flying round like litter on the wind. 'I heard tell the Huns were coming over in the middle of the night and women and children are being murdered in their beds.'

'It's best that you ignore scaremongering stories like that, Lottie,' said Anna, working at her efficient best to allay the wild rumours going round when she noticed wide-eyed customers hanging on to every word. Everybody had someone fighting in Flanders Fields and hearsay could become fact in the blink of an eye.

'Some of those reports are so outrageously ridiculous, I wonder how any sane-minded person could possibly believe them to be true.' Anna said knowing her Ned was doing his very best to stop the marauding enemy from storming up the dock road and ravishing any passing female. However, there were women like Lottie who believed every word. 'Are you sickening for something, Lottie,' Anna asked, 'you look a bit peaky.'

'I'm fine,' Lottie said with a shrug, 'just worry I suppose.' But she knew it was more than that. She hadn't 'seen' her monthly visitors since Jerky got out of prison in May, and it was almost the end of July.

* * *

Back at Ashland, Ruby, in her element with the busy bustle, giving out cups of tea and chatting to the patients. And Anna's cheerful performance back on the ward was a tribute to the courage these men had shown. How long she could keep up the charade, she did not know. She would have to find courage, too.

Ruby was not going to be pleased that she had volunteered to go overseas. She had to find her brother, Sam.

'She will go mad,' Ellie's eyes were glassy-bright with excitement. 'We will have to sneak out under the cover of darkness.' But there was no time to stand around engaging in idle gossip, They were kept busy with incoming casualties.

Later that evening they were dispatched to Aintree train station to pick up men from all over Great Britain: English, Irish, Scottish and Welshmen whose fierce pride had taken them to the killing fields and returned them home to recover, and after long talks with some of the young soldiers who had joined up to escape grinding poverty, they learned that some were taken from the workhouse to build the armies needed to fight the enemy. While many men had no choice but to go off to war, even before subscription came into force. They were obliged to accept the King's shilling to put bread on the table. Now they were coming back with limbs missing.

Some patients had been taken off the troop train at Aintree and put in an ambulance for Ashland Auxiliary Hospital, while others received necessary medical treatment at the First Western hospital.

'We'll soon have you in a nice comfy bed, soldier,' Ellie had said, and roared with laughter when one of the cheeky sods asked if she would care to join him. Nothing fazed Ellie, thought Anna.

'We went in the hope of a steady wage to feed our family, Nurse,' one man told Anna, 'but any hope of work is hindered now. Who is going to employ a man with half a leg and only one good arm?'

These poor men... Tired, bedraggled and looking less like conquering heroes than it was possible to imagine, tore at Anna's heart. Their arrival had drawn a crowd, as civilians gathered on the bridge at Aintree station to watch the wounded being stretchered to the ambulances. The crowd was so large, the ambulances had difficulty negotiating the road and had to be driven very carefully and slowly, allowing the throng of sympathetic devotees to follow at a pace to the gates of the First Western Hospital at Fazakerley.

Some wanted to catch a glimpse of the heroes returning from epic battles at Mons, Ypres and those who had fought at Marne. Places made famous by headlines in the local and national newspapers and Anna recalled some mothers pleading for information, wanting to know of their loved ones still fighting on the battlefields.

Some of the officers were transferred to Ashland Hall to recuperate, while nurses watching from sash windows pulled up high, waited for their new charges to arrive.

'This is a bit of all right, hey George?' an injured corporal, brought in with his commanding officer, said to the general in the opposite bed, who, deaf as a post after being too close to an exploding shell, did not answer. But his spirits were raised when he saw the ballroom was now lined with narrow iron beds organised in perfect rows a wall of glazed doors opening out onto the garden.

'Are we doing the right thing?' Anna asked Ellie. 'Patching up men to return them to the lion's cage. It must be terrifying for them.'

'They know what they are going back to,' Ellie answered, 'and that must be so much worse.' Reports in the newspaper told them the action was no easier at sea either, with ships torpedoed so food could not get to this country. 'The enemy are certain they will starve us into submission, according to the latest reports.'

'It's being so cheerful that keeps you going, Ellie,' Anna snapped. She did not want to hear about the fighting at sea. They had lost thousands of men, during the Battle of Jutland. She took a deep breath. The Royal Navy managed to scare off the Hun and their navy had not left enemy harbour since. Anna immediately regretted her retort. And she felt an icy shiver run through her, even though the room was warm.

8

May was glad her husband's funeral, paid for by the church, had commenced before Ruby, Archie and Ellie arrived in Scarborough. It was one less humiliation she had had to suffer because of Giles's underhand dealings.

'Penny for them?' Ellie asked seeing her deep in thought.

May, smiled, initially she felt sorry Ellie had missed the funeral, but was grateful she did not have to endure the hypocrisy of the sparse ceremony, knowing Giles rarely endeared himself to his parishioners.

Since she received the telegram, Ellie had had no time to grieve and if she was being honest, she had no wish to. The funeral had taken place in her father's church in Scarborough and her mother was now effectively homeless, because the rectory they lived in had been tied to her father's work with the church. Even though her father's death had little effect upon her, given that he had paid her so little attention other than to berate her for some minor misdeed, Ellie was surprised at how calmly her mother had actually taken the death.

'There is something I need to discuss with you in private after dinner,' May told her daughter quietly. Her husband's death had thrown light onto the murky extent his gambling debts had sank their money.

'He left me with nothing,' May told Ellie when they were alone, 'except a huge amount of debt. No home. No money. I am at the mercy of creditors!'

Ellie had never felt unhappier for her poor mother. The rectory, cold even though the day was warm, was sparse even by her father's frugal standards.

'I do not own one stick of furniture,' May told her, 'Giles sold everything. My jewellery, even the clothes in my closet.' She sat down heavily on a straight-backed chair, as if the necessity to stand was too great to bear. Lowering her head, May removed the wedding ring, which on closer inspection, Ellie could see had made her finger turn green, and she knew that her father's devout piety was a sham, a lie he had used as a stick to beat her mother with.

'Oh Mama,' Ellie cried, her throat tightening. She had grown accustomed to Aunt Ruby's lavish lifestyle without giving a second thought to her mother's silent distress. 'You are far braver than I could ever imagine.'

May seemed to brighten at her words, and her lips stretched to a gentle smile that did not reach her eyes. 'Two sisters who were closer than close, were prised apart by a controlling man who had no thoughts for anybody except himself.' May said, her voice full of regret.

'Because maybe, I was too wrapped up in my own wants and needs,' Ruby said from the doorway. Neither May nor Ellie had heard her approach. 'I neglected the one person who shared the same fears and worries I had myself.'

'No,' May said, feeling stronger now, 'I was old enough to know better.'

'You were lonely,' Ruby said, glad they had missed the funeral. 'I see that now, and you were ripe for Giles Harrington's plucking. He knew what he was doing.' Ruby ventured into the room not knowing if she would be welcomed or turned away. But she was made of stern stuff. She could handle everything life threw at her because she had a good, honest man by her side. 'Giles played the long game, his most exquisite gamble. The one that would see him through all the years of Ellie's rearing.'

'You are right,' May said, 'and if truth be told, I knew it from the moment I married him. Everything fell into place for Giles. A loveless marriage. My inability to have children of my own. The idea that one day Ashland Hall and everything that went with it would be his in all but name.'

'May!' Ruby stepped forward, knowing her sister had said more than enough. 'You are tired and distraught; you don't know what you're saying. You need to lie down before we make our way back home.'

'I know the whole story,' Ellie's voice was low and measured. 'Mama told me everything when I was young.'

Ruby felt as if she had been slapped in the face, she was stunned. 'But you never said a word.' The air was being sucked out of her. And not for the first time.

'I'm glad Giles was not my father,' Ellie said, 'and I love Mama dearly. I didn't know you personally. But felt I did by the hundreds of stories Mama told me as I grew up.' Tears began to form in Ellie's eyes. 'That day. When I came to tell you about the reading of Grandpa's Will, I did not know if you and Archie would turn me away or welcome me with open arms...' She gave a watery smile. 'Thankfully, Mama had told me so much about you I *knew* in my heart that you would not let me go a second time.'

'My darling girl,' said Ruby, 'I did not want to lose you the first time.'

When May returned to the Lodge at Ashland Hall, she was the one who played hostess to Ruby, Archie, Ellie and Anna. In this time of so much strife, she had never felt happier. They were all one big happy family once again.

'I am so glad the truth is out about my father's behaviour and my mother's circumstances, and we can put the past behind us,' Ellie told Anna when they were on duty in the small hours of the night. However, she did not tell Anna that Ruby, and not May, was her mother.

'Mama is thriving under Ruby's lovingly protective, and sometimes smothering, wing.'

'I think Ruby's mothering has now been transferred to Archie since his eye operation.' Anna gave a low, contented laugh.

Doctor Bea had worked a miracle with Archie's sight, but Ruby made sure the good doctor's rules were followed to the letter, much to Archie's frustration when Ruby would read him a section of *Pride and Prejudice* when he would far rather hear her read the latest news from The Front.

'No, Archie,' Ruby had said, 'Doctor Bea said you are not to get excited.'

'Well, I can assure you,' Archie said under his breath, 'there is not much chance of that.'

'Did you say something, Archie?' Ruby asked. Archie had gone through the whole procedure without even telling her, until after the deed was done.

'No, dear,' Archie said, 'I think I heard May calling.'

'She promised she would accompany me to the tank fundraising this afternoon. You don't mind do you, Archie?'

'Not at all,' said Archie. He loved Ruby with all his heart and soul, but when she had a mission of mercy, she threw herself in entirely. It could get a bit tiring. 'I was going to have a snooze anyway.'

'Good thinking, Archie. I will leave you in peace.'

* * *

'If I had known Archie was going blind, I would never have depended upon him so much, or let him drive the motorcar, or even his bicycle.'

'I think that was the notion, Ruby dear,' May said, casting off a new line of boot socks for the Royal Navy. Her time at Ashland Lodge had renewed her spirits and with her sister's support, she had grown stronger than she had been for years and much more inclined to share her thoughts. 'You know Archie isn't one to make a fuss.'

'Isn't it wonderful you can speak so freely these days,' Ruby's casual tone hid her delight at having her sister back in the fold. She had forgotten the sometimes spiky but fundamentally loving exchanges they both had shared from childhood, and Ruby was enjoying her sister's company enormously.

'Archie will be having his bandages removed today,' said Ellie, whose little bursts of joy echoed the feeling of everybody, that May was back where she belonged, albeit in the Lodge, something Giles Harrington would never have considered when he was alive. She never thought of him as 'Father' any more and no longer felt the stab of guilt she once had when she realised she did not love him, and she never had. Shuddering, Ellie remembered the times when he ordered her mother to sit in the wings and say nothing.

* * *

'I will go and read the newspaper to Archie over tea,' said Ruby when she got back from another successful fundraiser.

'Tell him I will pop in later,' said May, whose eyes now sparkled with the light Ruby had been so used to seeing, and Ruby smiled, patting her hand, knowing her sister could enjoy a life of her own choosing. Instead of meekly following in the long shadow of a greedy, overbearing husband.

When Ruby sat at her husband's bedside, she noticed the evening newspaper, obviously brought in by one of the orderlies, the old retainers who were too old or frail to join up and were as loyal to herself and Archie as they had been to her father. Picking up the newspaper, Ruby gasped in shock when she saw the headlines telling them of the fierce fighting in the North Sea.

Ned would surely have been involved in The Battle of Jutland. The huge-scale clash of battleships between the Royal Navy's Grand Fleet and the German High Seas Fleet. Ned was never far from everybody's thoughts, and she knew he was as vulnerable as any man on the front line. Not that he could tell her of course.

9

Izzy was shocked that Lottie had handed in her notice.

'Where are you going?' Izzy asked when she saw Lottie packing a cardboard suitcase.

'I don't know,' Lottie answered, 'all Jerry would say was that it is a surprise.' She trusted him and believed he was going to change her life forever.

Lottie was elated when she said her goodbyes to Izzy and left the charity shop for her biggest adventure yet. Dreams of bringing a new life into a different town filled her head and sustained her as seven o'clock came and went. She paced up and down the platform, Jerry could not leave her like this. She was expecting his child.

Trains came in and went back out again. Whistles blew and smoke filled the air. Servicemen from the troop trains were being transported to the ports. Most of them were in their twenties and thirties; but some were just boys in late teens.

Officially, they were meant to be nineteen to be sent overseas to fight, but obviously, given the young faces and bodies as yet not fully grown, some had lied about their age. Many had joined up in a fervour of patriotism with their pals or had shown up at the police station to enlist after being shamed with a white feather.

Eight o'clock... Something must have happened. She worried. *He has obviously had an accident,* Lottie thought as she sat on the bench to ease her weary legs, watching travellers depart and servicemen kiss their sweetheart's goodbye.

Nine o'clock... She was more anxious now. Lottie did not feel the keen desperation of a jilted bride. *Jerry loves me.* She never doubted him. Of course, he would wed her.

* * *

Anna nudged Ellie with her elbow and nodded to the forlorn-looking girl sitting on the bench on the other side of Lime Street Station, her suitcase at her feet.

'Isn't that Lottie, over there?' Anna asked, smart in her nurse's uniform like Ellie, dressed in a similar fashion as they waited for the troop train to come in.

She peered across the platform and nodded. 'She told me she was due to meet her chap here at seven o'clock.'

'Oh no,' Anna wilted, 'you mean Jerky Woods?'

'That's the fellow,' said Ellie. 'She told Ruby she was leaving the charity shop with immediate effect. Ruby was not impressed; I can tell you.'

'I am not surprised,' Anna replied as Ellie pushed her handbag up her arm, her gaze running the length of the platform, watching for the troop train.

'Excuse me, ladies,' said the doddery porter, 'do you know that young lady?'

Anna and Ellie nodded.

'You say she is waiting for her young man?'

They nodded again.

'If I'm not mistaken, he was taken by the military police earlier. Just before the young lady arrived.'

'Oh no,' Anna said, 'let's go over and speak to her, we have a few more minutes before the troop train comes in.'

'I think something must have happened to Jerry,' Lottie uttered when Anna and Ellie approached her. 'I was supposed to meet him here at seven o'clock.'

'The porter told us he had to leave suddenly. The military police took him,' said Ellie.

'He must be going overseas, if the officers came to escort him,' Lottie said, trying to hide the fact that she and Jerry where planning to run away.

'You must be so proud,' Ellie said, avoiding the truth that the porter had seen Woods wriggle like a worm on a hook when the military police caught up with him, but for as much as he jerked and pulled himself from their clutches, Jerky Woods did not live up to his name that time, and thrashed like a fish on a hook in his unwillingness to serve his country in any capacity.

* * *

'I must go back and face Izzy in the charity shop,' Lottie said, knowing she had been warned. She had been naïve where Jerry was concerned because she believed every word he said.

'Let's get you back, we pass the charity shop on the way to Ashland Hall so we can drop you off,' Anna said gently, as Lottie, head bowed, looked so lost and pitiful.

'We will not leave you stranded in a train station,' Ellie joined in and Anna nodded. She would not see her one-time neighbour on the streets. 'But we need to wait for the next train to meet the wounded troops who are to go to Ashland first.'

Heartbroken, Lottie told Anna the whole sorry tale on the

journey back to the flat over the shops, where Izzy took the sobbing girl in her arms and assured her everything was going to be fine. Izzy sighed and thanked the two nurses.

'Poor Lottie, I'll see she gets the care she needs,' she said as the two nurses made their way downstairs to the front door and the waiting ambulance. 'She is so gullible where that whipper-snapper is concerned.'

After they had left Izzy sat Lottie down, gave her a bowl of beef broth and a slice of fresh crusty bread and plenty of sympathy for the heartbreak her son had brought on this poor girl, who had so much going for her before Jerky came and ruined her.

'So, the authorities caught up with him, yet again,' Izzy said to herself after she had settled Lottie into her own bed. She had no sympathy for her eldest lad who, in her eyes, didn't have the sense he was born with. Always looking out for himself, like his father. And look where that had got Splinter.' Izzy was glad she was stronger now and in a position to help the poor motherless girl who'd had her head turned by her unscrupulous son. She should have been proud he was going to do his bit for his country, like Nipper, but the difference being was, Nipper joined up of his own free will, while Jerky was taken kicking and protesting.

'Izzy doesn't deserve a son like him,' Anna told Ellie, recalling the days, long gone, when he would terrify her with his boyish taunts and his suggestive remarks until Ned put him in his place. Jerky Woods was so different from his younger brother who, like his mother, always tried to do the right thing, no matter what. 'And Lottie certainly deserves a better husband.'

'What chance does she stand now?' asked Ellie wiping her

forehead with a lace handkerchief as the clammy July heat seemed to rise from the pavement. 'Given her predicament, she is in no position to pick and choose. But it's poor Izzy I feel sorry for, she will be so worried when she reads this morning's newspaper,'

'Why, what's happened?' Anna asked, taking the paper from Ellie that told them over nineteen thousand men had been killed on the first day of the Battle of the Somme. What the newspaper did not tell them was that the Accrington Pals had been effectively wiped out in the first few minutes of the battle.

10

The second day of the Battle of the Somme saw Nipper Woods sitting alone in one of the trenches that he believed stretched from the English Channel to Switzerland. The end of the pencil he was chewing had turned into a wet pulp of wood and every now and then he spat out a splinter, his mind searching for something to write and tell his mother about.

He knew he couldn't tell her that the war was not going well and large parts of France and Belgium were still under German occupation. It would never get past the censors. Nor the fact that Germany's modern weapons made killing on a grand scale more possible than ever.

The allies had agreed to join a summer offensive and the area they chose to launch their attack was this twenty-six-mile stretch of the Western Front in Northern France by the River Somme. That's what he would say:

Dear Ma,

I hope this letter finds you well. I am in good spirits as we have now moved from the muddy trench to some lush green pasture, where the ground is nice and dry, and the smell of chamomile fills the air with its apple scent. Some of the lads boil the chamomile in water and drink it like tea. They say it helps them sleep, but you won't catch me pandering to those daft ideas.

I did as you asked and told the Padre the truth about only being sixteen and you'll never guess, he said I had the heart of a lion, Ma.

Just to let you know there was a bit of a skirmish yesterday, and so there aren't as many tea-drinkers left but, being an agile lad who had to dodge his older brother many a time, I had enough nous to get out of the way of any strays being chucked my way.

See you when I get home, Ma. Look after yourself.

Your ever-loving son,

Nipper xxx

* * *

'I got a letter!' Izzy, behind the high pawnshop counter, waved the envelope in the air and the line of waiting women on the other side nodded, bunching up to hear her exciting news. 'Surprised the life out of me, I can tell you,' Izzy proclaimed, laughing as she spoke. 'I didn't know he could read and write.'

'He's a lovely lad, your Nipper,' said a woman from Ariel Street, 'he used to carry my shopping back from the market. Not like...' She stopped abruptly. No mother wanted to hear bad of her son, even if he was a badd'n.

'Yes, Missus?' Izzy said sharply. 'Not like who?' She knew nobody had time for her eldest lad, because he refused to go and fight like their boys did. But she would be a poor mother if she didn't stick up for her own.

'Nobody,' said the customer, 'I wasn't gonna say nothing about one of yours.'

'Glad to hear it,' said Izzy. 'I'd be so disappointed if the stuff you're hocking wasn't up to snuff.' She was not going to enlighten this lot that Jerky had joined up and was, at that moment, training out in Litherland.

'My sheets were all washed and ironed first thing this morning,' the woman countered, but Izzy was having none of her backchat. She was miffed.

'That's as may be,' she said, lifting her chin, 'but I'm the one who decides on the price.' She went about her business examining the wares that local women were here to hock, in the hope that they would get enough money to see them through to their old man's payday.

Who'd have thought it? Izzy considered the question that asked how she had arrived at such an exalted position – at her age, and she knew it was all thanks to Ruby and Archie Swift.

'When I finish here,' she said proudly 'I am going to go straight home and write my Nipper a nice long letter...'

'If your name is on the bullet, it will find you,' Nipper said to nobody in particular, 'so there ain't no point worrying, is there? Like the song says, what's the use?' He shrugged, accepting his fate, and resting his spade on his shoulder, he joined the line of men digging trenches in the soft mud and laying telephone wires. All German lines of communication had been cut the day before and he was feeling invincible.

'Fancy a game of cricket, anyone?' an officer asked when they finished digging and were told that they would not be going to the Front today because of the heavy rain.

'Oh, I see,' said Nipper, 'rain can stop the war, Sir, but it can't stop a game of cricket.'

'Spot on, Private Woods,' said the Lieutenant Commander

Rupert Bray, who had no wish to enlighten the young lad that there were rumours over twenty thousand men were killed at the Somme in the first hour of yesterday's assault to capture German trenches. Armed only with rifles and bayonets, the British soldiers were no match for the hail of heavy machine-gun fire that the enemy issued in the final insult to over a third of the advancing troops.

* * *

By the end of July, the casualty list had run into many thousands. Nipper and his unit had been waiting since the beginning of the month for orders to move forward and the waiting around was stretching some nerves to breaking point.

The sun was high in the pewter sky and the nearby fields were held in the glorious arc of a rainbow after a thunderstorm that was barely heard above the bombardment on the other side of the woods. Nipper imagined he could smell the faintest scent of chamomile and lavender. Then, as the perfume grew stronger, filling the rain-soaked fields, he watched the commander coming towards them and the whole battalion seemed to hold their breath. In minutes, the order came.

'Pack up, Men. We are moving to a new house,' Lieutenant Commander Rupert Bray ordered, and, with military precision, the trench was emptied of everything the soldiers would need for the next part of the operation to near the Front Line and the final push, to overtake the German trenches.

Ten kilometres along the road, Nipper saw wounded men being put onto stretchers by women.

Women? He was seeing things. He must be. Women couldn't carry men on stretchers!

'I've never seen the like!' Nipper watched two female medics dressed in military-style jackets and ankle-length skirts. And they were running towards a mobile hospital. The ambulance, with its huge red cross on the side, was taking injured men on board to be looked after by more women.

As they marched further on, Nipper saw more soldiers. They were lying so still he was sure they were already dead. A bit further still and he saw men without limbs, without faces, injuries that were impossible to survive. His stomach churned.

'Jesus. Mary and J...' He didn't have time to finish his sentence. Nipper didn't feel the mortar bomb blast that lifted his body from the ground.

11

'Don't worry, Bud, I've got ya.' The voice sounded American. But Nipper Woods knew he must be confused. The United States hadn't joined the party. 'You're one of the lucky ones, Soldier,' the voice told him as every bone in his body felt like it had been smashed with a tank driven by a malicious giant. Every muscle screamed, contracting and twisting in pain. He didn't know where he had been hit. He didn't know how bad his injuries were. Nobody would tell him. When he tried to speak, no sound came. 'You're one lucky son-of-a-gun, soldier. You bagged yourself a Blighty one, and I'm the guy who has the power to send you home. Yessir, you are one lucky son-of-a-gun.'

Nipper didn't feel lucky as the flap of canvas slapped his face. This must be the casualty tent, he thought, listening to the sound of nurses and doctors shouting orders.

'Bag him, tag him and get the next one on the table!' Nipper heard an impatient male voice issue orders with the same speed as one of those Vickers machine guns. Although he could see nothing for the mud that had glued his eyes closed when he fell into the shell hole and had now dried. What the hell had he been thinking of to sign up for this lot?

Mam will have a fit of conniptions when she gets the news. Nipper, thinking his days were numbered, tried to open his mouth, but his lips seemed to be glued shut. *Sorry Mam. I didn't mean to cause you this heartache.* He just wanted her to have a son to be proud of.

Someone lifted his identity disc, known to all as a dog-tag, which bore his name, rank, number, regiment and religious denomination. 'Liverpool Pals?' said the medic, 'That's my old hometown.'

'American?' Nipper could barely sound the word through the mud-baked grit in his mouth.

'Canadian,' said the medic, 'but Scouse runs through my veins. Do me a favour, Soldier, if they send you back to Liverpool, you tell the folks back home that Sam Cassidy said Hi.' Sam hoped that someone back in Liverpool might remember him, although he had no family there now, believing his sister Anna to have died of pneumonia before he was sent as an orphan to Canada.

Although Nipper could not see the medic, he remembered a lad called Sam Cassidy from Queen Street. How could he forget. That Christmas Eve, when the fire took most of the Cassidy family, would live with Nipper for the rest of his life.

'We found you hanging on a barbed wire fence, Soldier, you've breathed in a bit of gas and it's irritating your eyes,' said Sam as the stretcher was put on a hard surface, which Nipper supposed was the floor or a table. 'Lord only knows how you managed to climb out of that mud hole and find your way into no-man's land.' Sam Cassidy deliberately kept his tone upbeat, knowing the patient needed to be reassured when they had such severe injuries. 'But you can't keep a good man down, so I reckon you're going to be fine... Just, fine.'

Nipper didn't feel fine.

'This place has been manic for days,' Sam Cassidy said conversationally. 'The medics are sending patients to England as soon as possible, so they can get new patients in and fix them up. It's been one long continuous convoy in and out.'

Nipper did not know how long he had been stranded on the barbed bush that trapped him in its steely grip in no-man's land. All he could remember was the lances of stabbing pain shooting through his leg when he regained consciousness. Struggling to disentangle himself from the barbed wire only caused more pain, ripping his hands to a shredded mass of flesh. In the end he must have passed out again, barely still alive when they scraped him up and transported him to the casualty tent three miles back from the front line.

A shot of morphine gave him the first decent sleep he had experienced since he got to France.

When he woke sometime later, the dim light of a paraffin lamp hurt his eyes.

'They will be sore for a while, that mud dried like cement on your face, we will cover them with a bandage to help them heal,' a deep male voice told Nipper as a cool bandage was wrapped round his head, covering his eyes.

Taking the opportunity to sleep, he drifted off once more and only woke when he felt himself being moved again. His lips and ears were being washed, and then he heard the sound of gulls' cry. He flinched as the bird's cry seemed to be right on top of him.

'I imagine the mud made you partially deaf, but we have most of it out of your ears now, soldier.'

Nipper could feel the adrenalin course through his veins when the stretcher he was lying on tilted forward, and from the sound of boots on wood, he realised he was being carried up a gangplank.

'Don't worry, soldier, you are going back to Blighty on the hospital ship tonight.'

Nipper could not believe it. He was alive and he was going home!

* * *

Accustomed to the relentless rumble of bombardment, the boom of explosions and the dying groans of pals, Nipper could now hear only the gentle thrum of the ambulance engine rumbling through quiet roads and had no idea where he was. For months, he had known only the rural countryside of France and Flanders, where every living thing had been trampled and obliterated into the mud and trenches and shell holes. Being injured was a blessing, he thought. At least it got him off the battleground.

A Blighty wound allowed him to escape the death and destruction of war, but he did not allow his thoughts to drift to what the future had in store for him. Ignoring the nagging familiarity of soldiers whose injuries brought a new kind of terror. Fear for the future.

The prospect of never walking or never working again. The probability of unending pain, of lasting disfigurement. But for Nipper, the fact that he was alive was a godsend he could not ignore, for his mother's sake.

* * *

Sam Cassidy was squatting in an eight-feet deep trench after patching up another poor soul. Stopping only for a quick smoke, he thought about what he would write to his girl, Millie. He wanted to tell her how much he loved and missed her, and how he feared for her now that she had volunteered to join the hospital ship *Gigantic*.

But he could not write the words. He could not build up her hope that their relationship could be anything more, even though he cared for her in a way he had never cared for anybody else in his life. He was scared to lose her, petrified. But she would never understand his need to get back to Liverpool and see the faces and the places he had left behind and try to get some answers as to how and why his family died that Christmas Eve six years ago. And his sister, Anna died later in hospital after trying to save them. His whole family wiped out.

If truth be told, that was only one of the reasons, he didn't fear this war, although he did have a healthy distrust of those new tanks they were now using, and the power that went behind them.

He was more scared of his strong feelings for Millie, and whether she would want nothing to do with him when he told her he was not going back to Canada when the war was over. He intended to go back home to Liverpool and find out the truth. The need to know had sustained him over the years and had coloured his actions. Spurred him on to join the battlefield with his countrymen on both sides, English and Canadian. And made him proud to do his bit.

Only then would he be able to relax and raise a family, live a good life... But he could not bear the thought of settling down with any other girl except the pretty Canadian nurse whose father saved him all those years ago when he was on the brink of death. Because it was Millie who gave him the strength to believe life was good, and he grew strong again.

What if he could persuade Millie to set up home in Liverpool? he wondered. Would she? Could she leave everything she had ever known to be by his side? Sam questioned how he could he put his thoughts into words when they made no sense to him?

Millie would never leave Canada. Why would she leave a clean, vibrant country, for the dirt and smoke of a port city that got into your soul and never let go?

After a week at the busy end of intense fighting, Sam went down the line to pick up more casualties from the trenches that had been transformed from tranquil forests and bountiful farmers' fields into a wilderness of spent iron and rotting corpses that came to be called the Western Front.

The temporary ditches became multiple lines of dugouts, fortified with sandbag parapets, barbed wire and heavy Vickers machine-guns on tripods. Within these underground cities, their only means of relaxation was to recline into a dugout depression carved into the side of the trench, known as a funk hole, which was also a space for soldiers to keep out of the way of busy medics with stretchers, who came to collect the wounded.

'Want a smoke?' he asked when his pal, Alfie, finished bandaging the hand of another soldier.

Alfie was another Home Boy who had joined the Canadian Medical Corps when war broke out and shared his trench, called *Scotty Road* by its inhabitants, because that was where most of them came from.

Alfie shook his head and sat down beside Sam, tipping his tin hat to the back of his head, and closing his eyes against the glare of the afternoon sunshine. 'I'm trying to get a tan before we finish this holiday,' said Alfie, always the joker. 'Can't go home to the missus looking like a bottle of milk.'

'I don't think she'll care what you look like,' Sam smiled. 'Although, you might want to get a bit of a wash.'

'I'll book meself into the *Hotel Du Luxe*, have a bath and a shave – she won't be able to keep her hands off me.'

'That's the spirit, Alfie, old son,' Sam said, enjoying the respite. After last night's heavy bombardment, the casualties came thick and fast. There was no let-up until first light and even now there was still the odd distant boom in the background.

'I don't think I'll come back here for my holidays, next year,' said Alfie, 'it's a bit noisy.'

'You can say that again,' Sam agreed, drawing in a lungful of nicotine and flicking the butt of the cigarette onto the lime-strewn floor, grinding it out with the heel of his boot.

'Here, who was that pretty little blonde I saw you talking to last night?' Alfie asked and Sam could feel the heat rise in the trench. He turned to his oppo.

'Don't you go getting any ideas in that direction, Alfie old son,' Sam gave a friendly warning. 'You're a married man, and she is an ambulance driver. One of the finest and scariest drivers I have ever had the misfortune to travel with.'

'They're a good lot those ambulance drivers. Who'd have thought women could drive like that through shell and shot?' Alfie, too, looked to be enjoying the rare hiatus in the shelling. Burrowing into the ground they had become accustomed to the gaping, interconnecting holes there that saved their lives if they kept their head down. Generally dug six to eight feet down, they were then built up with sandbags stacked at the top by another two or three feet.

'She's called Daisy Flynn,' said Sam, staring into an azure sky watching the birds flying freely overhead. 'She came over to Canada with me when I was just a kid.'

'Wadda-ya-mean, just a kid, you're still a kid,' Alfie laughed and Sam raised an eyebrow, knowing Alfie was a good five years older and had joined the Medical Corps as soon as he could. 'You'd better not let your gal back home know you have been fraternising with old flames.'

'Daisy is not an old flame,' Sam scoffed, 'she's a good friend, and I'm glad we got the chance to catch up on the old days. Here, did you know she's a singer? A good one too by the sound of it. If you behave yourself, we can go and see her in the mess hall on Saturday night. She had the voice of an angel when she was a young'n' and used to sing to the other kids who were homesick, to cheer them up on our way to Canada.'

'I'll look forward to a good old sing-song, Sammy boy,' said Alfie. Then, lowering his voice he leaned a little closer to Sam. 'You wanna know where there's a good stash of rum?'

'You'll get us into trouble, you will,' Sam said. But the thought of a slug of rum would go down a treat after the week they'd had, the snifter they received this morning didn't touch the sides, and he would have welcomed another one. The dark, sweet, gooey overproof alcohol would be just the ticket after the battering their platoon had taken. 'Lead on McDuff, I don't mind if I do...'

Alfie led the way down the warren of dugouts, past Scottie Road, and down Marsh Lane. Becoming one with the earth was the only way to survive, and their nostalgia for home was evident in the names they gave to their trenches. Hunkering down in the mud, the soldiers carved the familiar on the irregular, turning to the names of local addresses from their pre-war civilian lives. Naming a space made it their place.

'Our boys have given good old Liverpool names to their trenches,' said Alfie when they'd first met.

'All the trenches look alike,' Sam had complained when, once again he had got lost in the confusing labyrinth cluttered with

ammunition boxes, cables, detritus, and all manner of supplies
required to shore up the trench walls and fight a war.

'We give the German trenches in front of us Canadian names
before we capture them, so that when we take them, they are
already ours.' Alfie had told Sam.

He had taught him a lot, Sam realised, especially when it
came to sniffing out the rum store. There was no getting out of a
trench to study a place in the landscape, knowing that to do so
would invite a bullet through your helmet or through your vest.
Handmade signs guided them to their destination, and Sam was
now familiar with the strange names given to their quarters by
the wags within. The Lettuce Inn, The Ritz Cracker, The Adel-
phinium.

'Be careful when we come up to Whizbang Corner,' said Alfie
when they reached Lovers' Lane and then continued onto a
trench sign that read Hell's Bells This Way, giving Sam a
cautionary instruction to crawl on his stomach, crocodile-style.
'Down here,' Alfie said, still leading the way to a cave by way of
clay steps going down to an entrance, covered by a heavy blanket
impregnated with chemicals to keep out most of the poison gas
fumes that were now common on the battlefield.

The dugouts with their rudimentary ventilation system, were
always fusty and overcrowded, the walls blackened by tobacco
smoke. With humorous, somewhat off-colour, ditties scratched
into the walls, a testament to their authors having passed through
the area to leave a lasting memorial of sorts. The soldiers' names,
units, and hometowns appeared alongside cartoons and jaunty
phrases or risqué images of alluring mademoiselles in flimsy
nightwear. Candles flickered a weak light so that men could read
and write. Soldiers, sprawled on the packed dirt floor on sandbags and duckboards, scrounged to create chairs or beds.

The backline dugout spaces were social places where the men

came to play cards, sing, or tell stories especially after a few shots of illicit rum. Someone was playing a harmonica and a fiddle, and Sam joined in with singing their own earthy version of the latest popular melodies.

'I'll be back in a minute,' said Alfie as he headed to the latrine, and Sam nodded when another medic brought him a tin cup half filled with dark rum.

'I'll say you could do with this after last night,' said the soldier. 'Bloody shame about your pal, Alfie.'

Sam's brows pleated in confusion. 'Alfie has just gone to the lavatory,' he commented.

'I doubt it,' said the medic. 'Didn't you hear? He caught the brunt of a toffee apple when he went over the top last night.' A *toffee-apple* was the trench mortar bomb, the Hun's favourite weapon, Sam knew. 'They buried him this morning.'

Sam downed the rum in one go and felt the hot trickle slide right down his gullet. He had no time to think straight when another medic came hurtling in. And when he caught sight of Sam he stopped in his tracks.

'Sam, my friend, did you hear? *Scottie Road* has just been hit. You are one lucky son-of-a-gun. You're the only one who got out alive.' He looked up to the sky and he said, 'Someone is surely looking over you, pal.'

12

AUGUST 1916

'How are you feeling this morning, my dear?' Ruby asked, knowing Doctor Bea had given Archie the all-clear to do light duties.

'That woman has done an excellent job of restoring my sight,' said Archie, 'even though the spectacles are taking some getting used to.'

'You look very distinguished, I think.' Ruby greeted both nurses who were joining them for breakfast and her bosom swelled with motherly pride, 'Where do you girls get your abundance of energy from, you were at the hospital so late and yet here you are ready to go and do it all over again.'

'No rest for the wicked,' Ellie's larking was interrupted when Mrs Hughes came into the morning room.

'My, my,' said Mrs Hughes who had brought a bundle of letters to the lodge from Ashland Hall, 'someone is popular.' She put the letters on the table and Anna's eyes widened when she saw every one of them was addressed to her and her hand flew to her lips to stem the gasp of excitement.

'They're from Ned,' she cried. 'And by the look of this lot, he must have written every day.' She and Ellie had been prevented from going overseas by the number of casualties coming in, the hospitals were bulging at the seams with injured servicemen and she promised Doctor Bea she would wait until the new doctor came to take over.

'Well, aren't you going to open them?' Ruby asked expectantly and Anna felt a small jab of disappointment. These were the letters she had been waiting for. Her impatience had bordered on desperation when she'd heard nothing from Ned for weeks.

'You want me to open them now?' Anna said while Ruby, in a state of eager anticipation, was obviously impatient to know how Ned was faring. 'But I have to go over to the Hall,' Anna said, feeling torn. 'Matron Meredith will not allow lateness for any reason short of a sudden death in the family.' Obviously, she was desperate to know what Ned had to say, but if she was being truly honest, she wanted to read his words alone. 'We have a large admission of wounded servicemen coming in today and are bound to be busy.' Her duty was to the men in her care.

'Open one at least,' Ellie said, 'I will go and get our cloaks,. Taking in Ruby's look of undisguised disappointment, Ellie was also eager for news.

Since taking part in the Battle of Jutland back in June, Ned had been involved in the largest full-scale clash of naval battleships so far, and everybody was on high alert for news. Serving in the Royal Navy's Grand Fleet under Admiral Sir John Jellicoe, Ned had not been home for two years and his cheerful good humour was missed by all of them.

'Perhaps just one and we will save the rest for this evening,' Anna said, ripping open the envelope with her thumbnail, aware Ruby had not scolded her for omitting to use the bone-handled letter opener... And as she began to read the words, her face grew hotter.

Hello beautiful girl,

Just to let you know I am lying in my hammock dreaming of the day we will be together again. The only thing that keeps me going is the thought we will be back together soon. I really miss you, Anna, do you miss me?

I cannot tell you where we are for obvious reasons, all I can say is that the locals speak very much like your new doctor, I imagine. Anyway, just a short one today as I am about to go on duty.

All my love and counting the days until I see you again.

Your ever-loving, Ned xxx

'Oh, Aunt Ruby...' Anna felt a sudden warm rush to her cheeks. 'He is fine or at least he was when he wrote this.' She watched Ellie leave the room to fetch their capes and could swear she had a tear in her eye. 'Do you think he is in Scotland?' Dressed in her pristine uniform, Anna's own eyes filled with happy tears that were always so near the surface these days.

'It sounds very much so,' Ruby said. She looked thoughtful and Anna wondered if she was thinking of a way to get him home.

'Scotland is not so far away, is it?' Anna was so happy she felt she would burst.

'I wouldn't like to walk it,' Ruby said, bringing a bit of sobriety to the waltzing nurse who was holding the letter close to her heart. 'Have you seen the time?'

'Oh no, I'll have to hurry... Ellie!' she turned and bumped into Ellie who was bringing in their cloaks. 'Oh, there you are. Did you hear Ned's news? I'll tell you on the way over, Matron will have our life if we're late.'

'Slow down,' Ellie smiled, she had heard every word, 'we've got plenty of time, you know Aunt Ruby always has the clocks ten minutes fast.'

'I put them to the right time when the authorities introduced the extra hour in March, to lengthen British Summer Time,' Ruby told them, secretly holding in a smile when she saw them scamper to the front door and scurry down the path.

Anna knew she really ought to pull herself together, but these were such emotive times, and she could not imagine what life was like before the war. 'Even if we had time, I dare not read any more before going on duty.'

'Knowing Ned's letters are waiting for you, will spur you on,' Ellie said, understanding that her best friend would love nothing more than to find a cosy corner and spend the rest of the day reading Ned's news.

'I know,' Anna answered, and for as much as she longed to linger on Ned's words, she must save that pleasure until later. For now, incoming servicemen depended upon her. 'Have you heard from Rupert?' Anna asked, not even a little breathless given the speed they were walking. Ellie had met Rupert at one of Ruby's fundraising dinners earlier in the year. 'He's quite keen by the sound of it.'

'He loves me deeply. Didn't I tell you?' Ellie answered. 'Although, we haven't got to the undying love bit yet.'

Anna laughed, knowing Ellie was a popular member of the Corby set. She threw herself wholeheartedly into everything that was going, and Rupert was just one of the many young officers who appreciated her company.

'Come on Florence Nightingale, let's hurry,' Anna beckoned Ellie to shift herself.

Matron Meredith called an emergency meeting in the dining hall, where every member of staff, auxiliaries included, was given instructions as to what they must do in case of an enemy attack and warned there would be severe reprimands for any nurse who was late for duty.

'From now on, we will have to be even more vigilant,' Matron told the gathered staff after news of attacks on the eastern side of the country were becoming more frequent. Anna and Ellie also digested the news that some of the VAD nurses who belonged to the Territorials would be leaving Ashland Hall for overseas work. They all knew what that meant, and there was a low buzz of excitement as the nurses who had been attached to Seaforth Barracks were sent for, only to return a while later, proudly waving their marching orders.

'Oh, you lucky thing,' Ellie declared as one of the nurses showed her brand-new military uniform. 'Do you think I could join you, too?'

'Be careful what you wish for, Harrington,' Ellie had not heard Matron Meredith's quiet approach. 'The fields of war are not like a Saturday night dance, you know.'

'No, Matron,' Ellie said, solemnly, aware that the majority of cases being brought to Ashland Hall were here for rest and recuperation before being sent back to the Front. As she watched the straight-backed figure of medical authority continuing along the corridor towards her office, Ellie said: 'Can't you just imagine all those poor injured servicemen dependent upon us alone.' She clasped her hands to her bosom. 'They would be ever so grateful...'

Anna reminded Ellie that she had promised Rupert she would write and maybe accompany him to a dance when he got leave. If he got leave, she meant.

'So, I did,' Ellie looked almost innocent but it was the devilish twinkle in her eye that told Anna she was not a girl who would be tethered by social mores.

Immediately, Anna could see the similarity between Ellie and Ruby, and she had more than a sneaking suspicion both women were carved from the same wood. Not that she would ever repeat her suspicions that Ruby and Ellie were more closely related than was common knowledge. But their resemblance and plain-speaking attitude were too similar to be merely that of aunt and niece, she was sure.

* * *

'Let me get you a glass of water,' Anna told young Private Daniels who was in the throes of a coughing fit. His face as dark as a plum.

'I wouldn't mind a cup of tea, Nurse,' he said when the coughing subsided and Anna had to smile when his neighbour in the opposite bed said in a jocular tone: 'Blimey, Nurse, young Sproglet here, was hardly making a sound all night. I think he's looking for a bit of sympathy.'

'Well, I would say he deserves a bit of sympathy. Private Daniels has been through a bit of a rough time,' Anna answered, knowing the young soldier had been rescued from a place called No-Man's-Land on the Western Front and sent back with what was known as a Blighty wound. He had had all the toes on his right foot taken off yesterday when gangrene set in.

'You're right, Nurse, getting caught in that rumpus must have been a bit of a shock to his system.'

'It was more than a rumpus,' said the young soldier irritably, 'I'm here for a bit more than an ingrowing toenail, you know.'

'Me too, Mucker,' said the older soldier, 'I 'ad me bleedin' leg shot off, excuse me French, Nurse.'

'Now, now, boys,' Anna said as she bustled back and forth with cups of tea, 'play nicely.'

'You tell 'em, nurse,' said Taffy through the bandages that covered his whole head and face. A Welsh miner, he had helped dig the underground tunnels and lay explosives under the German trenches ready for the Big Push back in July and was lucky to be alive when the sticks of gelignite he had been using blew up in his face. 'I'll have you know, boyo, I've had two fingers amputated. They were my best two an' all. The ones I used to salute the generals who never came near the trenches.'

The ribbing banter continued, and Anna knew they did it without malice, each one had horrific injuries but made light of them whenever possible.

'That'll teach you to stop biting your fingernails,' said mild-mannered Sproglet, so-called because at sixteen he was the youngest on the ward, and he gave a weary smile when Taffy threw his head back and filled the room with his loud booming laugh.

'Touché, Sproglet,' said Taffy. 'Some of those officers haven't got a clue.'

'Now, now, Taffy,' said Anna, 'don't let Matron Meredith hear you talking like that. Her fiancé is an officer.'

'They're not all bad, Nurse,' Taffy said by way of an apology.

'Matron says you might be getting your moving orders some-time this week,' said Anna and saw Taffy's shoulders droop as his mood changed from jovial to solemn in the blink of an eye, and she had an inkling that he had no wish to be sent anywhere, least of all home.

'I can see you might have a problem holding a rifle,' said the young soldier, 'so I imagine they will send you back to the valleys, to marry your sweetheart.'

As Anna put a cup of tea and a freshly made scone on his locker, Taffy returned to his usual cheery self.

'Don't be telling them that, Sproglet,' Taffy called to the lad in the next bed, 'the news will break this poor nurse's heart. The whole staff will be bereft when I'm discharged.'

'We won't miss your cheek, that's for sure,' said Doctor Bea who was suturing the hand of another soldier.

'You know as well as I do, Doc,' he said, 'they won't have anything to look forward to when my handsome physog is no longer here for them to admire and dream about each night.'

'How did you guess?' Anna laughed. 'How will we manage without you, Taff?' She tried to keep his spirits up, knowing he had lost more than his good looks and his fingers when his sweetheart's letters stopped coming.

'Any chance of a nice bit of bacon and egg for breakfast?' A voice called from the other end of the ward that had once been the Ashland Hall ballroom.

'You will get porridge, and like it,' replied Doctor Bea, opening the French windows as a VAD nurse tidied away the galvanised dishes and removed them to the sluice room that was once the flower room across the hall.

'Oh, and nurse,' said Doctor Bea, 'make sure that dressing is kept spotlessly clean and change it every day, no matter how much he assures you there is no need.'

'Yes, Doctor,' said a young volunteer nurse who had done nothing more strenuous than written party invitations before the war.

For some of the men, being injured was a blessing. A Blighty wound allowed them to escape the death and devastation of the battlefields. For others, their injuries meant a lifetime of pain and disfigurement. The prospect of never walking or never working again. They had suffered long and agonising journeys, having been scooped up from the battlefield by regimental stretcher bearers. Sometimes, after lying abandoned for hours in no-man's land before being shuttled back to casualty posts in tents and dugouts for basic first aid, a shot of morphine and perhaps a hurried operation. They had been transported in ambulance trains to one of the French ports, crammed into a hospital ship to cross the channel, then packed into Red Cross trains bound for any hospital where there was room. And Anna's heart wept for every single one of them.

13

Lottie took out her writing pad and a pencil from the sideboard drawer. Izzy was down in the pawnshop so she decided to close the charity shop and, it being her dinner hour, she would write to Jerry and tell him of her predicament.

Dear Jerry,

Please don't be angry with me, but I have got something to tell you...

Lottie placed a protective hand on her stomach. It had been several weeks since Jerry had joined training camp awaiting orders to be called overseas and knew, without any shadow of a doubt, that she was expecting. He would have to marry her now.

* * *

Lottie's words seemed to bounce round the page. Every muscle in Jerky Woods body was rigid. Expecting? She was expecting! Panic, like a balloon swelling up inside him, threatened to swallow him belly-first. He had never given a moment's thought to the consequences of his actions. A small click of his tongue on the roof of his mouth clipped the silence and Jerky swallowed bitter bile.

She planned this, he thought. *She's been trying to get me down the aisle for years.* And in a moment of weakness, he had finally been tricked into a wedding he wanted no part of.

If we apply for a special licence, we could be married in no time, she wrote. And he could hear her scratchy, high-pitched voice raking incessantly inside of his head. *We will say the child is premature. There is nothing else we can do.*

'Bloody woman!' he hissed under his breath and did not hear the sound of the barracks door closing.

'Trouble?' his oppo asked and Jerky could not help but blurt out the whole sorry tale. 'You lucky Barsted,' said his Cockney pal, 'you get special leave to marry, and while you wait for orders to go overseas, the army let married men go 'ome each night. And they pay you for the pleasure.'

'Never?' Jerky's mind began to work overtime, maybe Lottie had done him a favour after all. He could have his cake and eat it. He didn't give a stuff about fighting for his country. All he wanted was to go home and get paid for doing so.

Jerky Woods was given permission to wed his girl, and he sent a telegram immediately.

* * *

Lottie reluctantly accepted the telegram with a heavy heart, ignoring the look of sympathy from the woman who had taken the place of the postman fighting overseas. She read the words written, and then read them again to Izzy.

'*Get the banns up. Buy a ring. I'm on my way home.*' Lottie jumped on the spot, hindered only by her swollen abdomen. 'He's making an honest woman of me after all.' Lottie threw her arms round her future mother-in-law and hugged her.

'There, there,' Izzy said. She could hardly believe her eldest lad would do the decent thing and assumed Jerky would only do so if there was something in it for him. *He's up to something.* She could tell. Having got out of marrying Lottie once before, Izzy could not think why he was so eager to marry the poor girl now.

'Didn't I say he would do the right thing by me...?' There were tears of elation running down Lottie's pale cheeks as she hugged Izzy. 'Didn't I say he loved me...?'

Lottie's excitement oozed from every pore, and Izzy's sorrowful eyes gazed out over the River Mersey. Sadly, she shook her head, knowing Lottie's life from now on was not going to be the fairytale she expected it to be. Not when she was going to marry the second coming of Splinter Woods, and it was only Lottie's approaching motherhood, and the fact that she would not want any grandchild of hers born out of wedlock and Lottie's name dragged through the mud, that Izzy did not persuade the girl to run as far away from Jerky as it was possible to go.

The loosely tied apron covering Lottie's black dress did not hide the fact that she was pregnant. But it would be of no use trying to persuade the girl not to marry her son. Lottie was obviously besotted. So, there was no point in wasting her breath, thought Izzy. But of one thing she was certain, a life with Jerky Woods was not going to be easy for Lottie.

* * *

'Sometimes I wonder if this child is mine.' Woods told Lottie. 'Some girls try and trick soldiers into marrying them, so I've heard.'

Lottie's voice sounded like a strangled whimper when she said, 'Of course, this child is yours, who's else would it be? I have never looked at another man. You know you are the only man I have ever loved.'

But judging by his bleached pallor, the news seemed as welcome as rain at a picnic. Why would he tell her to get the banns up and buy a ring, if he felt that way?

'What about when I was inside, or away at training camp? Who was walking out with you, then?' He stepped forward and Lottie flinched, shrinking back from him when he put his hand out towards her.

'I wasn't walking out with anybody, you know how much I love you,' Lottie's tone held a pleading note, she didn't like it when he was in this mood. And suddenly he touched her cheek and his voice softened.

'Here,' he said as her subservient nature caused a stirring in his loins, and the frisson of power her anxiety gave him made him feel virile. It was time to do his bit. Show her that she could depend on him. 'It was just a bit of a shock, that's all. I'll look after you, girl.' He gave a half-shrug, watching her shoulders relax, then, putting his arm round her, he smiled when she leaned into him, knowing he had her gratitude. He liked his woman to be grateful. 'And I'll tell you what else I will do,' he said, brightening. 'As soon as we're wed, I'll ask for special permission to come home every night to look after you. What about that then?'

'You'd do that for me, Jerry?' Lottie jumped up and down with glee and then, standing on the tip of her toes, she threw her arms round his neck and kissed him full on the lips in a rare show of unconfined excitement.

'O' course I will.' He felt the power surging through his loins. 'There ain't nobody telling me I can't look after my missus.'

'Oh, Jerry, do you think they will let you come home each night?'

'Let me? Let me!' His eyes speared her with indignation and he obviously felt he had been insulted. 'I'll tell them straight, I will.'

'Oh, Jerry, you are so good to me. I don't know what to say.'

14

'Why don't we turn part of the house into sewing rooms,' May said. She was made to feel comfortable airing her thoughts, without fear of being shot down in flames. As she had been when Giles was alive. These days, she felt more like her old self and loved getting to know her sister all over again. It was like old times, she discovered. They still shared the same sense of humour. They combined the same ideas, rarely having to explain as each understood the other perfectly. They used the kind of mental telepathy they shared as children when they wanted to do something Nanny would disapprove of, like picking blackberries and distributing them to the Children's Home next door. The place her husband had lied about, when he told Ruby all those years ago that her child had been sent away to another country, knowing the information would be forbidden to public scrutiny and, more importantly, Ruby and Archie's tenacious investigations.

But now, Nanny and the governesses had gone, and so too the malevolent influence of Giles Harrington. And, for the first time since she naively married Giles believing he truly loved her, May, feeling the warmth of a loving family, was now living her own life on her own terms, and she was loving every moment.

'Yes, workrooms, what a good idea,' Ruby said enthusiastically. 'Seamstresses can make shirts and quilts for the soldiers.' Ruby was glad they were all living here in the Lodge, thrilled her family were all back together again, and glad to see the great hall was now being used to its full potential.

Part of the house and grounds were enjoyed by recovering servicemen: who played tennis, or bowls, rowed on the lake, painted down on the shore, sat writing letters, poetry or any of the other pastimes that aided their recuperation, while the rest of the house was used as a busy auxiliary hospital run by Doctor Bea, Anna, Ellie and the Red Cross VAD nurses.

'We could use the stables now that most of the horses have been requisitioned by the military.' Ruby, happy and relaxed in her sister's company, had encouraged May to take up fundraising for the troops and May had thrown herself wholeheartedly into every venture. Ruby was proud May had finally found her voice and was not afraid to use it.

'I was thinking that very same thing,' May replied, 'even a place where ladies can cut and roll bandages for the hospitals and for the Front.'

'Most certainly,' Ruby said, putting down her embroidery on the polished mahogany table, and realised, not for the first time, that her sister was much brighter and more creative than she had given her credit for in latter years.

'That way, Doctor Bea will have no room to complain about threads of material being walked all over *her* nice clean wards.' May's tone was a little constricted, but she was suddenly pleased to hear Ruby's easy laugh at her indignant observation fill the room. This was the sound May had longed to hear for years.

'If she replaced Doctor with Queen that would give you some

idea of how she sees herself.' The two women laughed again, something they had done so much in the past when they were younger. 'Why don't we hop to it, and see what can be done,' said Ruby. 'I like the idea of these workshops.'

'I am so glad,' May said, 'because I was thinking, so many women feel the need to do something useful, they will be happy to do their bit too.'

'This will be the first time some of the well-to-do women will experience the taste of gainful employment – on a strictly voluntary basis of course,' Ruby said. 'I would never insult the wives and mothers of influential businessmen with offers of money for their endeavours, as if they were kitchen staff or housekeepers.'

'The paid help, in other words.' May gave a knowing smile, aware that her sister would always be able to make a silk purse out of a sow's ear. Ruby squeezed her money so tightly it screamed. But she never slowed in her determination to gain what was needed for *her* boys, *her* hospital, or *her* nursing staff.

Ruby's eagerness to be at the vanguard of every charitable event kept May busy since she had returned to Ashland Hall Lodge. And May was only too glad to throw herself into the fund raising and the charitable events that Ruby had organised for her. All of the collection money went into helping those in need, unlike Giles whose charitable collections went straight into the pockets of his bookmakers and left May almost destitute. Her sister had a heart of gold, which was in contrast to her husband's heart of stone.

* * *

Later Ellie and Anna joined the two sisters before leaving for their night shift in Ashland Hall.

'I was just thinking how easily you have settled into life here,' said May.

'I enjoy nursing and have made a good friend in Anna,' Ellie answered. 'It was such a pity Father could not find a church nearer.' Given her mother's financial plight in the wake of his death, Ellie was not surprised Giles Harrington favoured a sleepy village where his absences in order to attend gambling dens, while using the excuse of visiting the sick or dying in outlying farms, could be explained away more easily than they would if he were part of a larger more easily accessible community.

'It was not to be,' May said, casting off grey wool from her knitting needles that contained another pair of mittens for the troops.

'At the time it did upset me that you had to go through the whole funeral ordeal without any of your family present,' continued Ellie.

'These things are becoming a common occurrence in wartime,' May answered. And Ellie nodded being practical, she knew they must accept these unavoidable changes.

Ruby, missing Giles's ceremony by hours, was glad. If there was one thing she could not abide it was hypocrisy, and the thought of standing at Giles's graveside pretending to appear sad at his passing made her bones jangle with discomfort and was relieved she had been spared the pretence.

After Giles was buried in a little graveyard near the cliffs at Scarborough, May made no secret of the fact she was eager to return to Ashland Hall. More than happy to share the yellow sandstone lodge set back in the grounds away from the 'big house'. The lodge was surrounded by what had once been a pretty flower garden, but which had now been turned into a vegetable allotment overlooked on all sides by the arched mullioned windows.

'See you both tomorrow morning.' Ellie and Anna gave the two women a peck on the cheek and a hug before making their way over to Ashland Hall auxiliary hospital for their night shift.

'You have done a wonderful job of bringing Ellie up,' Ruby said staring out of the window watching the two girls chattering and hurrying through the grounds; her heart was now overflowing with gratitude towards her sister, knowing she would not have lived the kind of life she had over the years, if she'd had a baby to raise. 'If anything, May, you did me the greatest kindness by bringing up my little girl while suffering an overbearing, grasping husband.'

'It was not a chore, I assure you,' May answered 'Ellie is my life, and I love her as if she were truly my own daughter.'

'I doubt Giles appreciated the effort you put in,' Ruby said, 'especially after he discovered Father had not left you this house in his Will.'

'I was so glad and very relieved,' said May, 'with such a large estate comes large responsibilities, and I do not feel I have the emotional wherewithal to run Ashland Hall.'

'You are growing stronger by the day,' Ruby declared. 'And I have an idea for the war effort, May?' Ruby had a gleam in her eye when she suggested that May might be happy to offer her sewing expertise. Sizing up blankets, sheets, and pillowcases for the narrow iron beds and nodding to the picture of the vast Ashland hallway hung here in the lodge. 'We could turn the mezzanine into another ward,' Ruby said as she gazed at the picture gallery shown in the painting. 'What do you think?'

May was genuinely taken aback her sister had asked her advice, even though she did not wait for an answer.

'I knew you would agree,' Ruby said. 'Did I tell you the mayor said Ashland Hall is one of the finest auxiliary hospitals on the coast?'

Gushing with ideas, Ruby reminded May of when they were young, remembering that Ruby always took charge, making May feel safe and secure. Especially in the days when they had only nannies and governesses to care for them. Ruby was her mainstay. Her protector. Her ally. The very reasons Giles would not allow her to see her older sister during the years of their marriage. Taking May and Ellie as far away as he could, so she was completely under his spell. But since moving to the lodge and for the first time in years, May experienced a complete lack of self-consciousness, which she had not felt for twenty years and she hugged her sister. Her heart was so full of love and deep appreciation for this wonderful woman who had been everything to her. And had been so cruelly betrayed by their father and her husband.

Ruby gave a small clearing of her throat, raised her chin, her shoulders went back, and her colour deepened before that familiar gleam of shared history shone from her eyes. 'Our brave boys will recover much faster in the sea air, don't you agree, May?'

'I certainly do,' said May, who knew Ruby's remark was a statement not a question. 'But I suspect they will not want to recover too quickly, and return to battle.'

'Maybe you're right,' Ruby said, 'in which case, they should have at least six weeks of rest and recuperation after being declared fit for duty. So, they can recover fully before returning to their units. I will have a word with Doctor Bea.' The doctor was a feisty woman who had offered her services in France at the start of war and was promptly told by the commanding officer that the battlefield was no place for a woman, to which she had replied that maybe he should tell that to Florence Nightingale, a pioneer who had nursed the wounded and dying soldiers of the Crimean War and had organised better conditions in Constantinople.

'I think that's best, my dear.' May nodded, knowing nothing

deterred Ruby when she put her mind to something. Being busy *sometimes* kept her out of mischief.

'The billiard room is being put to good use by the recuperating patients,' Ruby said. 'When I see the room being used, it reminds me of the days when father played host to the Empire builders.' Her eyes danced with excitement now.

'Those days are a lifetime away, but I remember them as if they were yesterday,' May answered, caught up in her sister's enthusiasm. 'Do you remember watching Archie train father's horses along the coastline?' May asked, relaxing in a way she had not done for many a long year. 'Then there was the weekend pheasant shoots in the summer.'

Ruby sighed. 'And the times when we used to go down to the shore and paint?'

'The shore has been covered in barbed wire to stop any invasion,' Ruby said, remembering with fondness the spectacular twilight sunsets she had once captured on canvas. 'Our brave Tommies can picnic nearer the house in the sand dunes, or maybe grow vegetables in the walled garden...'

'There is so much to organise,' May said. 'I don't know where you get your energy. If it is all the same to you, I will have a short afternoon nap.'

'Take as long as you like,' said Ruby, 'after all, this is your home.'

'I tend to forget this is mine,' May said, looking round the spacious but cosy lodge that was complete luxury compared to the parsimonious conditions Giles forced upon them.

* * *

'Your ideas to involve May in your plans seems to have done the trick, my dear,' Archie said later when May was having a lie down. 'The colour has certainly returned to your sister's cheeks.'

'I don't think she is strong enough yet, to nurse the sick and wounded, though,' Ruby replied, 'she is much happier doing the practical things, like teaching local ladies to sew blankets or knit boot socks.'

He knew the middle- and upper-class women, who were clamouring to nurse the sick and wounded, were not even close to being prepared for the sights they would eventually see. For them, the romance of tending military men in need of succour was the be-all and end-all. Ruby knew what she was letting herself in for and did nothing to shy away from what she saw as her duty.

'Remember when the Prince of Wales paddled in the sea,' Ruby asked. 'I even walked with him along the sand dunes, do you remember, Archie?'

Archie nodded. 'He loved to watch the horses exercising for the Grand National. Your father spared no expense.'

Ruby was quiet for a while and then, taking a deep breath, her mind made up she said, 'And none shall be spared now.' Standing at the lodge window that permitted plenty of light into the cosy room, Ruby looked out on the exclusive, panoramic view of the vast sea beyond, now lined with rolling coils of barbed wire to fend off marauding invaders, and watched a pewter sky meet the silver sea. 'Our boys will have everything they need, a clean bed, a warm hearth and a full stomach to help ease their pain.'

On days like this, she tried to banish memories of the loneliness she felt as a motherless child, who was not just a sister but also a mother and a protector to May. And in return, May had raised her daughter. What a crazy mixed-up life she had lived.

'Care to share?' Archie asked and one thing Ruby knew she would never regret was the years she and Archie spent as man and wife. She had found solace and all-consuming love in the arms of her father's groom. Archie, the man who was accused of being out of her class, was more of a nobleman than some of the so-called luminaries she had met. Archie was the gentlest man she had ever known.

'If you look at the seascape with adventurous eyes, my love,' he said, slipping his arms round her slim waist, 'you won't see it as stark, or lonely.'

They both watched the waves crashing over the tarry stones at high tide, knowing that when the water came right up over those large flat cobbles that lined the shore, nobody dared venture into its strong undercurrents.

'I love you so much, Archie. I do not know what I ever would have done without you.'

'You would have married a rich man and grew bored.' Archie laughed.

15

'Ma won't be so quick to stick her nose into my business when I'm a married man with a kid of me own on the way, will she?' Fancy your own mother telling your expectant sweetheart she deserved better. Jerky Woods was unable to keep the outrage from his voice. He had a forty-eight-hour pass for him and Lottie to marry the following day. Then his platoon were being sent overseas the following Monday. But if he had anything to do with it, the army were going to be one man short come marching time. 'What kind of a mother doesn't love her own flesh and blood?'

'That's what I thought,' said Lottie, relieved he sounded cheerier. Jerry might be a bit thoughtless sometimes, keeping her waiting when they had a date for the music hall or, occasionally, not turning up altogether. But things had altered now and once they were married, Lottie imagined she would change him. Jerry would provide for her and the child. He would show the doubters that they were wrong.

'I've fixed everything, I got a special licence to marry first thing tomorrow.'

'How did you do that?' Lottie asked, full of blinkered admiration as they walked out of the train station and onto busy Lime Street, bustling with omnibuses, horse and carts, and motorcars.

He put his arm round her thickening waistline and manoeuvred her across the busy road towards the beautiful gardens that surrounded Saint George's Hall. 'I said I was being sent abroad, and my girl was in a delicate position, if you get my meaning.'

Jerky's words made Lottie feel ten feet tall. She liked it when he called her *his girl,* and in her head, she thumbed her nose to the cynics.

'You're not really being sent abroad next week?' Lottie couldn't bear the thought of her man being sent overseas.

'You bet your life, I'm not,' he answered. 'I have no intentions of going overseas at all - ever!'

* * *

Anna, about to finish her afternoon shift, knew Ashland Hall was considered the best auxiliary hospital in the North West and that Ruby was paid the sum of one pound, four shillings and sixpence per week by the war office for each patient. The money covered treatment, food, and anything else her boys needed. Nothing was too good for Ruby's heroes, Anna thought when she saw Ruby come onto the ward armed with a basket of apples from the orchard and a large supply of *Blighty*, a new weekly magazine which served the servicemen's humour.

'You, Ellie and I have been invited to Lottie's wedding – tomorrow morning,' Ruby said, after dispatching a magazine to each bed and heading towards the exit.

'Tomorrow!' Anna and Ellie chorused as they left the ward and headed toward the staircase. The last thing Anna wanted was to see poor Lottie getting hitched to that conniving ne'r-do-well who had made her life a misery in days gone by.

Anna knew none of them were looking forward to the wedding. Not because they didn't like Lottie. They liked her very much and did not want to see her rush headlong into a marriage she would one day regret.

Nipper Woods felt himself being lifted from the stretcher and was told he was on the final leg of his long journey from France. Given a jab of morphia and having been out cold for most of the trek, Nipper did not find the jaunt uncomfortable, until he was transferred from the hospital train at Aintree Station to a waiting ambulance.

'Do you think we could nip into The Old Roan, Nurse?' asked a cheeky wag, who was soon given short shrift by the ministering ambulance nurses.

'You will do no such thing, Corporal. Visiting public houses and drinking alcohol is strictly against Matron's rules.'

In moments, they were on the road and Nipper drifted into a welcome sleep.

Accustomed to the relentless rumble of bombardment, the boom of explosions and the dying groans of pals, Nipper could now hear only the gentle thrum of the ambulance engine rumbling through quiet roads and had no idea where he was. For months, he had known only the rural countryside of France and Flanders, where every living thing had been trampled and obliterated into the mud and trenches and shell holes. Being injured was a blessing, he thought. At least it got him off the battleground.

He had been collected by a band of female volunteers who smelled clean and fresh, making him even more aware of the putrid stench that still clung to his clothing aware that his wounds may have been tended but his clothes were something else entirely. There were too many soldiers in need of treatment or triage at least, that there was no time to worry about a spot of mud on your khakis.

Inhaling the fresh scent of soap as they had put him into an ambulance, Nipper had asked, 'Where am I?' His throat was dry, and his tongue felt too big for his mouth. The voice did not sound like his.

'You are in good hands – that's where you are, Soldier.' The voice was gentle yet had an unmistakable air of authority. And Nipper thought that he must have died in his sleep and gone to heaven. Which wasn't so bad after all, he decided.

'Don't worry, Soldier,' said a female voice. 'Your war is over. You're going to Ashland Hall Auxiliary Hospital.'

The words were like music to Nipper's ears. Feeling no pain after another jab of morphia, he did not have the energy to wonder how long it had taken to bring him home to British Soil, ensuring his fighting days were over.

* * *

Nipper was aware of the hushed, almost reverential tones of busy women and realised he had been relocated from a world of men and was now surrounded by a soap-scented circle of women.

The smell of disinfectant mingling with heavy-scented freesias permeated the ward and gave Nipper a strong sense of contentment after seeing the horrors of hell unleashed by men in France and elsewhere.

The maternal tone of the medical staff was a comforting reminder of his life in Queen Street with his Ma, especially when he overheard the other patients talking fondly of their own mothers, sisters and sweethearts.

'Women nurses are one thing,' Nipper heard one of his travelling companions say, knowing many of the men had already had their wounds dressed by women back in field hospitals and ambulance trains, 'but women doctors is something else entirely.'

Nipper was unperturbed about being treated by women; they were much gentler than those hairy-arsed medics back on the battlefield. And suddenly, without knowing why, the thought brought stinging tears to his eyes and Nipper was glad his head and face were covered in bandages.

None of the patients had been treated by a woman doctor in civilian life. The idea of women giving medical aid to men was unheard of; plainly it was because they had the inclination to make grown men cry.

'Women doctors should not be employed into the army,' another patient said. 'I mean to say, like, some of us have wounds in places even our wives haven't seen.'

'I heard tell, a woman doctor gave Toddy the unpleasant results of his encounter with a French dancer. Apparently, she had left him with more than a reminder of her foxtrot.'

'I expect he's taking home a lot more than is good for him,' said another soldier, who obviously came from the Welsh valleys. 'I expect he'll have a lot of explaining to do when he sees his missus.' There was a ripple of laughter round the room and Nipper surmised there were quite a few servicemen installed in this particular establishment.

'I'm convinced we've been sent here to die, Taff,' another voice sounding about the same age as himself, Nipper thought, taking in the sounds of a busy ward. 'Why else would the army dispatch us to a place run solely by women.'

'And not just any women,' Taff answered in mock-conspiratorial tones, 'but suffragettes! Former enemies of the state?' The reputation of some of the VADs went before them.

'You'll have the young'uns running for the hills, Taff,' Nipper heard a nurse saying.

Then there was a bit of a commotion and the young lad, sounding most indignant, cried, 'Here! What you playin' at?'

Nipper could hear the young man's indignant voice clearly. He was obviously in some distress and he wondered what on earth was going on to make the soldier so shocked.

'Right, soldier,' a broad Scottish voice said, so close Nipper could smell a mixture of disinfectant and lavender now, and this one also sounded like she was taking no prisoners. 'Let's have a good look at those beautiful baby blues, shall we.'

Nipper felt the bandages being loosened round his head and when they were removed, he held up his hand to block the light that temporarily blinded him. Slowly, he opened his fingers and pepped through, allowing a bit of light into his eyes at a time.

'They're more of a cocoa colour, to be honest,' she said with a grin as Nipper took in the blurred vision of rust-coloured frizz in a white coat and a stethoscope looming into sight. Behind her he could see two nurses waving soap, towels and a bath chair. Nipper soon realised that all the commotion was coming from the bed opposite.

As his eyes adjusted to the light, he could see the panic in the young soldier's eyes when the VAD nurse tried to remove his vest.

'I'm not 'avin' this,' the young soldier said clearly, making the other male patients smile. 'I'm puttin' in fer a transfer!'

'Not before you've had a bath you're not,' Doctor Bea's determined voice sailed across the room as she peered into Nipper's eyes, 'and *you* will not sleep in one of my clean beds until you have been bathed either.'

'Consider yourself told, Private,' the nurse smiled to the soldier who had accompanied Nipper from France and helping him into the bath chair, she marched him off to the bathroom at the end of the ward, where she left him to undress in private, calling through the rapidly closing door. 'Deposit your uniform in the sack, which is here, outside the door. It will be taken away, fumigated and laundered ready for when you are fit enough to leave us.'

When he came out of the bathroom a good while later, Nipper noticed the young private was all pink and shiny and smelled much better than he did when he went in. And looked much more cheerful after his long soak.

'Maybe I was a bit hasty when I said I wanted a transfer,' he said to nobody in particular. 'I think I'm going to be happy enough here.'

'I'm glad to hear it, soldier,' the VAD said, briskly coming on to the ward. 'You will be pleased to hear that nobody wants to leave Ashland Hall when they get here.'

'Too right,' said another male patient. 'When you're feeling up to it, there's a billiard table in the games room.'

'And the library is stuffed with lots of lovely books,' said Taff. 'You're lucky to be here, you need a letter from God to get in here.'

16

Father O'Connell looked down his elongated nose and took in the congregation of just seven people. Standing at the golden-curlicued altar rails was young Charlotte Blythe who had been coming to Saint Patrick's since she was born, with her poor departed mother, *God-rest-her-soul.*

Lottie's husband-to-be, a rather cocky jack-the-lad, called Jeremiah Woods was fidgeting uncomfortably, as if he expected a sudden calamity to befall him. This young man was going overseas, so he had been told, and was on special leave to marry Charlotte and, given the evident bulge in the front of her dress, was not a minute too soon.

The young doe-eyed bride was obviously besotted, given her adoring expression.

God bless her and save her, thought Father O'Connell.

The pale blue chiffon dress, which Izzy had rescued from the bag of *unclaimed pledges,* had seen better days, but she had managed to remove the creases by hanging the dress over a boiling kettle. The steam also killed any fleas, or 'hopping lodgers' as Archie used to call them, that may have been lurking in the seams but, unfortunately, did nothing to hide Lottie's imminently expectant arrival.

Father O'Connell breathed deeply and let out a silent sigh. He was not given to the liberalised view of some, who believed pleasure must be taken as and when it was offered given that some of these young men may not see another home leave. Nevertheless, he felt that Charlotte might be better off without a husband like this one.

Dressed in the uniform of The Pals Regiment, Woods looked reasonably decent, unlike his best man who wore a pair of grey flannel trousers that looked like they had been slept in, an off-white shirt and grey tie that was almost obscured by a too-large waistcoat and brown corduroy jacket that had seen better days long ago and he wondered why this man was not in uniform as Woods looked nervously behind him towards the large wooden church door.

If he dare try a hasty retreat before he makes an honest woman of this poor girl, Father O'Connell thought, *I am prepared to initiate my famous seminary rugby tackle.*

'At least the boozer will be open when we get out of here,' Woods said slyly to his pal, and Father O'Connell's glare left him in no doubt of his intention. Woods shifted uncomfortably and the priest noted that his friend looked equally uneasy in the House of The Lord.

'Do you take this woman...' Father O'Connell was not surprised when the best man gave the groom a timely nudge.

'Sorry, Your Honour, could you repeat the question, please,' Jerky Woods said, while Lottie stared, embarrassed, at the feet of the statue of the Virgin Mother on the alter.

Father O' Connell said a silent prayer for the Good Lord to keep a special eye on Charlotte, for the sake of her poor departed mother, a devoted and regular churchgoer before she died.

Anna rolled her eyes. Jerky Woods, true to form, was making a show of his mother and his future wife. Where did he think he was? In court! *Your Honour indeed.* She viewed the ceremony with an ominous feeling of foreboding. Lottie was worth ten of Jerky Woods, a bully and a coward, who took after his indolent father where drink was concerned. She imagined Lottie would have to struggle or want from now on if she had to depend on him to look after her. And she would stake her life on Jerky Woods being the worst husband a woman ever had the misfortune to marry. He would sell his mother for the price of a pint, she was sure.

She wondered how Jerky Woods had managed to wangle leave to marry when her Ned, and more than likely her beloved and much-missed brother, Sam, were fighting for their King and country.

'Jerry's expecting orders to go overseas,' Lottie said later, when they attended the wedding breakfast over the shops. The wedding breakfast was a sit-down affair for the few people who had been invited and the pristine white tablecloth was obviously one of Ruby's best, as were the crystal glasses and fine silver cutlery.

Izzy, after asking Ruby's permission to borrow the fine items, looked proudly across the table as her son got up to make a brief mumbling speech and the most ungrateful expression of gratitude to everyone for coming.

'Anybody would think he had a gun in his back,' Ellie whispered, causing Anna to give a small cough to cover up the burst of sudden laughter that threatened to escape.

There was a decent spread of a boiled ham salad with trifle for afterwards. The tea was poured into dainty porcelain cups by a neighbour who had come to '*wait-on*'. And each place had a glass of sherry for the ladies and a whisky for Jerky and his best man, who looked as if he was itching to get out of there. Izzy had paid for everything, knowing her son did not have the means or the inclination.

'I hope you ladies don't mind if me and Spike, 'ere, go and wet the horse's head,' Jerky Woods said, standing up. 'We're off to jolly old Flanders on Monday and want to say our goodbyes.'

Anna lifted her chin, silently thinking that if Jerky Woods ever set foot on French soil, she would eat her best new hat.

Everybody complimented Izzy on a good spread, and she took the compliments with a nod, knowing it was what was expected. Dockside women were prepared to give their all, no matter how or where they got the money from, and Izzy was no different.

Hospitality was her middle name, Izzy thought, and luckily, she was relatively prosperous these days, being in regular employment in the busy pawnshop, as well as being in receipt of money sent to the post office each week from Nipper. For the first time in her life, she was in a much better position to splash out than most of her neighbours.

'I hope he doesn't come back steaming drunk,' Izzy said. Dressed in a huge hat with a scarlet feather, she looked every inch the proud mother.

'Anyone would think she was Lottie's mother – they would have no idea Izzy was the mother of the groom,' Anna whispered to Ellie, who nodded in agreement. 'Poor Lottie.'

'I see what you mean about the husband,' said Ellie, who had never met Lottie's intended before today.

'This has been such a wonderful day,' Ruby told Izzy and Lottie, who had invited a few of the more respectable neighbours into the flat, 'but unfortunately, we have to head back to Ashland Hall. We had a new intake of soldiers come in late last night.'

'No rest for the wicked,' Anna gave a false, half-hearted, laugh and everybody joined in.

'Tell your son he must look after Lottie.' Ruby told Izzy as they headed towards the door and Izzy nodded, feeling relieved he was doing his duty for his country, at last. 'And I do hope all goes well for your son *and* Lottie,' added Ruby, rarely using Jerky's name if she could help it. 'Did you say where they were going to live?'

'Aye,' said Lizzy, knowing Ruby would not give houseroom to her eldest son, and she didn't blame her. Izzy would have been like a cat curled up near a hot fender, worrying that Ruby's beautiful possessions would tempt her light-fingered son. 'They have a cellar dwelling in Primrose Cottage.'

'I really can't understand why those ugly cramped courts were given such pretty names,' said Ruby, relieved Izzy didn't ask if her son could come and live here over the shops. 'But nevertheless, you will have bigger worries to add to your burden come Monday when he goes off to war.'

'I'm sure the Hun have more to worry about when they hear he's on his way,' Izzy laughed and Anna could see she must have had more than one sherry to talk so flippantly about Jerry, who, even though he had brought her nothing but trouble, was still her son.

'Will Lottie move back in with you?' Ruby asked and Izzy shook her head.

'Jerky won't hear tell of Lottie coming back here now they're married,' Izzy informed the three women in hushed tones. 'He also made her leave the charity shop and she loved that job.'

'I know,' said Ruby, 'but given the circumstances, she is better off her feet in her condition and there are plenty of volunteers willing to take her place.'

'She's not ill,' Izzy said, her eyes widening in astonishment. 'Women round here don't get to put their feet up when they're in the family way, they have to get on with it. I suppose Lottie will be back and forth when Jerky goes overseas.' And even though Izzy had little time for her eldest son, she did feel a pang of regret that he too was going to France with his battalion so soon after getting wed.

'I only wish my Nipper could have been here to be best man for his brother. I would have been so proud to see them both standing at the altar in their uniform.' Izzy's nostrils flared and she sniffed, like she had a bad smell under her nose. 'Not like that daft ha'porth he chose to be his best man – I haven't got a clue where he dug him up from.' Neither Izzy or Ruby had any idea that Nipper was back in the country and so close by.

17

'You smell like a rose garden, Nurse,' Nipper gasped. His chest tight from the phosgene gas he had breathed in and his lungs felt like they were going to burst out of his chest, as if he were breathing through a tiny hole and not getting enough oxygen. Stretching his upper body, he was desperate to catch more air, but it was no good. His lungs were exhausted.

Anna took in his ashy blue-grey complexion, his voice barely audible, and she could see he was becoming more distressed, his lungs gurgling, his breathing extremely laboured and noisy as he fought to cough up the gluey mucous.

Putting a white enamel bowl under his chin, Anna was relieved to see him bring up copious amounts of stubborn yellow-green froth that had been threatening to drown him and when he could expel no more, he lay back on his pillow, exhausted.

His eyes were re-covered in bandages to give them a chance to heal when the light caused him so much discomfort and pain, and the morphia jab Anna gave him to ease his pain made him sleepy.

'You rest now and get your strength back, Soldier.' Anna felt sorry for these young men who went to France mere boys and came back heroic men. She was angry they were patched up and sent straight back into battle when pronounced fit for duty. But this soldier would be going nowhere near the battlefield again given his injuries. 'I appreciate the compliment.' She said about to take the bowl to the sluice room.

Although they had been advised not to get too friendly with the patients, or side-tracked by sugar-coated words, she liked to let them know their praise was appreciated, otherwise what would be the point.

'But make sure Matron doesn't hear you saying such nice things to the nurses, she'll confine you to bed.'

Anna knew some young soldiers would tenaciously survive no matter what they had been through. And she hoped this young fellow was one of them, for his mother's sake if nothing else. Despite the bandages covering his eyes, Anna thought she recognised this young soldier as Izzy's youngest son.

He gave her a weak thumbs-up, and Anna sighed.

Nipper was far too young to fight in battle. Hell, he wasn't old enough to vote, or drink, or even marry without his parents' permission, but he was expected to die for a cause he probably knew little about. Anna wondered at the thought processes of the recruiting officers who could obviously see a boy, no matter how eager, was too young to serve his country. Simply, boys who came back – if they were lucky – after seeing things no man should ever see, and her heart swelled with compassion for what he must have been through.

'I know you. You're Anna?' he said, his voice was barely audible, so Anna had to lean forward to listen, looking at him closely for the first time, her brow pleating.

'I am, yes, and you're Izzy's lad.'

'Your... Sam... said... Hi,' Nipper whispered, making Anna's heart lurch so hard she almost dropped the bowl she was holding.

'Sam! My brother, Sam?' Anna desperately wanted to know more. But Nipper did not answer, he had drifted into oblivion once more, so she continued to gently remove the bandages that covered his eyes, which were changed daily. He winced when the dressing was removed completely and half-opened his painfully swollen eyes.

He lifted his thumb as if the effort to do so was almost more than he could manage, and his eyes closed once more.

* * *

'Nipper says he saw Sam in the field hospital,' Anna told Ruby and Archie when they sat down to afternoon tea later.

'Never!' said Ruby, her eyes wide with wonder. 'Although it's not impossible, I imagine,' she offered when she saw Anna's expression change from hopeful to dejected.

'What are the chances of that happening?' Archie asked, and Anna nodded.

'Do you think he would be in France?' she asked hesitantly, knowing she didn't want an answer.

They were all silent for a moment and then Ruby, who could not abide what she called library atmospheres, poured more tea, and said: 'I almost forgot to tell you about poor Lottie.' Ruby was trying to take Anna's mind off her worries. 'That rapscallion, Jerky Woods has gone AWOL...'

'Nothing surprises me about him,' Anna said, not really interested in anything he was up to, but her concern for Lottie made her curious. 'How did you find out.?'

'Izzy told Archie when he went to fetch her to come and see Nipper.'

Anna shook her head wondering what Lottie saw in Jerky Woods that persuaded her to marry him. Because as far as she could see, he had no love in that cold black heart of his. If he did, he would not put his wife and his mother through the agony of worry and conflict.

'Izzy's with Nipper now,' Anna said, remembering the shy boy who always seemed to be in the shadow of his obnoxious brother, knowing the burns injury caused by the gas exposure would last for an awfully long time, maybe years, but one thing was for sure, his fighting days were over. 'Izzy is so thrilled Nipper is home.'

'I don't think she expected him to be in such a perilous state, though,' Archie said.

* * *

'At least you're home safe,' Izzy whispered in the quietude of the ward, where men were reading or sleeping, and chilled to the bone at her much-loved son's appearance. *Please, Lord,* she silently prayed, *let my boy live and grow strong, but not too strong before this bloody war is over!*

'I'm not sure about safe,' Nipper whispered, the burning in his throat making it hard for him to be understood, 'not the way my chest hurts.'

The ghost of a smile spread across Nipper's parched lips and Izzy dipped her fingers into the glass of water on the bedside cabinet and gently wet them.

Suddenly he was gasping for air. The gas that damaged his lungs was still working and he could feel his chest heaving.

'Nurse! Anna! Please help him!' Izzy cried and although Anna felt her own heart race at Izzy's distress, she remained outwardly calm and composed. Putting her arms around Izzy's shoulder she led her to Matron's office at the end of the ward while Doctor Bea tended to Nipper.

'Let's make you a nice cup of tea while doctor does her work,' Anna said when she saw Doctor Bea attaching an oxygen mask to Nipper to try and give him some ease.

* * *

'I remember your face,' Nipper said in the small hours when everybody else was asleep. Anna had sat by his bedside all night in case his health should deteriorate, and Nipper whispered as if he had only just seen her for the first time. 'I know you, don't I?'

Anna nodded, realising that the lack of oxygen had made him forgetful, as she wet his lips with a sponge.

'You're Anna,' he gasped, obviously needing to get his words out. 'Your family... perished in a fire?'

Again, Anna nodded, still unable to bear the memory that always came with the stab of despair. She was the girl who was not strong enough to save her family.

'I was ten years old...' Young Nipper was fighting valiantly to make her understand, struggling for every breath, and Anna could see the deep hollow under the laryngeal prominence, known as his Adam's apple.

'Shh, just relax.' Anna put the oxygen to his face and stroked his hand, easing his distress with soothing words. 'Just breathe slowly. In... and out. In... and out. That's it. Much better,' she whispered, her words allowing him to ease a little more.

'Is anything the matter, Sister Cassidy?' Matron Meredith asked, nearing the bed.

'No, Matron,' Anna answered with a smile, 'he's fine now.'

'I will take over. You go and get a cup of tea and ask Nurse Weston to assist me.' Matron, like Anna and Ellie, was a dedicated regular nurse, while Nurse Weston was a VAD, who, although vigorously eager, was not qualified to tend the severely wounded alone, no matter who her politically ministerial husband, father or brothers were.

'Are you sure, Matron?' Anna did not like leaving Nipper like this. 'I can finish off here.'

'You have been on those feet since yesterday.' Matron gave a tolerant smile, 'So go and rest them before your arches fall.'

'Yes, Matron,' Anna smiled, knowing she could do no good with fallen arches.

'An empty sack can't stand, Nurse,' a young soldier, in the opposite bed, said gruffly, lifting his thumb.

'Do you need anything?' Anna asked him in hushed tones so as not to wake the other patients.

'How about a goodnight kiss?' He grinned when she gave a gentle tut.

18

SEPTEMBER 1916

'Ned's coming home!' Anna's eyes lit up the following day when she opened the letter which had been delivered to the Lodge that morning and, hardly able to get the words out, she breathed, 'He is getting leave!' Her eyes scanning the room, she tilted her head, as if listening to music only she could hear, and then closed her eyes, imagining her Ned walking into the lodge where she would run into his arms and welcome him home.

Ned's coming home. The words that had been so long coming kept going round inside her head. The news was like a miracle. It *was* a miracle. Better than her birthday and Christmas all rolled into one. Slapping her hand over her mouth, Anna tried to stifle the giggle that was bursting to break free. Her one true love was coming home.

'Oh, darling, that is good news,' said Ruby, 'I hope he's home for his birthday.'

'His birthday! Of course.' Anna's excited eyes widened, and she laughed. 'I must go into town and collect his birthday present.'

'Is it all right if we eat breakfast first?' Ellie asked, delighted in her friend's good news.

'We could go to Lord Street.' Lord Street was the main shopping street in fashionable Southport, once home for a brief period to Prince Louis-Napoleon Bonaparte before he became the French Emperor, and it was rumoured that Lord Street was the inspiration behind the tree-lined boulevards of Paris, yet today was more likely to see fundraising women who had once rallied for the emancipation of women's suffrage. An avenue of exclusive stores where neither Anna, nor her family, would have been able to afford to shop in days gone by, but given the generous allowance from Ruby and Archie, when she first moved into their home above the pawnshop, Anna had managed to save enough to ensure she could shop in select stores.

The thought brought a pang of guilt when she remembered her brother, Sam, hovering round the doorways of magnificent stores waiting for the grand ladies who would be laden with bags and boxes and would pay him coppers to carry their purchases to their carriages or even down to the pier head and the ferry terminal.

She was so deep in thought she only caught the latter end of Ellie's words. '...Shall we go in the motor, you can drive.'

'Rather!' Anna brightened immediately. Archie had taught her to drive in the grounds of Ashland Hall and before the war she liked nothing better than getting the car out for a leisurely ride. 'We'll be back in plenty of time for Ned's arrival.' His birthday present was ready for collection and she was thrilled she could now give it to him in person, instead of posting it in the hope it would reach him. 'I love driving,' Anna said, her eyes lighting up at the prospect of driving Ellie's beautiful motor.

Anna took the wheel and drove with the hood down in the glorious September sunshine. Winding down narrow lanes with the golden beaches bordering the Irish sea on her left and the Lancashire countryside on her right, she imagined Ned's home-coming and sang at the top of her voice. Ellie joined in, too. A world away from war and shattered bodies.

Anna's first stop was the jewellers, along Lord Street's fashionable boulevard where she had something put away for Ned's birthday. Collecting her parcel, she arrived back to where Ellie was drooling over a peacock-blue cocktail dress in a shop window near the parked car, noting the glances of passers-by, who openly admired the gleaming motor.

Anna slipped into the driver's seat, enjoying the disbelieving expressions from people, seeing two women in the front seat of the car and one actually behind the wheel. Women drivers had been practically unheard of before the war. Nevertheless, it was becoming more common now, as the chauffeurs were all at the Front. The thought of war filled her with trepidation. All those young lives, gone.

'Sam would be old enough to fight,' Anna said, feeling sad, wondering, as she did so often, if he would ever come home again. 'Nipper said he saw him in France.' Quickly brushing away a stray tear, Anna checked there was nothing coming up behind her as she pulled away from the kerb.

'Nipper has been through so much, he could be mistaken,' Ellie said. 'I pray he will grow stronger.

* * *

Later that evening after finishing her afternoon duties and relaxing with Ruby, Archie, May and Ellie in the sitting room of the lodge, Anna heard the distant rumbling of an engine. It grew louder and Ruby put a hand on her arm. Anna took a deep breath, trying to keep her composure. However, no matter how she tried, she could not keep still. In moments she was hurrying outside.

A nurse opened the door to the hall, momentarily shining a dim light on three trucks, like shadows, rolling up the drive. But all too soon, the blackout blinds were pulled way down, and it was hard to see whom she was addressing. A shadowy figure emerged from the first truck and went round the back. He may have been unrecognisable in the blackness, but the voice was as familiar as her own. 'Are you going to stand there all night?'

'Ned!' Anna could not stop herself from letting out a squeal of delight. Running into his arms, she felt his lips on hers. Probing. Urgent. If she could have climbed inside his skin, she would. Eventually they reluctantly parted as a point of decency. Their eyes, now adjusted to the matte black of the night in the silvery moonlight, were only for each other.

'You stink to high heaven,' Anna said adoringly, as Ned's right hand spanned her slim waist, while the other, she noticed held a walking stick. Gone now was the sweet scent of hay that used to follow him round when he worked in the stables, instead he carried the scent of the sea that clung to his navy-blue great coat.

'You say the nicest things, Anna.' Ned had heard the army truck was coming to Ashland Hall when he got off the troop ship and had begged a ride from Liverpool docks. He had waited over a year to see Anna and did not want to waste another moment and hold her in his arms. The soldiers, some only half-conscious, were in dire need of a bath.

However, such luxuries were far from their minds when they held back the enemy line. After a gruelling battle where many men died, their offensive was called off, while smaller skirmishes continued. Their attempt to capture the village of Hooge resulted in many wounded. Since then, they had battled on relentlessly, only now, many months later, seeing their homeland for the first time. During the most horrific battle of the war so far, the Bosch headed their attack with the introduction of poison gas. French and Canadian forces had suffered heavy casualties, but Ned was not going to worry Anna with the news.

He may skirt over the sinking of his own ship, off the Dardanelles after the second battle of Ypres, sure Ruby and Anna would not want to hear about such things.

'I could do with a tidy up,' Ned said in the marbled lobby where stretchers were being installed into wards and the walking wounded hobbled towards an anteroom where they would give their particulars if they were able.

'I will show you where the bathroom is,' Anna said. 'We have plenty of soap and hot water.'

'Sounds like heaven,' Ned answered, keeping his tone upbeat even though the pain screaming through his thigh was almost unbearable. But he was not going to give his darling Anna cause to worry on his first night back.

'Aunt Ruby will lay an egg if she sees the state of these men.' Then, as if the sound of her name made her appear, Ruby was moving forth like a ship in full sail.

'Ned! My darling boy,' Ruby said in a voice only a smidgeon calmer than Anna's, 'there is so much we have to catch up on – after your bath.'

'I want the doctor to have a look at this leg, too, if that's possible.'

'Doctor Bea is a treasure,' said Anna, encouraging a raised eyebrow from Ned. 'And even managed to acquire an X-ray machine.'

'An X-ray machine?' Ned asked, noting how fetching Anna looked in her nurse's uniform.

Anna drew her gaze from Ned, knowing she must concentrate

on why she was here. There were a lot of soldiers ready to be admitted and she had to pull her weight.

Anna smoothed a strand of pale honey-coloured hair that had escaped her white headscarf tied at the back. Her face growing hot, she patted the stiff collar, wishing she could remove it. Anna took a deep, heart-slowing breath, glad that Ned was home at last.

As the demand for auxiliary hospital beds increased, Anna knew these boys would not be here for long. VAD nurses and other Red Cross volunteers were on hand to deal with the incoming patients. Ashland Hall, which had become Ashland Auxiliary Convalescent Hospital, was now under military control and a fully functioning hospital establishment, for recovering soldiers. Anna understood they were to expect more admissions, but looking at the beleaguered bunch of men, she knew it was going to be a busy night. Thank goodness she was still in her pale blue uniform. All she needed to do was put on a clean white apron. Some of the men were in bandages, several in splints and a few were unconscious, lying on stretchers.

'I thought you were chosen to escort the casualties, but I can see you weren't *chosen*,' Anna said to Ned, leading the way to the large anteroom where the soldiers would be assessed for the amount of care they needed, before being admitted to the most suitable wards.

'It's nothing,' Ned said, dismissing his obvious wound. 'A slight graze with a piece of shrapnel in the thigh,' Ned replied and began to undo his buttons, 'here, I'll show you.'

'Not here!' Anna said, cutting off any view from prying eyes, and she saw that mischievous smile she had fallen in love with all those years ago back in Queen Street where they grew up together. 'So, you're not on leave. You're here to recuperate?'

* * *

When the formalities had been gone through, and the huge front door of the hospital closed for the night, Anna found Ned sitting quietly in the private sitting room, used only for family gatherings. When they were alone, he lit the gas mantle.

'Why didn't you tell me you had been injured?' Anna could feel her throat tighten when she noticed the black circles under his eyes, which told their own tale. He was thinner now too and his once vibrant eyes had a haunted, tired look. Although there was still a ghost of misbehaviour when he took her in his arms and Anna's heartbeat raced. 'Ned!' Anna said reluctantly as he pulled her closer, 'someone might come.'

'Good old English reserve.' Ned laughed, letting her go, although, his laugh was not as hearty as it used to be, she noticed. 'We picked up some navy lads from the military hospital in Fazakerley,' Ned told her, filling in the heavy silence that ensued.

'The First Western?' Anna asked, feeling unusually shy in his presence, and he nodded. They were just making small talk. Both knowing what they wanted. Each could see it in their hungry eyes. If only they could be alone, thought Anna...

'I couldn't wait another moment, I had to see you.' Ned's words tumbled from his ever-so-kissable lips, and Anna imagined herself melting, just sliding onto the carpet in a puddle of lust as her cheeks grew hotter.

The feeling made her vulnerable, just thinking about their entwining limbs gave her sharp palpitations that, in any other situation, would need the attention of Doctor Bea. As every hair on her scalp stood to attention and every skin cell tingled when his finger brushed her cheek, Anna knew if he took her now, she would not object.

'I have missed you so much it hurt,' Ned told her. Standing up and reaching out, he caught her waist and drew her to him, caressing the arc of her hip bones with his thumbs, his lips melding with hers, and Anna felt as if she had a runaway horse thundering inside her. Or maybe that was Ned's heartbeat she could feel. Then suddenly he pulled away, holding her at arm's length. 'Let's get me fixed up,' he said, his voice raspy with desire, his rapid breathing told Anna he had far more willpower than she did, because she knew, if he had lingered a moment longer, she would have... she would...

Quickly coming to her senses, Anna knew what could have happened and the thought terrified her. What if...? What if...? No. She could not think that way. Ned was away at sea for long months. The sea was his life. He always said he wanted to see the world. And she could not jeopardise his ambition. She had a career in nursing and even though her vocation was hard and sometimes heartbreakingly sad, she loved her work and knew she was not ready to give it up, as she would have to do if...

But Ned *was* her life. He was the air that she breathed, the light that led her way forward, and if he asked her to walk into the fires of hell to be with him, she would do so. Willingly.

* * *

'We have a fully equipped operating theatre,' Anna said, slipping into her usual nursing style as she had been trained to do in awkward situations, while she led him along the corridor towards Doctor Bea's examination room, desperately trying to stop the scandalous thoughts that were running through her head. 'Ashland Hall is complete with trained nurses, as well as volunteer nurses and we also have the wonderful Doctor Bea who will have you on the mend in no time at all.' Anna knew that treating him like a patient was the only way she could cope. 'And we have wonderful amenities to help in your recuperation...'

'Wonderful,' Ned repeated, his dancing eyes causing her cheeks to fire up once more. 'I'll take it.'

'Pardon?' Anna asked, stopping to make sure she had heard him properly.

'Your sales pitch was spot on, I'll put down a deposit on the house forthwith.' Ned threw back his head and laughed when he saw her forehead crease in confusion and, when she realised he was joking with her, Anna cuffed his arm with the notes she was holding. 'Nevertheless, I am your man if you need your vegetable gardens sorting or your stables mucking out.'

'There aren't many horses left since the military requisitioned them,' Anna said, 'and you will not be tending any patches until we've had a look at that hip.' His limp was obvious now. She continued to chatter inanely, avoiding any kind of intimacy. If Ned looked at her in that special way he had, she would give herself body and soul. So, help her, she would.

'I suppose this Doctor Bea is ninety-nine and suffering from dementia,' Ned offered, as they reached Doctor Bea's door.

'She is nothing of the sort,' Anna said, amused, when he raised his eyebrows in disbelief.

'A woman?' Ned questioned his hearing and when Anna nodded, he said: 'This is only a flesh wound, nothing serious. I don't need any fuss or bother.'

'Are you sure?' she asked, looking pointedly at his walking stick.

'I doubt I even need it,' he said with bravado, 'but I must admit, it does encourage lots of sympathy from pretty nurses.' When he saw Anna's wry expression, he laughed out loud. 'Well now I've heard everything, a woman doctor. Is she beautiful, like you?'

'Wait and see,' Anna added mysteriously before knocking on the consulting room door, and she was amused to see Ned's surprised reaction when he realised that Doctor Bea was not the meek and mild woman he had in mind.

'Drop your trousers and get on the bed,' Doctor Bea instructed, and Anna stifled a giggle as she left the room, knowing that being brusque was the good lady doctor's way of putting some servicemen firmly in their place.

* * *

Her examination completed, Doctor Bea ordered a wheelchair and told Ned he may take a bath before getting into bed, which he was looking forward to doing. Having travelled from Plymouth in the early hours of God-knows-when, his head could not hit the pillow fast enough.

'I'll be in the bathroom if you need me,' Ned told Anna, bashing the wheelchair into the door frame. 'This thing is not as easy to manoeuvre as a horse – or a ship,' he grinned.

'Here, let me help you,' Anna said, expertly directing the wheelchair. Looking at the back of Ned's strong neck as she pushed him towards the bathroom, Anna recoiled in horror. 'You have a louse crawling down your neck!' No matter how much she loved him she was not going to share him with headlice, 'Your hair is walking with them.'

'They'll have come off the PBI,' Ned said. 'They say the trenches are riddled with them.'

'I don't care if you got them off the Poor Bloody Infantry or the King of Timbuktu, you are not getting into a nice clean bed without getting rid of every last one,' Anna said, hanging the 'in use' sign on the handle outside the bathroom door. She then locked it behind them and quickly unbuttoned Ned's shirt. Dragging his singlet over his head, she began filling the bath with hot water. 'Remove your trousers,' she ordered, and Ned thought all his birthdays had come at once. However, his hopes were dashed when she said, 'I am having no lodgers on my ward, not even the six-legged kind!' She turned quickly when she heard Ned roar with laughter.

'I am capable of undressing if I take it slowly, Anna, but if you insist.' He began to unbutton his navy-blue uniform trousers, and Anna realised what she had done. In her haste to delouse him, she forgot the implications of being alone while he removed all his clothing!

'Oh, my goodness!' Anna exclaimed. What *was* she doing? Her actions could have led to... could have led to... Her pulse was like a runaway train. 'I could get a severe reprimand for this!' she said quickly, trying to cover her embarrassment. Even though the thought of making love to Ned here in the bathroom was tempting beyond words, Matron would have her shot by a dawn firing squad, she was sure!

Quickly she opened the cupboard, took out a bottle of Sassafras oil, and a block of carbolic soap. Then, placing them on the side of the bath, her face hotter than the running water, she said, 'Of course you can manage!' *Whatever was I thinking*? 'I'll leave you this. Use as much as you like. We have plenty! And there's more if you need it.' Mortified, Anna knew that if he had been an ordinary patient, she would not have batted an eyelid at the cheeky insinuation in his smile, but Ned was anything but ordinary. He was her Ned.

'Put your dirty uniform in the sack provided and I'll arrange for clean clothes to be sent straight away!' Anna did not look back as she hurried from the bathroom. Even when she was halfway down the corridor, she could still hear Ned laughing.

* * *

'Aunt Ruby, stop fussing, we will sort everything out. Wear a nice frock. We're going to have a surprise birthday dinner for Ned,' Ellie said. 'Standing on ceremony has become so outdated since war began, but I know some of the older generation cannot ignore the social etiquette.'

'Older generation!' Ruby's eyes widened. 'If I didn't love you, Ellie, dear, I would have you banished to the barn.' They all laughed and the happy atmosphere in the lodge was music to Ruby's ears. This was something she had dreamed of for years. Her whole family around her.

'It may be September, but the evening is lovely, shall we take the celebration out to the garden?'

'Oh let's,' cried Ruby. 'I am so excited to see Ned's face when he sees what we have done.'

Anna was thrilled when she wheeled Ned into the garden and saw the table, set for six, with all the silver and crystal proudly displayed. 'This is nice.' She had exchanged her stiff collar and cuffs and looked exquisite in a dress of pale lemon lace. The high collar made her look demure.

Ned looked so handsome in his navel uniform as he regaled them all with funny tales, while keeping the more gruesome details from the women. 'The nurses at the Front are doing a sterling job. We picked up so many casualties to take to the hospital ships,' he said. 'The conditions are not ideal, up to their knees in mud that clings better than any glue, but they never complain.'

Anna, rapt, listened with a hint of envy. It had never crossed her mind that Ned would be around other women. Other nurses... Looking at him now, she was not so sure she was being silly. However, she did know a green-eyed monster was lurking somewhere inside her. No matter, she thought, he was home now. He was all hers.

'The Red Cross set up a hospital in a deserted school, and

soldiers were arriving before the staff even had time to unpack equipment,' said Ned.

His tales were thrilling, exciting Anna, who wondered what it would be like to see battle first-hand. She had planned to go and try to find her brother. And Ned's exciting stories did not diminish her ambitions.

'Did you know,' Ruby exclaimed, 'income tax has doubled to pay for this awful, bloody war! So much for it being over by Christmas,' she continued, 'but the authorities failed to tell us which Christmas they were talking about!'

'Have a word with the Lord High Admiral when you get back, Ned,' said Archie, his eyes twinkling.

'Oh don't.' Anna did not want to think of him going back to sea, especially now. She knew so much more about the battles. 'You must be so worried.'

'I don't mind,' Ned lied, 'but I'll try not to get in the way of U-boats, next time.' He did not tell Anna that the superstructure that fractured his hip had killed the young sailor fighting beside him. Half an inch to the left and he would not see this birthday.

'We don't want such talk today,' said Aunt Ruby. 'It must be present-giving time, surely.'

'Oh, yes!' Anna pushed back her chair and took out a long, brown leather box from her bag and handed it to Ned with a kiss. 'Happy birthday, my love.' Her eyes shone as she handed him the beautifully wrapped box.

'You shouldn't have,' Ned said, rubbing his hands together excitedly. 'But I'm glad you did.' All smiles, he carefully unwrapped the paper, savouring Anna's anticipation, an impish smile making his lips twitch as all eyes wanted to see what his gift was, as did he, but he was enjoying their curiosity just as much.

'Come on, slowcoach,' Anna said, 'it'll be dark soon.' And

when he opened the brown leather box his eyes widened in surprise.

'It's one of those new wristwatches!' Ned said and Anna nodded.

'Waterproof for many fathoms, the jeweller told me.'

'How clever!' Ned exclaimed, turning the wristwatch this way and that, admiring the white-faced dial encased in a dark brown leather strap.

'Look at the back.' Anna could not hide her excitement. 'There's an inscription.'

Ned read the dedication on the back of the watch, and his face split in a wide, appreciative smile. 'There is not a chance of me getting lost now that my name and date of birth is inscribed in such fancy letters. I love it,' he said, proudly strapping it to his wrist, 'but you shouldn't have spent so much money on me, these watches are expensive.'

Anna knew it was worth every penny just to see the look of pleasure on his handsome face.

'Do you think they'll catch on after the war?' asked Archie, admiring the watch.

'I'm sure they will.' Ruby sniffed and Anna gave Ned a little reminding nod.

'And these handkerchiefs are absolutely the best ever, Aunt Ruby, thank you.' He wheeled his chair across the lawn and warmly kissed her upturned cheek.

Ruby smiled indulgently. 'Think nothing of it,' she waved away the acknowledgement, relaxing visibly.

* * *

'Shall we go inside?' Ruby asked. She loved the outdoors but was not as fond of the forthcoming autumnal evenings, which grew a little chilly when the sun went down.

'Let's walk for a while.' Ned said to Anna, catching her hand as he stood up with the aid of his walking stick. 'And don't worry, I won't fall. Your Doctor Bea is very thorough in her ministrations, even if I did think differently at first.'

'She is one of the best,' Anna said, 'we are so lucky to have her.' If this war had taught many doubters one thing, it was that women were not just pretty things to look at and treat like precious china dolls, they were as clever and as forward-thinking as any man.

Nevertheless, they also liked to be kissed and when Ned put his finger gently to Anna's lips and then brushed his lips on hers, time stood still, and all thoughts of anything that was not her soulmate and one true love sailed right out of her head.

This time, Ned's kiss was not the frenzied passion of a starving man at a feast as it had been earlier. Instead, his lips met hers in a languorous, undulating connection she never wanted to end.

'Evening, Sister,' said a volunteer nurse who was escorting a hobbling patient on crutches through the grounds. They were accompanied by the dying echoes of a nightingale's song and gave Anna and Ned a respectful nod as they passed, quickly followed by another nurse pushing a man in a wheelchair.

'It's like Lime Street station.' Ned sounded a little impatient and led her to the summer house.

Closing the door behind them, Ned stood, just looking at her, saying nothing for a moment. Then he made all her dreams come true in eleven words.

'Anna, when this awful war is over, will you marry me?' He held out a powder-blue leather box and placed it in her hand.

Her heart hammered in her chest and she found it hard to breathe. This was the best moment of her life! She loved him above all else. She always had.

'Oh yes, Ned,' she breathed, 'you know I will. But why do we have to wait until the war is over?' Opening the box, her eyes widened through a haze of happy tears and Anna's heart flipped when she saw the gold band with the Hebrew letters, *MIZPAH* engraved around its circumference. These rings had become a symbol of eternal love between serving men and their sweethearts since the beginning of the war and Anna felt her heart skip when Ned lifted her hand and gently kissed it.

'*Lord watch between me and thee when we are absent one from each other,*' Ned said paraphrasing as he slipped the ring onto the third finger of her left hand.

'Oh I do hope so, my love.' Anna looked up to him and her eyes were full of happy tears.

When Ned took her in his arms, he vowed they would be together forever and Anna sighed, content she was the luckiest girl in the whole wide world.

However, there was little time to enjoy their newfound happiness when the rumble of a truck sounded outside the door. Quickly inserting the ring back into the plush velvet interior of the box knowing she was not allowed to wear jewellery on duty, Anna slipped the box into the deep pocket of her pale lace gown.

'Here we go again!' she cried, giving Ned a quick kiss on the cheek. There was no time to change into her uniform. Who knew what the next convoy would bring?

As she reached the wide gravelled driveway, the orderlies were already bringing the stretchers from the Red Cross ambulance and casualties were coming thick and fast now.

'It is not often that casualties are met by nurses in evening gowns, with diamonds at their throat,' Ellie said as they hurried to meet the ambulances. There was no time to discuss the matter now, as the wounded were quickly dispatched to appropriate wards. One soldier, hobbling unsteadily on crutches, was making his way unaided when Anna hurried to help him into the building.

'I can think of better ways of bringing home Boche souvenirs, Tommy,' Anna said brightly, quickly discovering he had come home with shrapnel damage to his leg.

'So can I, Nurse, but I didn't have a suitcase handy!' He grinned through the inevitable screen of cigarette smoke, 'I 'ave t' say, though, it was worth gettin' in the way of the guns, if I'd a known I was comin' to such a classy establishment.'

'Glad you approve,' Anna laughed. She felt as if she was walking on air, and not only for the sake of the injured man arriving tonight did she remain cheerful.

'This place must cost and arm and a leg if the nurses wear lace frocks!'

Anna laughed. 'Go with the orderly, we will soon have you comfy and on the mend.' Nevertheless, the heroic men now arriving certainly brought the war closer and even though her heart was light, she couldn't help worrying. When Ned was eventually pronounced fit for duty and returned to his ship, the guns and U-boats would not discriminate. They killed newly engaged fiancés too.

* * *

Anna woke the following morning and could hardly believe that she and Ned were engaged to be married. Then, stretching luxuriously in her bed, she outstretched her hand before her, and giggled the gentle laugh of a girl in love.

'Thank you for saving him, Lord.' Anna hugged her left hand

to her and offered a little prayer to the cerulean sky beyond the open window. Then, it being her day off, she dressed quickly, keen to show Aunt Ruby and Archie the gold ring that Ned had given her the night before. Excited at the prospect of spending the whole day with her beloved Ned, Anna did not want to waste a second of it.

Her light, quick tread on the sweeping stairs came to a sudden halt when she saw Aunt Ruby waiting in the foyer. Looking up to where Anna now stood, she spoke with more than a hint of sadness. 'He has gone, my dear, Ned has gone.'

'No!' Anna did not trust herself to say another word. She recalled their last kiss, the way he held her for so long, saying nothing... Just holding her. Then he let her go as she hurried away to the ambulance which had arrived at that moment. She thought... she expected to... A dry sob escaped her lips. How could he! 'He is injured!' Anna cried, too distraught to hide her tears.

Aunt Ruby came to the bottom of the sweeping staircase and took Anna's hand. 'He is a serving officer. The Royal Navy will take care of him now.'

'He did not give me any indication that...' Anna could not finish her sentence. Last night he gave her a ring and asked her to marry him. He made her the happiest girl in the world. She went to bed, her head full of hopes and dreams of their future together. Why would he go off in the middle of the night without telling her?

'Obviously, he is a man who cannot say goodbye.' Ruby was unable to divulge the conversation she heard between Archie and Ned before he left. They did not know she was listening in the hallway of the lodge, when Ned told Archie he had been given special leave to see his family.

'That can only mean one thing. You are on Special Operations?'

said Archie, then more quickly he said, 'I'm sorry. I know you are not allowed to answer questions. Forget I asked.'

'I only wish I could tell Anna, but I did what I came back to do, and I asked her to be my wife, but keep it under your hat. I'm sure she will want to tell you herself.'

'I'm sure he had good reason to leave so suddenly,' Ruby said as Anna looked at the woman who had given her and Ned the security which they both needed and who, she knew, would forgive Ned anything.

'You would say that!' Anna's tone was terse. 'He can do no wrong in your eyes and I thought so too, until he sloped off without so much as a goodbye. What about his wounded leg? Did it miraculously get better?'

'I understand how bereft you must feel.'

'Bereft?' Anna's eyes flashed anger as she hurled the words across the room. 'Bereft? I don't think so, Aunt Ruby. I am far too angry to feel bereft!'

There was a sudden heavy silence and Ruby said nothing, her face devoid of any expression. And Anna realised she had been unbelievably nasty. Her hand flew to her lips in an attempt to stop another outburst as the enormity of her words dawned on her.

'Aunt Ruby, I am so sorry, that was uncalled for.'

'I understand your reaction, my dear,' Ruby said, but her empathy did nothing to assuage Anna's embarrassment, in fact, it only made her feel even more irritated, but with superhuman effort, she managed to keep calm. But his leaving proved one thing. She had to do what was right for her, and the war – the same as Ned did. And when she saw Doctor Bea later, she was going to tell her that, yes, she would be going to France if she was still needed.

19

Anna was changing Nipper's dressing when he took a sharp breath as she began to clean the wound. Aunt Ruby was not at all pleased earlier that day when Anna revealed her intentions. So when she came on duty, Anna was not feeling on top of the world.

'I'm sorry, did I hurt you?' Anna said as Matron Bray, a no-nonsense, often unapproachable stickler for rules and regulations, entered the ward.

'He can't understand you, Sister, he is away with the fairies on morphia,' Matron snapped, and Anna took in a slow stream of steadying air. Sometimes, she wondered if this particular matron actually had a heart, when the poor lad's effort not to cry out in pain was thwarted as she began to remove the blood-dried bandages covering his hands. 'They must be scrupulously cleaned,' Matron said, 'there is bound to be some fear, but the most important thing is not to let their distress distract you.'

'Yes, Matron,' Anna said, knowing she cried if she got a splinter in her hand, God alone knew what she would be like if she had two of her fingers shot away.

'I am happier here than dodging German whizzbangs,' Nipper smiled as Matron moved onto the next bed, and Anna smiled too. He had heard every word.

Anna soaked his bandaged hand in a white enamel bowl of warm saline water, which did a fine job of loosening the dried blood and helped the bandage come off easier. Gently, applying the new dressing, Anna made him much more comfortable, before moving onto the next bed, where a mud-soaked, blood-soaked soldier was sitting in a wheelchair awaiting orders to move, when Doctor Bea came onto the ward.

'The most important quality for a nurse is compassion, and I am pleased to say, Sister Cassidy, you certainly have that.' She looked round the ward to the beds, each one tidy and filled. 'When you have done that, you might want to give out the tobacco allowance. There are some here who look like they could do with something to cheer them up. Carry on.'

When Matron Meredith came to take over from Matron Bray, everybody breathed a sigh of relief.

Doctor Bea went over to have a word.

'You look tired, Matron,' she said in that low Scottish burr that could soothe or scare patients and medics alike depending on the situation.

'I am a little tired,' Anna heard Matron Meredith say and she knew the older woman had been on duty longer than anybody. 'We have had a few busy nights this week.'

'I know that, Matron, but perhaps your spirits will be lifted when I tell you that Professor Burns is arriving to join us very soon.'

'Really? And why is Professor Burns visiting?' Matron Meredith looked puzzled. Professor Burns, consultant from the First Western Hospital, was well known to the nursing staff and much-feared due to his brusque manner, deafening voice and often unreasonable expectations.

'He's not visiting, Matron, he is coming to take over from me,' Doctor Bea told Matron of her intentions to go to France to tend wounded soldiers.

And before Matron could say any more, the girl from the local post office came onto the ward pushing a trolley.

'Here we go, Boyos. Here's the post.'

Everybody brightened, and one of the more mobile soldiers went over to the trolley and took a bundle of envelopes to hand out to the other men, who cheered and eagerly opened their post, but Anna noticed one young soldier, who had not received anything.

'Maybe if you let your family know where you are, they would write to you,' said one of the old soldiers, and Anna realised that she had never seen the soldier read or write.

'I'm no good with words,' said Sproglet.

'I imagine it will take time to settle down after what you have been through.' Anna saw him nod, grateful for the excuse. 'Would you like me to write to anybody? Let your family know how you are, perhaps?' She saw his eyes light up and he looked relieved.

'That would be good of you, Nurse. I'd be so grateful.'

'Of course, as soon as I've finished my duties, I will get a pen and paper.'

Later on, she drew up a chair and positioned herself. 'Right now, you tell me what to write and we can get this posted tonight.'

'Right... erm... Dear Mam... I hope you are all well. I am doing champion and you wouldn't believe how grand this hospital is. You might have heard of it. Ashland Hall it's called. It is like a palace. Better than a palace and you can come and visit if you find the time...'

* * *

'I have been watching you, Nurse Cassidy,' said Doctor Bea when Anna left the ward to go and post the letter, 'you have such a calming effect on the men. You notice things that others are too busy to notice.'

'Just doing my job, Doctor,' said Anna, enjoying the frisson of pride Doctor Bea's observation gave her. 'Some of the men don't like to admit they can't read or write.'

'Exactly,' said Doctor Bea, 'but you picked up on the fact and you did something about it, making a soldier's day that little bit brighter. Imagine how many soldiers are on the battlefield and have no way of getting word to their families.' She paused for a moment. 'Men can be strange creatures. Enormously proud, obviously. And sometimes, very silly. Have you given any more thought of serving overseas?'

'I have, Doctor,' Anna answered, 'I am still pondering.'

Doctor Bea nodded but said nothing as she made her way towards the stairs and Anna, heading to the sluice room, wondered why she had hesitated. She had been so certain she was going to go earlier.

Ellie came in with another batch of bedpans. 'Skiving, I see,' she laughed. 'I don't blame you; you should see what I just had to clear up.' She wrinkled her petite nose and shuddered dramatically, making Anna smile.

'I am not skiving,' Anna laughed. Drying her hands on a clean towel, she too wrinkled her nose, 'I would rather not know what you cleared up, thank you.' Ellie enjoyed keeping up the spirits of the injured men with her risqué banter, out of matron's earshot, of course. However, the men certainly cheered up when she was on duty. 'My stomach thinks my throat has been cut, I am so hungry,' Anna said, lifting a clean stack of bedpans. The hours were long, and they saw sights a woman should never see, but Anna loved her work.

'What's for luncheon today?' Ellie asked and Anna shook her head.

'Too late,' Anna said, watching the military porters carrying another young soldier in on a stretcher and saw Ellie's shoulders slump. 'You go. I'll finish here.' Anna smiled, knowing Ellie, although tall and very slim, loved her food as much as she loved dancing. 'And make sure they save me some before I drop down dead with starvation.'

'Are you sure you don't mind?' Ellie was already halfway out of the room, heading quickly towards the door and, by the look of it, had no intention of coming back to help.

Anna shook her head and smiled. Ellie was incorrigible.

* * *

Ellie was in the staff section of the large dining room, which had once been the servants' hall, where energetic, opinionated and intelligent women now cooked and served food to staff and patients of every class.

Anna took the seat opposite Ellie.

'You will never guess what one of the soldiers called us nurses, even the strictest sisters, Matron and Doctor Bea?'

'What did he call us?' Ellie asked, pushing away her empty plate, her hunger satiated.

'He said we were his Mersey Angels,' Anna replied, eager to tuck into the boiled egg, lettuce, tomato and radishes collected fresh from the garden that morning. Ashland Hall was self-sufficient in garden produce, which was tended by servicemen who were on the mend. Expert diggers given the number of trenches they had dug in Flanders fields, now they enjoyed digging for pleasure and not for safety and shelter.

When they finished their luncheon, Ellie and Anna returned to their work and Anna sat at the table in the centre of the long ward, writing her notes. When she finished the latest report, she would arrange afternoon tea for the boys. Looking up, she noticed Nipper had woken and was struggling to sit up.

Knowing she would not get any more reports done as one by one they woke from their afternoon nap and were now eagerly awaiting a cup of tea, she put away her notes.

Nipper had been relieved of his facial bandages as Doctor Bea felt his eyes needed to adjust to the light, although she had kept the blinds of his window closed so that the September sunshine did not make his eyes sore. Anna knew it was customary for these young men to adjust and get their bearings after spending so long in the trenches.

'Are you feeling any better after your snooze, Nipper?' Anna asked, pouring him a little water from the jug and allowing him a few sips.

He nodded. His eyes haunted by who-knows-what awful sights he had seen.

'Here, let me make you a little more comfortable,' Anna said, lifting his pillow and giving it a jolly good thumping, and she noticed him smile for the second time that day.

'I see you've still got a good right hook,' he said in a husky whisper and Anna stopped what she was doing, when he said, 'you gave my brother Jerky a right go-along, one day... He said he'd never had a whack like that off a girl before.'

'I remember,' Anna said. How could she ever forget? He was no good to anybody, especially Lottie.

'He's a bad lot,' Nipper croaked. His throat still badly scarred three weeks after his arrival.

'You must get some rest,' Anna said, unwilling to get into conversation about her nemesis. The embodiment of every nightmare she had ever known. Taking a glass thermometer, she popped it into his mouth even though she could see his temperature was high. 'I have a surprise for you Nipper,' Anna knew Izzy was so proud of this son.

'A surprise? For me?' Nipper sounded doubtful. 'I haven't had many of those, Is it a good one?'

'The best,' Anna said, 'and I will probably break every rule in the book, but I don't care. I have someone who will be thrilled to see you without your bandages.' She turned, leaving Nipper to wait for her return.

He decided to close his eyes, just for a moment, to rest them.

When he opened them again, he thought he was still dreaming when he saw his Ma standing beside the bed, and she had tears in her eyes. With his bandages off, he could see the deepening lines on her face, as tough as old boots. She didn't cry for nothing or nobody, but now she was wiping her nose on a clean handkerchief and sniffing past herself.

'It's so good to see those lovely chocolate-coloured eyes again?' Izzy's voice was as soft as a kitten's purr. 'How are you feeling?' Her heart went out to her son who looked like he had been in a fight with one of those tanks the fundraisers were so eager to buy.

'My hand's a bit sore, like,' Nipper said with his usual understatement, 'but apart from that I'm tickety-boo. But don't tell the doctor, Ma, they'll be shoving me out the door and back on the battlefield.' He grinned, knowing he was a long way off being sent back to the battlefield, but he didn't want his Ma worrying over him. 'I love being here and you visiting every Sunday. Ashland Hall is another life from the battlefields, and I felt sorry for all those poor men still out there.' He started coughing and wheezing. He had talked too much.

'I'll get the doctor,' Anna said, fearing he had overdone it. The damage to his throat caused by gas burns had blistered and she worried they may become infected, even though she had been scrupulous in her care, but Nipper still looked a little flushed. 'We will have you up in no time.' Anna's voice was upbeat, even though she was worried, feeling heartsore for the lad who was so young and vulnerable, she saw the pain etched on his face, even though he tried to hide it with a lazy grin. But Izzy could not hide her worry. 'Doctor Bea will come and have a look at your hand, just lie back and have a little rest.'

'Diya think they'll cut it off, Nurse?' Nipper's eyes were wide in alarm, and Anna knew it was a consideration if his wounds became gangrenous, but she had to keep him calm.

'Not before tea.' Anna's words encouraged him to relax a little.

As she turned to go and fetch the doctor, she heard him say to his mother in a throaty whisper, 'She's a real angel you know, Ma. If anyone can fix me it's Anna.'

'Rest your voice, Nipper,' Anna said soothingly. And when he began to cough, she hurried back to his bedside, offering him a drink of water. 'You're going to be fine.' Anna smoothed his sheets and patted his good hand while Izzy sat by her son's bedside, having been allowed to stay at Ashland Hall for the night. 'I will make sure of that.' There was not a lot Anna could do for him, but human contact and gentle words were a comfort at a time like this.

'That night...' he struggled to speak, and she gently shushed him. However, she could see he wanted to go on. 'The night... of the fire...'

'The fire?' Anna asked, her heart plummeting at the thought of that Christmas Eve six years ago when her life changed forever.

'Jerky got riled... you'd got the better of him, see...' Nipper took a deep breath, 'you, putting him on his arse like that... sorry for the language...' Nipper closed his eyes as if trying to block out the memory. But Anna realised he needed to speak out. To make his peace. Because there was no telling what he might say. 'He went and got rags... and paraffin...' Nipper was talking about the night her mother and two of her three brothers perished when their house was on fire. The police never did find out who started the fire.

'What did he do then...?' Anna was afraid to ask, but she needed to know. She held her breath and listened to the young lad.

'He lit the rags, and...' Nipper was obviously exhausted now, slumping back on the pillow.

'Go on.' Anna's mind could barely take in what he was telling her. His face was solemn. His words, halting. Nothing prepared Anna for what she heard next.

'He waited until you'd gone with the big fella... Kincaid... Then he went back to your house. He thought everybody had gone to church and he stuffed the lit rag through your letter box.' As if all the energy had been sucked out of him, Nipper shrank into the bed as a chill of iced water ran through Anna's veins. She stood at his bedside with Izzy.

His mother gripped Anna's arm, 'Oh Anna,' Izzy gasped, 'I am so sorry.'

'Are you telling me your brother murdered my family?' Anna felt numb. She could not voice the terrible thoughts of revenge that were crashing through her mind.

Nipper barely nodded. That night changed her life forever. She lost her whole family. Her mother and two younger siblings died and Sam was taken by the church and sent to Canada. Anna had not seen him for six long years.

She saw Izzy's tears rolling silently down her cheeks.

'Jerky's a downright badd'n, and Nipper hasn't got anything to do with him. Please don't think that, Anna.'

'I'm no angel, Izzy,' Anna said, 'and I promise you this, if your oldest lad ever has the misfortune to cross my path, I will not be held responsible for my actions. But I will do everything in my power to save this young hero.'

* * *

For the next few days, Anna felt as shell-shocked as the soldiers coming in from the battlefields. She kept going over and over the revelation in her head.

'It's my fault,' she told Archie when the information became too huge to keep to herself. 'If only I had not challenged Jerky Woods. If I had gone straight home... given Ned the money to take back to Ruby. If only I had gone to check on Michael and James first.'

'It was not your fault, Anna,' Archie's tone was determined as he headed out of the door to begin his daily duties, 'don't you dare think that.'

* * *

When Anna arrived on duty a couple of days later, she found the ward unusually quiet. The young soldiers, always eager to hear news, were all in their beds, quiet as cherubs.

'What's the matter?' Anna asked Ellie, who was closing the curtains round young Sproglet's bed.

Ellie shook her head, and Anna's heart lurched. Popping her head through the curtains, hoping to see him sitting up at least, Anna saw the sooty lashes of the young soldier resting on marble cheeks and she knew immediately this young Sapper would not be going outside today. Or any day after that. He had passed away in his sleep.

'He had a smile on his face,' said Ellie, 'as if he was glad to meet his maker.'

Anna was surprised at how sad she felt. Young Sproglet, as she too had come to call him, could not read, and write his own mail he had jumped at the chance when she offered to write to his family, to let them know he would appreciate a visit. But he took a nasty turn when the infection in his leg became uncontrollable, and he was moved nearer to Matron's office, swapping beds with Nipper.

'The poison travelled quicker than anyone could have foreseen, it knocked the life right out of him.'

'Why do the good ones have to go first?' Anna asked, unaware of the tears running down her cheeks.

20

'Are you off duty this afternoon?' Anna asked, catching Ellie coming out of the long ward, where the more boisterous, recovering soldiers were singing round the grand piano.

'...What's the use of worrying, it never was worthwhile...' The rousing chorus of military voices filled the mezzanine and Anna sighed. It had been a busy morning and she wanted to get away from the house for a while.

Ellie nodded, yes, she was off duty.

'Oh good. Do you fancy a train ride into Liverpool?' Anna loved her vocation, and she valued being back at Ashland Hall. Nevertheless, her head had buzzed with thoughts of Ned all day. She had forgiven Ned for walking out without saying goodbye knowing she could never stay mad at him for long. Especially when the stories, bandied freely round the wards, were so bloodcurdling. They were beginning to set her nerves on edge, because she knew whatever these brave men had been through, her Ned and Sam would be experiencing the same thing.

'One of the Tommies told me there was a cracking film on at

the Scala,' Ellie said eagerly. 'It's been extremely popular by all accounts.'

'Is it a comedy? Is it Charlie Chaplin?' Anna threw the words over her shoulder as she led the way into the sluice room. 'I don't fancy watching *The Perils of Pauline* again,' she said, handing the bedpan to the VAD nurse standing nearby.

'No,' Ellie said eagerly, 'it's called *The Battle of The Somme*. It was premiered in London.' She watched Anna's grim expression. 'Apparently, in the last six weeks of general release, twenty million people have seen it!'

'Twenty million?' Anna's eyes widened. 'And it shows real soldiers, not actors?'

'Real soldiers,' Ellie repeated, 'in a real battle.'

Seeing what their men had to endure would give Anna a better understanding of what this awful war was all about, because, as things stood now, all they saw was the result of the fighting overseas, not the cause.

'Oh yes, let's,' Anna said and Ellie, always up for a train ride into Liverpool, smiled broadly.

'I heard the soldiers talking about it, and they say it is incredibly graphic.'

'Is it?' Anna looked doubtful, and when Ellie nodded, she said, 'I'm not sure I want to see that... Is there a Mary Pickford on?'

'Don't be such a wet blanket, Anna,' Ellie laughed. 'I heard that King George has given it his approval.' Ellie looked even more eager now, and grudgingly Anna agreed to go, if it was good enough for the King...

'As long as it is not all dead bodies and buildings being blown to pieces.'

'Certainly not, dear.' Ellie laughed. 'Who wants to see all that kind of thing in a war film.'

* * *

The picture house would be full to bursting, given the size of this queue, Anna said, doubtful they would even get a seat. Ellie agreed as they queued outside the Scala, dressed smartly in jaunty hats and good woollen double-breasted coats to keep out the early October chill.

A moment later they heard their names being called.

'Is that you, Nurse Anna! Nurse Ellie?'

The two nurses stood on the tips of their toes to get a good look at the owner of the commanding voice.

The doorman, in full khaki uniform had his right arm missing.

'Alfie!' cried Ellie. 'You got out then?' Alfie was one of her Tommies from her days at The First Western. He had been in a right state when they admitted him, but he rallied quickly and soon became the life and soul of the ward. Ellie looked after him from the beginning, even when he was moved to Ashland Hall and she used to lark about, calling him her shadow. 'I'm ever so glad to see you looking well,' she said when he ambled along the line.

Alfie edged back the crowd of onlookers, and beckoning the two nurses forward, said to the muttering crowd: 'These are our ministering angels... The women who fix our boys.' He looked proud, as if he had personally brought them to the line when a cheer went up.

Anna could feel her face grow hot, but Ellie was loving the attention.

'You didn't have to move us to the front of the queue, Alf, we were quite prepared to wait our turn,' Anna said as they were ushered into the brightly lit foyer.

'Speak for yourself,' Ellie answered, giving Alf a nudge of thanks with her elbow.

'If I know anything, you two have been on your feet all day. You need a good sit-down.'

'Thanks Alf,' Anna said, buying some sweets at the kiosk. 'Here, take these as a thank you and give them to your children.'

'Oh Miss, you shouldn't 'ave,' he tugged the peak of his cap, 'but I 'ave to be honest, the little ones will be right pleased.'

Anna and Ellie managed to get a seat near the front of the picture house and settled down to watch the flickering black and white images on the big screen. Through a pall of cigarette smoke, they were entranced. Soldiers, sweethearts, mothers, and wives gazed up, their mouths agog as the film showed the new horrors of war... poison gas, flame-throwers and tanks aimed at the men.

Unable to rip her eyes from the screen, Anna gripped the seat. Her stomach churning at the battle horror now showing ceiling high. Wounded soldiers on the shoulders of their brave brothers-in-arms. Others resting in the muddy trenches, writing, sleeping, and smoking to pass the time as explosions erupted behind them. There had been a lot of footage on the big screen, but none as 'real' as this.

Viewing 'The Big Push', which took place last July, the film showed the joint offensive of English and French armies hoping to break through the German lines to achieve victory on the Western Front. But that was months ago.

Anna's heart was beating so fast she could hardly breathe. Everywhere was bare and stark, not at all like the posters, now papered on every street wall. She recalled the days when the men, fuelled with nationalistic fervour, thought they were marching off to the dawn of Britain's greatest glory, the images of loyal mothers and daughters stood at neat windows, patriotically waving to their boys as they cheerily marched off... To this.

'The women of Britain say go...,' Anna whispered, repeating a familiar slogan, as tears rolled down her cheeks. 'To this hellish place!' Clearly now, in her mind's eye, she saw Lord Kitchener's forefinger pointing to England's bravest, enticing them into the army, and now he was dead too.

Another camera angle showed a soldier carrying his wounded oppo on his shoulder through the trench. A close-up showed his cheery smile, his laughing eyes, and soldiers all round them. Suddenly Anna grabbed Ellie's arm when she saw a familiar face. It couldn't be him. Could it?

'Sam!' The name of her beloved brother burst from Anna's lips when she saw him smiling out at her.

'Are you sure?' Ellie asked, knowing it had been six long years since Anna had seen her brother.

'It's Sam! I know it's him.' Anna was on her feet and the audience turned to watch her, almost dancing with contained excitement and pointing to the screen, as a rousing chorus filled the picture house. 'What's the use of worrying...' the audience sang, 'it never was worthwhile... so... pack up your troubles in your old kitbag... and smile... smile.... Smile...'

Laughing now, thrilled at seeing her beloved and much-missed brother again, and with tears streaming down her cheeks, Anna knew what she had to do...

'I've got to go and find him, Ellie!' Anna had to shout to be heard above the singing. After Nipper told her that his absconding brother Jerky Woods had caused the fire that changed Sam's and her life so dramatically, she was determined. 'If the Good Lord spares him, I am going to bring my brother back home to his birthplace, back to Liverpool.'

'And I'll go, too!' Ellie put her arm round Anna's shoulder, and with a new determination, they both joined in the singing.

'What's the use of worrying, it never was worthwhile so...'

But Anna could not help but worry.

21

Dusk was descending when they left the picture house, and they were in no hurry to face the patients back at Ashland, after having seen how they got their wounds.

'I told Aunt Ruby of my intentions to nurse overseas, but I don't know what she will say when you tell her you're going too,' Anna said, when Ellie declared that she was going as well. 'She is not going to make it easy for either of us to go.'

Nevertheless, Anna brightened when Ellie laughed, and said impertinently, 'I know, we could take her with us.'

'She could be England's secret weapon,' Anna quipped, holding on to her hat as a gust of September breeze threatened to whip it from her head.

'The Germans would run a mile if they saw Aunt Ruby stampeding towards them.' Ellie doubled up with laughter at the idea of Aunt Ruby stampeding anywhere.

'Oh, Ellie,' Anna wiped the tears of laughter from her cheeks, 'you are outrageous.'

'She wouldn't mind,' Ellie said, 'Aunt Ruby can take a joke, look how she wiped out the old gardener when he tried to tell her she could not demolish the rose garden, to make way for a vegetable patch. That was a sight to see and proved Aunt Ruby is not for the faint-hearted.'

'Look at that,' Anna said, 'those women are trying to give that fellow a white feather.' It had become a widespread practice for some women to issue men out of uniform with the commonly acknowledged sign of cowardice.

'Let's not get involved. Who knows what the situation is?' Ellie answered.

Anna shook her head at the ferocity of the female race, her mind returning to the amazing footage of the soldiers which they had just seen and the heart-stopping moment when she saw her brother for the first time in six years. Anna wanted to talk about it at length with Ellie, discuss every detail of the film in the teashop, but she noticed that it was already closed. One thing she did not want to do was to interfere with suffragists dishing out their own reprimand to men who would not fight.

Scarcely glancing across the road, Anna immediately recognised the man yelling and cursing at the two women from the public house doorway.

'That's Jerky Woods,' Anna gasped, 'Archie told me he was still AWOL! And according to Izzy, her son only married Lottie so he could return home each night from the training camp and be paid for the privilege.'

'Didn't he go absent without leave when he found out his battalion were on standby to go overseas?' asked Ellie and Anna nodded.

'Yes, he said he had an affliction,' she told Ellie. 'It is called cowardice.' Since she had known what he did, she had dreamt of getting revenge on Woods for what he had done to her, her brother and their family all those years ago. 'I'll show him what people from the dockside do with murdering cowards.' She was about to cross the road when Ellie grabbed her arm.

'No, Anna, don't sink to his level,' Ellie said, 'at least we have an idea where he is and can report him to the police. They will know what to do with him. There is no point in putting yourself in danger. It is obvious he has no compunction to strike out at a woman.'

'Don't you think we should help those two women?' Anna asked.

'I think they are doing quite well,' Ellie answered, 'given the merciless brandishing of their umbrellas.'

They watched as Woods escaped his attackers and disappeared into the nearby public house, and Anna suspected if Jerky Woods, was anything like his drunken father, he would stay there until throwing-out time.

'I've a good mind to call a policeman and have him arrested,' Anna said. Why should he roam the streets when men like her brother were in the firing line every day? She refused to entertain the idea that Sam could have been injured by now, like young Nipper, knowing the film showed the fighting on the Somme, which had begun back in July. That was three months ago. Anything could have happened between then and now.

'Seeing we have the evening off, why don't we go and see Lottie,' Ellie said. 'We haven't seen her since August when she married that scoundrel.'

It would be interesting to see how Lottie was faring. Jerky Woods had always been a stranger to hard work and judging by what they had just seen they had no reason to change their opinion of him now.

'Have you heard from Ned?' asked Ellie as they headed

towards the wall-to-wall courts of Scotland Road, and Anna shook her head. She didn't want to talk about Ned right now. Not after what she had just watched, knowing that the war at sea was just as fierce.

'Watch your step, here,' Anna said by way of an answer as they made their way through a litter-strewn alleyway, and her friend's reaction was as she suspected. Never having experienced anything like this, Ellie was holding a gloved hand to her nose. Clearly, she was trying to prevent the overpowering smell of open middens and decay from assaulting her nostrils. 'Not one of the most salubrious places, at any time of day,' Anna said, remembering when she was younger. Running through these backstreets without a thought did not seem so bad.

However, going through Olden Passage towards Primrose Cottage brought back other memories. The day she should have met Sam but encountered Jerky Woods instead. That day, Ned gave her the courage to fight back... The day her family perished.

'Keep walking,' Anna said, moving forward. She could not turn and run this time, no matter how much she longed to do. 'If anybody comes near us, we have our brolly.' She heard Ellie's muffled laugh behind her gloved hand. However, knowing these streets as Anna did, she had never been more serious as the early dusk enveloped the dockside streets. Even though she had lived in a better street, with clean steps and tidy curtains, she knew every back alley in this part of Liverpool, too. She knew the hidden nooks and crannies. But the mind plays funny tricks on your memory, she realised. The soot-blackened streets and disease-ridden courts in her head were nowhere near as bad as the reality.

Pulling the sleeve of Ellie's coat, Anna hurried through the worst of the depravation, knowing this was a place where sailors came straight off the ships, lived it up for a time, everybody was their friend when the money and the ale was flowing. Then, when it was gone, their poor wives lived hand to mouth with their large gaggle of underfed children, and the sailor was nowhere to be seen. Anna recalled many a foreign sailor who set his seed and buggered off before the result of his effort was obvious.

'Oh, my word,' Ellie shrieked with fright, bringing Anna out of her shocking contemplation.

'It's just a dead cat,' Anna answered, somewhat taken aback at her own detachment. She had seen the sight many times, and despite the better conditions in which she now lived, Anna realised she had not become so genteel as her shocked friend. Furthermore, if she were to follow her desire to go and nurse overseas, she felt she would need some of the dockside toughness, just to get by. 'Don't worry,' she said as if in some way apologising for the state of the substandard, run-down courts where callous, money-grabbing landlords exploited the deprived and the wretched, 'I won't let anything happen to you.'

She could smell Primrose Cottage long before she reached the three squalid, poverty-stricken buildings adjoining each other, which bore no possible resemblance to small flower-strewn houses. And Anna knew that in the daytime well-dressed people would avoid passing through if at all possible and at night the courts were considered unsafe to anybody except the poor wretches who inhabited them.

The air was thick with smoke and fumes from the large gasworks and coal-burning railway locomotives on their way to the docks. Coal dust coated everything, including the residents' lungs and the dilapidated houses swarmed with rats, cockroaches, fleas, and bedbugs.

Anna knew areas like this lay at the heart of the Industrial Revolution, and the war had offered many women from the area work in factories to produce the weapons needed, while the crowded tenements offered the manpower required for the trenches. But Primrose Cottage, the lowest of the low, was a battlefield of a different kind.

A fizz of trepidation coursed through Anna's veins, slamming into her heart, making her breathing rapid. The memory of the day she was confronted by Jerky Woods in an alleyway just like this. She blamed that confrontation on the horror that followed. Of losing her mother and her young twin brothers in that nightmarish house fire. Of losing Sam who had been lifted off the street by the church and sent away to Canada. The fear that constantly lurked at her shoulder had never quite left her. But she fought, as she had always done, to push the anxiety deep down inside her. Maybe she *was* tougher than she suspected. Her formative years with her cherished family, along with those spent with Aunt Ruby, had imbued her with courage.

Hurrying through a badly lit alleyway, Anna felt the heat rise to her cheeks, because it was not so dark to block out the sight that met them. A dockside prostitute was plying her trade with a black seafarer who gave a low growl of displeasure at the interruption.

'A tanner to watch, dearie,' the doxie said in bored tones over his tightly curled head.

'Don't look, Ellie,' Anna said as she pulled her friend towards the end of the alleyway towards Lottie's ramshackle dwelling. And in the flickering light of a gas lamp, Anna's heart sank at the sight and she wrinkled her nose at the overpowering stench of beer, tobacco and misery emanating from an open sash window.

'How can people live like this?' Ellie asked from close behind Anna, who knew that Lottie, even in her poorest days, would never let her home get into such a disgusting state.

'Not all the women round here are like this,' Anna answered

as she knocked on the half-opened door that slowly creaked open like a beckoning phantom and sent shivers down Anna's spine. 'The lock is broken.'

The splintered wood surrounding the lock showed the door had obviously been forced and was now swinging precariously on its hinge. As the rising wind grew stronger, it whistled through the large crack in the window.

There was no answer to her knock and Ellie silently urged her to go forward. Anna stepped inside the bleak interior.

'Hello,' she called, 'is anybody here?' She crept into the dim passage and, even knowing Jerky Woods was not here, she was nervous. *I beg you, Lord*, she prayed silently, *please do not let him come home now*.

She stopped for a moment as a low animal-like groan came from the top of the bare wooden stairs. She listened. Ellie too. Silence... Then, there it was again.

'Hello, Lottie?' Anna held her body taut, unable to ignore the sound of obvious pain, yet not wanting to witness the cause. Knowing she must go on; she climbed the stairs with hasty steps toward the noise.

'Lottie? Lottie are you in here?' Anna's voice was a low whisper and she gingerly pushed open a door to a darkened room, the ancient floorboards creaking beneath her feet as she ventured forth. The only light in the room came from the gas lamp on the wall outside, which cast an eerie yellow glow.

'Who is it?' Lottie's tortured whisper was barely perceptible in the murky gloom as Anna and Ellie edged into the direction of her voice.

'Lottie, it's me, Anna. Ellie is with me,' she said, able to make out the bed. She could see the figure of a woman lying amongst the struggle of bedclothes and her back stiffened. The place reeked of something she could immediately determine.

'Gas,' Lottie groaned as she tried to lift herself from the bed, but she was too weak, 'thank the Lord the money ran out. Otherwise, I wouldn't be here,' Lottie said. 'It went out yesterday, along with my husband, I did try... I did...' Suddenly her voice cracked, and the bed creaked under the force of her sobs.

'Did he do this to you?' Anna asked, her eyes growing accustomed to the dim light, and she could see that Lottie was lying on a blood-soaked mattress. *Jerky Woods ought to be locked up, who would leave his wife in this condition?*

'It wasn't his fault,' Lottie took a deep shuddering gasp of air, 'he's out looking for work.'

Oh no he isn't, Anna's thoughts remained unspoken as she and Ellie exchanged knowing glances. They could see Lottie was distressed and right now she did not need to have the truth waved under her nose like a musty old cloth.

Anna beckoned Ellie towards the bed and kept her voice low. 'Lottie needs all the help we can offer if she's going to see another night,' Anna said as an exhausted whimper alerted her as she knelt beside the bed, taking a deep breath, unprepared for the sight that met her. 'Oh Lottie,' Anna was heartbroken to see the cheeky girl, who paid no heed to kindly warnings, lying here all alone, her eyes full of the terror she had gone through and in her arms, she cradled the tiny stiff body of a stillborn baby girl. 'We will see to you now,' Anna said, grateful for her medical training, not just because it enabled her to help Lottie, but because it masked the revulsion and the turmoil, she was now experiencing. Turning now to Ellie, she whispered: 'If she does not get proper medical attention, soon, she will die.' Ellie's expression told Anna she had no doubt. 'I'll get some hot water and Lysol to clean her up.' They were already removing their coats.

'I 'aven't got no money for the meter,' Lottie's words came out in a breathless rush, 'nor no disinfectant... none for days.'

Anna took her purse from her bag and found the coppers for the meter. She did not hear the footsteps on the stairs. Nor did she hear the door open...

'What's goin' on 'ere?' the surly male voice asked, and Anna whipped round to see the menacing figure of Jerky Woods standing in the doorway. But she was no longer afraid of him. She was too disgusted at his callous, neglectful conduct to be fearful.

He left Lottie here, alone, to give birth to this beautiful baby.

Anna stood up, her back straight and she faced him. Her chin tilting upwards in the same way she had seen Ruby's lift many times before. Her shoulders adjusting to her daring stance, knowing what he was capable of doing to anybody who showed weakness. Something he would readily take advantage of.

'Your wife needs help,' Anna's tone was edged with the kind of steel she hardly recognised. 'We need hot water and disinfectant.'

Ellie handed him some money, 'Please hurry.'

Anna watched him turn and hurry from the room and heard him descend the stairs in two jumps. A practiced measure he had no doubt performed many, many times. To be able to exit so quickly, she imagined, was proof of his eagerness to escape capture by military or even civilian police.

When he had not returned half an hour later with the disinfectant or the money, Anna knew without a doubt he had fled, probably to the nearest alehouse.

She and Ellie made Lottie as comfortable as possible, while Ellie swaddled the baby in a sheet and said a little prayer, tenderly placing the tiny female in the dresser drawer perched on a straight-backed chair.

'The rogue has hopped it with the money!'

'I can't say I'm surprised,' Anna replied, 'although he has sunk to new depths this time.'

'Seeing us here, he obviously felt relieved of all responsibility,' Ellie answered.

'Well, we will soon see about that.' Anna's tone was full of outrage, knowing human life was cheap to him. She tore off down the stairs, almost hopping over the heads of grubby children sitting at the bottom. *Why did he not fetch help for Lottie? A midwife, a neighbour?* Anna thought. Unable to see Woods, she went into the local shop and bought the necessities. Disinfectant, tea, milk, and sugar to keep Lottie's strength up.

'He won't allow anyone into the house,' Lottie was reluctant to talk against her husband at first, knowing everybody had been right to warn her. But she wouldn't listen. Sipping the hot tea laced with sugar, she began to thaw a little. Anna knew it did not take much imagination to work out the reason Jerky Woods was shy of visitors and understood perfectly why a coward like him would be so secretive. He should be fighting overseas, not battling in the street with suffragettes. 'He's got a good heart,' Lottie whimpered, 'he's staying home to look after me.'

'Lottie don't defend him! He left you for dead.' Anna could not believe this girl still thought better of him. 'He did not give you a second thought. He never has. You deserve a better life than the one he has given you.'

Lottie looked to the drawer on the chair that held the body of her baby girl and wept uncontrollably.

Anna nodded to Ellie, who went to the local hospital to summon an ambulance to take them all back to Ashland Hall. Offering her another cup of strong sweet tea, Lottie gratefully took it. Over the next few minutes, she told Anna the whole story.

'Jerry enlisted but due to the lack of accommodation, he was sent home,' Lottie said, 'and because he'd served a day with the colours, they let him come home to take up normal employment until he were needed.' She shrugged hopelessly, 'But, in Jerky's case, it meant having money in his pocket to go drinking and gambling and when he were called, he refused to go.'

'How do you manage to live?' Anna tried to keep the disgust from her voice and Lottie sighed, her once vibrant eyes now dead as a day-old cod in the fishmonger's window.

'The first day they give him one shilling and ninepence,' Lotte said, 'he thought he was king of the midden.' She took a sip of tea, 'Then every day after that, until he was called up, proper like, he got what they called *a retainer*, sixpence a day. He thought he was in God's pocket, but I never saw none of it.'

'Surely they must have somewhere for him now?' Anna asked, knowing the military were not going to pay men to be idle at their expense.

'He said he didn't like the infantry... said he wasn't going back.'

'Surely the money stopped?' Anna asked.

Lottie nodded, but said nothing and Anna suspected he would stoop to stealing to pay his own way. But she did not broach the subject with Lottie. The girl had gone through enough already. Unwilling to risk his freedom, he was prepared to let his wife die along with their premature baby daughter. Anna could have cried for this once proud girl who had sunk so low, so fast because she was lonely and married the first man to show her any attention. Even if that consideration was not the kind she had been looking for.

'How anybody could be so callous is beyond me.' Anna was growing even more angry. Woods did not care who he hurt, so long as he got his own way.

Having used the police telephone to call Archie, when she went for supplies, Anna was not too surprised when she heard a commotion in the lobby downstairs. Cries of disbelief. Scurrying feet and cursing drew Anna to go and investigate. Leaning over the bannister, she saw two policemen. One, a burly six-footer, easily overpowered a wriggling Jerky Woods who had returned to the house.

'We've been waiting for you,' he told Woods.

'He stole Ellie's money,' Anna pointed an accusing finger.

'It weren't me,' Woods roared, 'she's a liar.' He was struggling under the constable's firm grip, 'I ain't done nothin' wrong.'

Anna knew different.

'This aint right,' Woods cried as he was led to the police van in handcuffs, 'what have I done?'

'You're a deserter, a dirty little coward,' Anna called over the bannister as she made her way back to Lottie. Then she noticed Lottie's eyes close. She had lost a lot of blood.

As the police van which had come to take Jerky Woods to his day of reckoning left, a horse-drawn ambulance arrived amid much curiosity. This was a notorious area, Anna knew, where police were not welcome, and horse-drawn ambulances were something of a myth. If people were sick round here, local women tended them.

'Let's get you back to Ashland Hall, Lottie,' Anna said to the girl who had paid a huge price for her reckless moments. 'That selfish husband of yours will get what's coming to him.'

Ellie agreed as the ambulance pulled away from the dilapidated door of Lottie's home.

'The authorities will deal with Jerky Woods, I'm sure,' Anna's feisty nature had come to the fore once again when faced with her childhood foe: a deserter, thief, murderer and arsonist who left his wife to die and deliver her stillborn child. Anna could not think of anybody more evil than Jerky Woods and she couldn't wait to hear that he had been given his just deserts. But one thing she knew for sure, the blight of her life did not shatter her determination all those years ago, and he certainly had not done so now. 'Don't you worry, Lottie,' Anna told the stricken woman, as she smoothed damp hair from her brow, 'you are in safe hands now.'

22

It took weeks for Lottie to get her strength back. However, thanks to Anna and Ellie, she recovered well and went back to live over the shops with Izzy, who took her motherly care very seriously, keeping Lottie's strength up and making her comfortable. Lottie was the daughter she never had and the two of them got on very well.

'You will always have a place here, Lottie.' Izzy was washing a few pots, her back to Lottie, and still unable to look the poor girl in the eye, feeling the stab of shame at what her son had done. Lottie was a decent girl who had come from a good home, and had a kind heart, which her unruly eldest lad had not hesitated to take advantage of.

'I was thinking of going back to work in the Emporium... I mean the charity shop,' Lottie answered wrapping the remains of uneaten bread in paper and putting it on the kitchen shelf. She wanted to do something. Anything. To stop her contemplating the horror she had been subjected to in her marriage to Jerry. 'I need to get back to work.'

'You don't have to worry about that just now,' Izzy answered, knowing Lottie's plight had been the talk of the community and that the girl would become something of a target for some who engaged in morbid curiosity.

'I can't sit around doing nothing all day,' Lottie told her mother-in-law, 'it's not in my nature to keep still.'

After a couple of weeks behind the counter of the charity shop, the polite enquiries regarding her 'health' petered out and life began to get back to normal for Lottie. She enjoyed her work and mixing with people who had known her all their lives and she realised that even though there were some outright busy bodies, on the whole this was a close, kind-hearted community that strived to help out anybody less fortunate, even if the help was just a kind word and a bit of encouragement because they had little else to give. And as the weeks passed, she found herself thinking less of her own nightmare marriage to a no-good shirker who left her for dead, to deliver her stillborn daughter alone, and began to concentrate on others who were not as fortunate as she had been to have the support of a woman like Izzy.

'Do as you would be done by, that's my way of thinking,' said Izzy as she set the table for the evening meal, 'I think the world would be a better place if we all thought that way.'

'I hear poor Mrs Dingle's lad died when his ship hit a mine,' Lottie said, and a shiver ran down her spine. She knew Jerry was an orderly on a Royal Navy ship. The magistrate decided he would be of no use in prison, nor would he be given the chance to abscond, as he was sure to do if he went back to the infantry platoon. He was much less likely to wander off, Lottie though, if he was in the middle of the Atlantic.

* * *

'I overheard one of the patients telling his next bed neighbour that he knew someone who deliberately shot himself in the foot, just to get sent home.' Anna was knitting seaboot socks for Ned.

'A bit extreme, don't you think? Although talk of Blighty Wounds is a popular topic of conversation among the patients,' Ellie responded, knowing how worried her friend was about her Ned.

Anna knew such a wound would be serious enough to bring him home, but not grave enough to kill him. 'I know,' she said, 'and try as I might, I cannot get the niggling hope from my thoughts.' She looked out to the far distance. 'I am so wicked to have such thoughts.'

'Not at all,' said Ellie, who was far more open-minded. 'It is human nature to want to preserve and care for those you love.'

'I miss him so much. I don't think my heart can cope.' Waiting for his letters had her nerves in shreds. Not knowing if there would be another tormented her daily.

'You have the heart of a lioness,' Ellie said, 'and to see you keeping up the spirits of the men who have seen enemy action close up is a lesson in courage.'

'What I am going through is nothing,' Anna said, 'compared to their suffering.' Catching a glimpse of her pinched expression in the window, Anna knew she had to put a brave face on things for everybody's sake. The men in her care had been through a living hell, the proof of which she had seen on the enormous screen at the picture house. Yet, she had to remain strong. Perhaps it had not been a good idea to go and see the film. Sam, her beloved brother who was snatched from her six years ago and sent to the other side of the world by the church, was there in front of her, on the big screen.

Anna marvelled at how much he had grown. He was now a

man. His boyish good looks were replaced with a rugged appeal. She would know him anywhere.

She wanted to go over to France and see him for herself. She wanted to help the wounded. Brave men like her brother, who were doing their bit. Perhaps she would even meet up with Sam? The idea taunted her, and she could not get it out of her head. She had already told Ruby and, of course Ellie who'd wanted to come too. She had even told Doctor Bea who had encouraged her to go.

23

'We got no warning that Professor Burns was coming here,' Ellie hissed as she came on duty, the place suddenly becoming a hive of activity in preparation for his rounds.

'He is replacing Doctor Bea when she goes abroad after Christmas.' Anna said expertly straightening bedclothes. and plumping pillows. While Ellie cleared side cupboards that suddenly looked as neat as a proverbial new pin. VADS swept floors and windows got another going-over before being opened a little wider and Anna noticed Ellie escape out of the ward like a bullet from a gun, not to be seen again for some time.

Anna could hear the professor before she saw him. His enormous footsteps storming through the corridors, as usual leaving sisters and junior nurses scurrying up to the second floor. Matron, the only one who could usually put him in his place, was not around either.

VADs ran for cover to the sluice room and surprisingly were no longer concerned about cleaning dirty bedpans. Anna knew the probationers dreaded accompanying the professor on his rounds, having questions thrown at them with the power of a force nine gale Those who had been unaware once did not make the same mistake again. The only solution was to stay in the sluice room until he had gone. Nearing the end of a relentless shift, Anna hoped she did not attract his attention, as the other nurses had gone on first tea. There was nobody else around.

'Oh, here he is,' a soldier in the end bed whispered, 'the great man himself.'

Looking round quickly, Anna could see there was nowhere for her to disappear to. Professor Burns was heading straight toward her. Ellie, sauntering up the corridor after coming back from her afternoon break and realising the prof was still on the prowl, dove into one of the side-wards. Anna made a silent vow to have words later. This was the second time she had been caught by the huge, barrel-chested man whose plum-coloured nose could sniff out an unenthusiastic nurse at sixty paces.

As he marched towards her with long determined strides, she saw Matron arrive on the ward, scurrying in his wake along with a young VAD. Anna suddenly felt sorry for them both.

'Follow me nurse,' The Prof said, his booming voice all but shook the bedsteads and woke the inhabitants, who were having their pre-tea snooze. However, Anna could see the young debu-tante was completely out of her depth.

Just in time Doctor Bea who had a soft spot for the professor came to her aid, and she was saved the ordeal of his wrath.

'That will be all, nurse, I will escort Professor Burns from here. Continue your duties,' she told her.

'Yes, Doctor, thank you, Doctor.' the nurse scurried back to her patients, relieved, and when they began pleading for a cup of tea, she agreed immediately.

Anna felt restless. Her fingers curled round the unopened letter that had finally arrived from Ned. She had hoped to read it when she got a break. But there had been no time up to now. His letters were quite sporadic... She missed him so much...

'Can I go down to the garden, Sister?' Nipper who was in a bed close by interrupted her thoughts. His eyes were wide with excitement. He had lost his fingers and was now in the bed nearest the open window, battling a raging temperature. Anna thought it was highly unlikely that Nipper would be allowed to go down to the garden tomorrow, but she never gave up hope.

Pushing patients round the grounds, where verdant lawns were now vegetable patches, was a tonic to those who had been seriously ill and were now on the mend. The ones who could take a bit of fresh air. However, Anna knew Nipper was nowhere near ready to go outside yet, and feeling a tinge of guilt, she said in a low voice, so Matron could not hear. 'I'll see what I can do.' It seemed such a shame to dash his hopes when he had been so poorly. The news seemed to lift his spirits, and he put his thumb in the air as he settled under the covers, a huge grin on his face, no doubt dreaming of getting outside for a short while.

24

'When are you going?' Ruby asked, stirring her tea continuously, a sure sign she was agitated.

'Not until spring,' Anna said it in such a way as to brook no argument.

'Well, at least you will be here for Christmas.' Ruby was unfamiliar with defeat, Anna knew. 'The matter appears to be settled, Archie.' An uncomfortable silence ensued, broken only by Ellie, who seemed deliberately impervious to Ruby's whims.

'Anna is a treasure, Aunt Ruby, you should be proud.' She gave Anna's arm a determined hug, 'it is a wonderful thing we are doing. Do you not think it wonderful, Aunt?'

'I think it is madness.' Ruby gave Archie and her sister May a beseeching, questioning glare. They both said nothing, enraging her even more, 'Is there nothing we can do to stop this foolishness?'

'Aunt Ruby it is not imprudent to want to serve your country, when the brave young men are out there offering their own lives.' Ellie did not want to be dissuaded by common sense.

'I am as patriotic as the next person,' Ruby said, 'I send

regular parcels of food and clothing to the front and raise funds. Nevertheless, I cannot say that this latest turn of events has brought out the enthusiast in me.'

'If anything were to happen to you, I would die. Do you hear me, I would die.' May's theatrical tone of voice rose accordingly, and Ruby's brow pleated in pragmatic censure. Her sister was not helping matters by coming over all hysterical.

'Oh Aunt Ruby,' Anna's vague smile wobbled, 'you will soon get used to us not being here, and it won't be for long. We'll be home soon.'

'We most certainly will,' said Ellie, 'we will be amongst the finest of nurses in England. It's not as if we will be sent to the trenches alone, Doctor Bea will be with us as well as some VADs.'

'You could both be sent to the trenches?' Ruby's eyes widened in horror, silently pleading with Archie to intervene, but he shrugged helplessly.

'It appears there is little we can do now, Ruby, my love.' He looked to Anna and Ellie who mouthed a silent, 'thank you.'

'I could, maybe, pull a few strings,' Ruby offered tentatively.

'No, you mustn't,' the two girls chorused, determined, 'we must all do our bit, and if that means being sent to the Front, then so be it.'

'I know you feel you must go,' May told both girls, 'and that is a credit to you, but Ashland Hall needs you too.'

'I'm sorry,' Ellie answered as Anna sighed quietly. They really did not want to discuss the matter in any more detail.

'We've done all we can here.' Anna did not reveal her burning need to find her brother. But what if Ned should come back on leave and find her gone? The thought was fleeting. If Ned had spent less than forty-eight hours on leave in over two years, she doubted he would be given leave just when she went overseas.

'I know I don't have the right to try and stop you both,' Ruby had that pained expression she adopted when she was not getting her own way. But she could not contain her martyred air any longer and resorted to pleading. 'You must both see sense. I could not bear it if anything happened to you.'

'I would die of a broken heart,' May joined in.

Anna smiled. She knew if Aunt Ruby could not get her own way by barking orders, she would try the other tack and play on their sympathy. But it would not work this time.

'Right. That is enough.' Ellie held up her hand. 'The war waits for no man or woman. Everything is under control here and our country need us.'

'I should have known,' Ruby replied. 'If Ellie wants to do something, she will find a way to do it, and it will take the wrath of the Good Lord himself to change her mind.'

'Who does that remind me of?' Archie asked and everybody laughed, except Ruby who did not have a clue who he could be talking about.

'That's the spirit,' Anna said briskly, defusing a possible sombre table of breakfast eaters. Ruby was pushing scrambled egg round her plate, eating nothing, while May, slight as she was, ate everything put before her. Since her husband's demise, she had become a new woman which included having a bigger appetite.

Anna felt she should be doing more. Also, since seeing the film her need to find her brother burned within her. And if that meant going to the Western Front, then so be it.

'I'm sorry you've taken the news so badly, Aunt Ruby, but it is something we have to do. They need good nurses to collect casualties and bring them back to England.'

'I agree with Anna,' said Ellie, 'we are a force to be reckoned with during these trying times, among the very finest nurses in the whole world.'

'What does this trip entail?' Ruby's dark eyes were worried.

'Travel, courage, grit and determination,' Ellie laughed, her stomach churning with excitement.

'To name but a few,' Anna interrupted warily, as if stepping into a bear pit without a gun.

'It's too dangerous,' said May, rolling her napkin, obviously worried.

'Of course, it is dangerous,' argued Ellie, who had been a staunch suffragist before the war. 'But it all sounds thrilling, Aunt Ruby,' she exclaimed, nodding to Anna for back up, her heart racing with excitement. Then she caught sight of Ruby's downcast expression and she gently patted her arm. 'We'll be there and back before you know it.' Ellie had that gleam in her eyes that reminded Anna so much of Ruby when she was determined to do something.

'Is this what you really want to do, my darlings?' asked Ruby and both girls nodded. Anna was determined to go to the battle-field. She would find Sam, and she would bring him home to Liverpool. Where he belonged.

'I feel we are shirking our duty by not going, so much needs to be done, we must assist.' Ellie, too, had heard valiant tales of nurses at the front, whilst plucky women travelled Europe in their quest to bring back injured men.

'I feel we have done nothing for the war effort,' Anna said, 'except patch men up and send them back. I feel so guilty that they are going back when we could be of greater service over there.'

'What are we sending them back to though?' Ruby asked, throwing down her napkin.

'We won't be anywhere near the front line, Doctor Bea said so,' Anna assured Ruby and she could see that May was considering the news she had been given.

'You won't be anywhere near the actual fighting?' May asked and the girls assured her they would not. 'We will be a few miles back in the beautiful French countryside nursing men who need our immediate attention,' Ellie assured her mother and her aunt.

All Anna knew was what she saw at the cinema and what Doctor Bea had told her. She felt such a fraud when she told a brave Tommy he was doing a grand job, and then hearing later that he had not made it. How could she tell brave men, that their country was proud of them and then send them back for more of the same from the comfort of a grand country house?

'This is our chance to see for ourselves,' Anna told Ruby, touching the ring that Ned had given her, and the pendant Sam had purchased for her mother all those years ago, which were on a gold chain round her neck. They gave her courage and determination.

'I don't like this one little bit, Archie,' Ruby said, looking to her husband, a font of all wisdom, standing with his back to the fire, dressed in his police uniform, hands clasped behind his back and rolling on the balls of his feet.

'This may be our only chance to do what is right for our brave soldiers and for our country.' Ellie could see Ruby stiffen and she knew instinctively, if Ruby and May had been younger and they had been given the opportunity, they would be in France like a bullet from a Vickers machine gun.

'My mind is made up.' Anna was resolute. She was not going to let anyone persuade her that she was doing a foolish thing, then a thought struck her. 'Will we need a letter of recommendation?'

'No,' replied Ellie. 'Doctor Bea is taking the new batch of nurses after Christmas; we will join them later and that will not pose a problem.'

'Of course,' Anna said, 'given our excellent qualifications, we will be an asset.'

'Such modesty is so becoming,' Ruby smiled, relieved they would be here for Christmas at least.

'I received your recommendation of good character from the Chief Constable,' Archie said, knowing that if they were hellbent on going, the situation must be prepared thoroughly. He avoided Ruby's murderous glare.

'We are meeting on the hospital ship, *Gigantic,* when it comes back to Princes Dock, so you have us for a good while yet.' Anna was a lot more confident now they had Archie's backing, and hopefully, in time, they would have Ruby's and May's approval too. She looked to Ellie who raised a conspiratorial eyebrow.

PART II

'Hold that ship, my good man.' Ruby's vociferous vocals echoed round the dockyard. 'Yoo-hoo! Don't sail just yet.' Her voice grew louder as she climbed the gangplank quickly followed by May.

Anna and Ellie exchanged curious glances as they looked over the ship's rail.

'They're boarding the ship,' Anna said, craning her neck, and Ellie hooted with laughter as they saw the two women speeding towards them, waving an umbrella.

'Do not raise that anchor just yet!' Ruby called in most unladylike tones to the sailor checking the ropes on the quay, whilst May did her best to keep up.

'Can you believe this?' Anna, Ellie and the rest of the travellers ogled the spectacle. 'Surely they're not coming too?' Anna could not imagine Aunt Ruby slumming it with a hundred other nurses. Ruby got seasick just watching the boats on the lake.

'There you are, my good man,' Ruby told the captain, 'permission to come aboard, I won't be a tick!' Then, panting as she boarded the ship and handed Anna the umbrella, 'You forgot this.' Patting the arm of a well-mannered sailor, who moved over allowing her to squeeze in, she said: 'If it hadn't been for Archie bringing me in the motorcar, I'm sure I would have missed you.'

Anna and Ellie both knew this was her way of waving them off, knowing Ruby did not like goodbyes any more than Ned had all those months ago.

'You shouldn't have,' Anna said, 'but I'm so glad you did. It gives us a chance to say goodbye properly.' She wasn't sure if Ruby had overslept or if it was an attempt to avoid the inevitable goodbye. 'The ship will be sailing soon but thank you so much for bringing the umbrella.' She tried to keep a sudden feeling of guilt from her voice. And was saved the emotional send-off that would surely come, when a cheeky Tar said in a jaunty voice:

'Why don't you come along with us, Ma?'

'Ma?' Ruby's eyebrows shot to her hairline. 'Who are you calling, Ma?' Ruby looked round and saw Ellie who was hooting with laughter. 'Just because there is a war on, it does not mean you may be impudent, young man,' Ruby admonished, 'and I forbid you to take advantage of two perfectly innocent young nurses.'

'Don't be such a spoilsport, Aunt Ruby,' Ellie rolled her eyes and Ruby raised her hands in mock despair before hugging them both.

'I'm sure these two can take care of each other,' May said, squeezing them tight before she and Ruby meandered off the ship, waving as they went, not looking back.

'Right, off you go,' Ruby called from the quay, waving energetically, as if giving permission for the ship to leave.

'She told me she did a stint in the Crimean War, did you know?' Ellie said, settling down for the journey.

'Would that be on the day the Emporium was closed?' Anna asked with a wry smile, not believing a word. Ruby was a lot of things, she thought and most of them were admirable, but a nurse in the field was certainly not one of them. But she doubted Ellie was paying attention, she was too busy listening to a couple of inebriated sailors who were singing some very salty sea shanties.

'We've been on leave in Liverpool,' the matelots informed them, 'although we cannot say which hostelries we visited. That is top secret.' They tapped the side of their noses with their forefingers while Anna nodded, wondering if Ned ever caroused the drinking establishments of foreign lands, and also if Sam felt this excited when he went off into the great blue yonder.

Ned. What did he feel when he took his first journey away from home? They shared an all-consuming passion she only dared think of fleetingly. She worried about him, like thousands of other girls, and even though they wrote to each other, it was not enough. The letters were patchy and infrequent at best, which was not surprising given the Atlantic U-boat campaign back in February, when Germany announced its U-boats would resume unrestricted submarine warfare, rescinding the 'Sussex Pledge'.

'I've got a girl in every port.' She heard the sailor chatting to Ellie say and realised that, in a destructive climate, a lot of men married within weeks of meeting a girl, solely because he thought he was never coming back. She had also seen men, like Ned, who wanted to wait until the war was all over. Ned told her it was not fair to tie her down if he should come home maimed and knowing Anna would feel obliged to nurse him for the rest of their days, he told her in his letters that she was free to do as she saw fit if this should happen. He was not going to hold her to the promise she made to marry him the last time he was home. Anna had replied, telling him she would be honoured to nurse him as his wife and would always be here waiting for him.

'You are under no obligations, while we are not yet married,'

Ned had told her. His comment, although meant kindly, hurt her more than she could say. Even if, God forbid, Ned was wounded she could never bear the thought of another woman looking after him and it didn't go unnoticed that only last week, German warships attacked British naval patrols off the Goodwin Sands, sinking HMS Paragon, Ned's last ship before he had been transferred. The war was coming closer to home by the day.

Lost in a world of her own, Anna gazed out over the rail. A thousand and one goodbyes had already been said in homes across the country, she thought, looking out to a muted grey sky that joined the far horizon, her hometown no longer visible as she eyed the white horses topping the swell of the sea, caused by the ship's forward sail. And she suddenly wondered if Ned would be willing to care for her if anything should happen to her in Flanders. Her heart said yes, but her head wasn't so sure.

'Well,' said Ellie interrupting Anna's thoughts, 'we've packed our stays and are about to enjoy untold escapades in the service of our country.'

Despite the official resistance towards Doctor Bea and the rest of the female medical staff who had been ordered to go home and sit still, Doctor Bea decided she knew better.

'We will show them,' she had told Ellie and Anna resolutely, as detailed discussions of various adventures went back and forth around them and even though they faced danger and suffering they also looked forward to a huge adventure.

There were scores of intrepid nurses heading across the Channel, not only to Belgium and France, but also to Serbia, Egypt, and Mesopotamia to nurse injured men who were fighting their cause. Anna could understand perfectly why these women felt a burning need to go to do their bit. She had even heard of women who galloped to the rescue on horseback, scooping up wounded soldiers and proving themselves indispensable in the field.

'Did Florence Nightingale think only of her own comfort when she nursed men in the Crimean war?' Doctor Bea had asked. 'No she did not.'

* * *

'Right, ladies,' the leader of the little band of nurses, shouted in a voice, so strident it roused a sleeping sailor from his slumber. 'I have checked the itinerary, we disembark at Le Havre, so, make sure you have all your belongings.'

'All she is short of,' declared an auxiliary nurse in petulant tones, 'is telling us to move in single file in complete silence She's got a voice worse than my father and he was a Sergeant-Major.'

Anna smiled, looking forward to her first voyage on a ship.

Thankfully, the U-boats had stayed home today, and as they headed towards France, the sun obliged by coming from behind the clouds and chased them away so they could enjoy sunshine on deck and the two girls looked forward to the new adventure with renewed optimism.

The ship was crowded with military men, some of whom had already been to France and once injured were now well. Some seemed a bit reluctant to go back for more and both nurses could understand why. Although others laughingly said they really missed the place.

When Anna and Ellie disembarked from the ship at Le Havre, they were greeted by the sight of a working dockyard filled with uniforms of every country, horses, wagons and ambulances waiting to dispatch men to Red Cross hospital ships, Anna could not see what there was to miss.

* * *

'Cheeky bugger,' a voice said as the ambulance door catapulted violently into a tree, encouraging a flurry of leaves to flutter onto the ground. Anna and Ellie had stayed in a little château near the dockside for the past two days in readiness for their orders. Now they were sitting on their suitcases watching the continual ebb and flow of khaki-clad men and women. Soldiers, Sailors, Airman, Nurses, Ambulances. The jetty was a moving unit. Never still.

'I beg your pardon?' Anna said, looking round, surely this khaki-clad woman was not talking to them?

'You must be Annie and Ella,' the ambulance driver called from the open window near the driver's seat when she heard the English accent and saw their uniforms. Her impatient grimace spread busy freckles as she looked up from the sheet of paper and met Anna's gaze.

'It is *Anna* and *Ellie*,' Anna said as Ellie picked up the suitcase upon which she had been sitting.

'I'm always getting bloody names wrong,'

'Excuse me, young lady?' said a passing officer of the King's Regiment, just off the ship and not yet accustomed to ripe language from a female, especially one so dainty in stature amid a fizz of military motors, Red Cross ambulances and speeding cars careering through the streets.

'Not you, Mister!' The girl had an accent Anna recognised immediately. It carried the inflection of her youth in Queen Street. 'That idiot of a sergeant major stepped right in front of me *ambolance,* and nearly got himself killed.' Nodding to a pale-faced officer now sitting in the middle of the road, the girl continued determinedly, 'He must think he can fight my Bessie,' she tutted loudly for all to hear, 'I ask you!'

Anna noticed the armband on the driver's sleeve clearly showed this girl was part of the Canadian Expeditionary Force, and judging by her rapid pace, she was in no mood for pleasantries with sergeant majors.

'Matron in charge asked for a couple of nurses to go to Number 33 Military Hospital at Le Treport,' said the ambulance driver to Anna and Ellie who had been volunteered while the other nurses went elsewhere by bus.

'Where are we going now?' Ellie asked. 'And who's Bessie?'

'First to Boulogne; it's under British occupation,' the girl said in answer to Ellie's question as she climbed out of the vehicle. 'And Bessie's me *ambulance*.' She nodded to the military first aid vehicle with an expression that seemed to suggest Ellie had gone quite mad, for not knowing.

'Righto,' Anna said, eager to be on the move and find out all about France.

'I'm Daisy, by the way.' She was dressed in an ankle-length uniform skirt, three-quarter jacket nipped in at the waist and was wearing a khaki-coloured hat resembling a soft-topped muffin. Her bright blonde hair was tucked severely under it, but it was her eyes that Anna noticed most of all, not the colour but the lofty, uncompromising expression. It was obvious that this young woman was nobody's fool.

'Can you smell that heavenly lavender?' Ellie inhaled leisurely, while Anna grabbed their belongings and threw them into the back of the motor vehicle.

'All I can smell is diesel and horse shit,' said Daisy. 'Lavender seems to have evaded me.' The ambulance driver shrugged, not quite knowing what to make of these two clueless arrivals. 'Come on now.'

'I don't take kindly to being rushed,' Ellie said, feeling tetchy, 'not after waiting nearly two days for your arrival.'

'Do you not?' Daisy answered wryly. 'That's a shame because you are going to be rushed off your bloody feet soon enough.' After Ellie and Anna settled themselves for a sedate journey through the French countryside, they watched the ambulance driver force the contrary gears with a gawky start, and manoeuvre the juddering vehicle, 'I'm sure they fill this thing with bloody kangaroo juice.'

'Is there any need for such language?' Ellie asked, but the driver ignored her, saying instead,

'Bessie takes a minute to warm up; she'll soon get going again.'

Then, Anna and Ellie were hanging on for dear life, as the revving ambulance catapulted into action, flinging them from one side of their seat to the other. Fortunately, it seemed most foot soldiers were well aware of the dangers of mad ambulance drivers and kept out of this one's way.

'You'll soon get used to that,' said the diminutive driver, 'there's no time to stand on ceremony out here.'

'So, have you been here long?' Anna was sure that she was on their side, no matter what her initial temperament dictated.

'Too bloody long,' she said. Her left hand was on the steering wheel while the right scratched her head for all it was worth, 'Looks like one of the patients shared more than was good for them.'

'In what way?' Ellie asked while sliding right to the other side of the ambulance seat as the ambulance turned a corner.

'Lice,' Daisy said matter-of-factly, 'they bring the little buggers in from the trenches.'

Ellie shuddered and Anna stifled a laugh; lice were an everyday occurrence in Queen Street. 'Ned brought some back with him on his last leave,' Anna said, 'it had been years since I last saw headlice.'

'Oh, they're much bigger than headlice,' Daisy informed them, 'and they don't just wander through your head either.'

'Where else can they wander?' Ellie's innocent eyes widened; most of the soldiers had been cleaned up somewhat by the time they got to Ashland Hall. Then, for the first time, Anna heard Daisy let out a laugh that was more common along Liverpool's dock road.

'You'll soon see...' Daisy howled with laughter. 'Welcome to the Front.'

Ellie was more than a little put out, at Daisy's lack of reverence for her lofty station, but it did not take long to discover that Daisy had little respect for anybody, especially authority, when she gave a passing general a one-fingered salute when he was slow to get out of her way and almost crashed into the front of her ambulance.

'Do you have to drive so fast?' Ellie did not like being thrown about and found it difficult to speak over the noise of the engine. 'I really do think you enjoy driving like a madwoman.' She held on to her headdress and promptly slid to the floor. 'We would like to be in one piece when we get to the hospital, you know.'

Anna had tears of laughter running down her cheeks and tried many times to help Ellie up, but to no avail.

'Maybe she's safer on the floor,' Daisy called, she doubted she was going to see eye to eye with Ellie. She had the measure of her all right. 'Oh, by the way, now you come to mention it, we're not going to a hospital.'

'Not going to a hospital?' Anna and Ellie chorused.

'We should be so lucky as to have a real hospital anywhere near here.'

'You're worrying me now, Daisy.'

Quietly, watching the countryside zip past, they travelled through the French landscape en route to Belgium at breakneck speed and sometime later Daisy told them, 'We have to pick up soldiers from a field hospital in Boulogne.'

'Is that not a real hospital?' Anna asked, feeling confused as they rounded another corner. 'There's no sign of war here.' They jolted and bumped along a stony excuse for a road. She and Ellie exchanged a quizzical look. It was certainly quiet as they travelled to their destination.

'You'll see when we get there,' Daisy said mysteriously as the sky darkened, low with the promise of rain to come and the angry rumble of thunder. 'Here she blows,' Daisy muttered as a jagged fork of lightning lit up the leaden sky, which then split and let loose rods of torrential rain. The long journey seemed endless. Would they ever see terra-firmer again? Anna wondered.

* * *

Daisy called over her shoulder: 'You'll soon get used to this,' before coming to a screeching, sliding halt near a skeletal tree bearing a white flag with a red cross. This was where they were going?

Anna had not known what to expect, but certainly not this.

Daisy jumped out of the ambulance and beckoned for her and Ellie to follow.

'We'll get soaked,' Ellie cried, but Anna was already halfway out of the vehicle and the rain on her face was a welcome respite. Shown to a tent, they picked up two wounded soldiers.

'Sometimes we pick them up from the side of the road.' Daisy informed them, 'poor buggers left lying there, what thanks is that, hey?' Anna gave an incredulous look to her companions and Daisy nodded in confirmation, 'Come on, we'll get these two back to the C.C.S. and then I'll show you to your billet.'

'C.C.S? Billet?' Ellie asked.

Anna had heard the soldiers back at Ashland Hall talking like this so she knew all about casualty clearing stations and that a billet was the place where they would get their head down and sleep.

'But don't expect Buckin'ham Palace,' Daisy said pointedly to Ellie, 'because you won't get it out here.'

* * *

Stiff uniforms rustled round her, as nurses went efficiently about their business. A medic, wheeling an empty bath chair, stepped back to minimise his chance of permanent injury when Daisy, with green eyes blazing, swung into the yard of a shabby-looking hotel now used as a clearing station and proceeded to drag Anna's heavy suitcase from the ambulance and across the newly scrubbed floor, cursing all the way.

'Well,' exclaimed the medic drily, 'have you ever heard the likes?'

On hearing the commotion, a serving hatch in the wall opened.

'Can I help you?' asked a stern-looking nurse in a white apron emblazoned with a huge red cross, her hair covered in the same wimple-styled headdress as Ellie and Anna. She leant forward and looked disapprovingly at the baggage. 'I would advise you to try and carry that thing,' she said, glaring at it. 'Sister will not be best pleased if you mark her clean floor.' She sniffed and looked directly at Daisy, 'This is not the kind of establishment that encourages riffraff to drag their belongings in off the street.'

'Really?' Daisy's deadpan expression made Anna quietly giggle, but not within sight of the nurse. They were not stupid.

Daisy smiled to Anna and Ellie. 'You'll get used to Sister Blake; her bark is far worse than her bite. Hello, everybody, this is Anna and Ellie,' Daisy told the rest of the new nurses gathered in the foyer when Sister went about her business. 'They have come to help us,' Daisy laughed, 'in the mistaken belief they will single-handedly win this war, and send all the good boys home to their mothers...'

'We all thought that at one time, didn't we, nurses,' a Canadian nurse declared to nobody in particular.

Sister returned, clapped her hands for silence and took in a long, pained stream of disinfected air.

Ellie, unfazed, turned to Anna and said in a voice that carried, 'Would it hurt her to crack a smile now and again?'

'What's your name?' Sister asked Anna as Daisy dragged a chair from under the much-scrubbed table, plonking herself down. Sister gave Daisy a fleeting look of dismay.

'Anna Cassidy.' Anna's smile too was fleeting, given Sister's frosty countenance.

'Daisy, do behave,' Sister said in a *you-always-get-one* tone of voice. Then turning to Anna, she said briskly, 'Matron told us you were coming earlier.' She looked accusingly at Daisy, who was now gazing out of the window, innocent as a newborn babe, 'Were you supposed to bring them earlier, Daisy?'

'We were a bit busy, Sister,' Daisy said as the nurse scanned Anna and Ellie's letters of recommendation. Then, without another word, Sister, folded the letters and put them in the pocket of a pale blue dress under her pristine apron. She stood up, her movements quick, alert. 'The fact that you have recommendation from the Chief Constable means nothing out here.'

'Why did we have to obtain it, then?' Ellie asked, confused. All she wanted to do was to be shown to her room, soak in a bubble-filled bath and have an early night.

'Follow me,' the older nurse nodded to the luggage littering her spotless foyer and Anna, lifting her suitcase, followed her and Daisy at a run down the winding stone steps.

'I can take that if it's too heavy,' Daisy called over her shoulder and Anna got the distinct impression that mischief laced her words.

'It's no bother,' Anna answered, suspecting imminent damage to Sister's polished floor.

'Hurry along now,' Sister called over her shoulder, rushing on.

Anna, not slow at the best of times, wondered if Sister was speeding up intentionally, just to show who was in charge. Nonetheless, Daisy, easily keeping pace, turned, and winked at Anna, who was fascinated with the busy energy of the girl at the end of a demanding shift. Nothing seemed to slow down round here, and Anna suspected she was not even seeing it at its most busy.

* * *

'Take a seat,' Sister told all of the new nurses who later were gathered together, some, like Anna and Ellie, were qualified nurses, and some were VADs.

Daisy, however, was not upper class. Nevertheless, she displayed highly qualified talents and seemed a force to be reckoned with. 'You'll get used to me,' Daisy said heading towards the door, 'see you later.'

Half an hour later, with Sister Blake's increasing list of do's and don'ts ringing in their ears, the girls were greeted once more by Daisy, whose knowing grin was a sure sign she had toddled off deliberately.

'Has she finished yet?' Ellie asked and Anna nodded, sighing when Sister barked instructions for them to go to their quarters and change ready for duty.

'I thought we would at least start tomorrow,' Ellie said as they crossed the hotel grounds and headed towards their billet. Then, when she saw Daisy dressed in a feather boa, she said incredulously, 'What *is* she wearing?'

'Do you like it?' Daisy's tone suggested a compliment had been paid her, when in fact it had not. She twirled unashamedly in the middle of the room, showing off her hobble skirt, 'Sister said it reminded her of a horse she once tethered to stop it running away.' Daisy gave a burst of effervescent laughter.

Anna was sure that not many people could get away with wearing one of those narrow skirts, so tight at the ankles you could only totter in short steps.

'I've been dying to wear one of those, but Mother doesn't like them,' Ellie said.

'I have to admit, it is a bugger to run in, but it's never stopped me...'

'Young ladies do not run unless they are being shot at, especially in this hospital,' Sister replied, catching the tail end of the conversation.

'Do they not?' Daisy's brows met in a disbelieving crease. 'I'd better practise walking then, hadn't I?'

Leaving the small hotel, requisitioned for recovering soldiers, they headed towards rows of white tents, and Daisy watched their expressions with interest. Most newly arriving nurses expected that they were going to be put up in the hotel. However, they were wrong.

'I come from a long line of nurses,' Daisy said confidently, keeping a jovial conversation going while waiting for the inevitable shrieks of incredulity, 'going right back to Florence Nightingale herself.'

'You are related to Florence Nightingale?' Ellie asked, showing a sudden interest.

'By God, no,' Daisy laughed, 'but I had an aunt who met her once.'

Anna had immediately liked this effervescent young woman, who positively fizzed with energy and good nature, and took obvious delight in confusing Ellie.

'What's this?' Ellie's jaw dropped and all merciful thoughts disappeared into nothing when she caught sight of their new home for however long they may be here. 'Surely, we are not expected to sleep in these things?'

'You will get used to it – or my name's not Tallulah Starr,' Daisy said with the obvious delight of one who had become accustomed to her circumstances and was now having a fine old time watching their apparent shock.

'But you said your name was Daisy Flynn?' Anna asked, bemused, looking to Ellie who shrugged.

'Yes, I did,' Daisy sighed theatrically. 'Tallulah Starr is my stage name. I sing you know.'

'Fancy.' Ellie appeared not to be the least enthralled.

Anna now knew Ellie had a different kind of adventure in mind, where she ministered cool cloths to fevered brows of handsome soldiers and listened to their tortured tales of heroic battle. Although she had worked with severely injured soldiers at Ashland Hall, she did not expect to tend men with missing limbs who were delirious with pain in a tent and have to sleep in one too. If Anna was honest with herself, nor did she. Nevertheless, now that they were here, they might as well do the job properly.

* * *

'Canada?' Anna jumped when a cat-sized rat scurried over her foot. She hadn't seen one that size since she lived near the Mersey docks.

Daisy nodded, not speaking now. They had quickly become friends. Anna liked the girl, who, on the face of it, appeared harum-scarum, but to anybody who cared to look closer, she was a caring and thorough medic.

'I don't usually talk about my past; some people might get jealous,' Daisy said in a half-hearted attempt to be frivolous. Nevertheless, Anna felt privileged to be her confidante. The young woman was not treated the same as the other VADs, even though she was more knowledgeable than some who thought they knew it all.

'Which part of Canada are you from? My brother went to Canada, on board a ship called R.M.S Sunshine.' Excitement hummed through Anna's body and her hopes soared, but they quickly dashed when Daisy began to laugh until tears ran down her pretty powdered cheeks. Anna looked towards Ellie, who shrugged, her brows pleated now.

'R.M.S. Sunshine?' Daisy wiped her eyes and stopped laughing. But still the tears continued to roll down her cheeks. 'We were the chosen ones, they said. We were the children of the Empire who were going to build a new world, they said...'

'Daisy...?' Anna went towards the young ambulance driver, who was usually so cheerful, always singing and making people laugh, who now looked bereft.

'We were the orphans, the deserted children, the kids who had no family, we were the street *Arabs*. The children that nobody wanted.'

'My brother must have thought the same thing?' Anna said.

'That was who we were,' Daisy nodded as if to supplement her words with some kind of obvious confirmation, 'to the child exporters we were cheap labour...'

'We were told he was heading for a new life, a good life.' Anna could hardly get the words out, 'I've seen my brother on the big screen at the cinema. That's why I chose to come out here. He's a medic, and he's here in Belgium.'

'As are many home children,' Daisy said, 'prepared to travel through the jaws of hell and risk our lives for a country that did not want us.'

'Surely you were wanted, Daisy,' Anna cried.

'As soon as Ma had enough of this little nuisance, she had me shipped out of Liverpool...' Daisy offered a mirthless laugh, then she said quietly, 'Not just me, there were a hundred other nuisances.' She was not talking to anybody in particular, but the expression in her eyes had a quiet, seething anger about them now.

'I didn't mean to open old wounds, I'm sure you weren't a nuisance, Daisy...' Anna said, 'and neither was our Sam. He was not. He was not...'

Daisy looked to Anna, as if waking from a dream and seeing her for the first time.

'Sam was my friend's name, too.' Daisy looked wistfully over the shell-shocked horizon. The rain had not stopped, but it was less torrential now. '"*We will always be pals, Dais,*" he had said just before we were separated again in France, as we were in Canada.'

'Where was he from?' Anna's heart hammered in her chest. Was it too much to hope for?

Daisy informed Anna that Sam was from Liverpool. Anticipation caused Anna to cease breathing. There were more Sams in Liverpool than her brother.

'It couldn't be him,' Daisy said with certainty, shaking her head, 'his name was not Harrington it was Cassidy.'

A stuttered intake of breath nearly choked Anna and she spluttered, coughing and wheezing. When she could get the words out, she gasped

'That's Ellie's name, Eleanor Harrington... My name is Anna Cassidy...'

'Sam is your brother...?' Daisy covered her mouth with her hand as if to staunch the words she was about to say, but no matter, they came out anyway. 'You are Anna? Anna who died?'

Anna nodded, her eyes wide, and Daisy shook her head as if to clear it.

'But you are a qualified nurse.' Daisy sounded incredulous, 'you live in a big country mansion. Your parents are richer than the King.'

Anna shook her head. The girl obviously had her information mixed up. 'No, Daisy, I am an orphan, I was taken in after my family were killed in a fire.' She did not want to use that word, *murdered*.

'Sam... My friend Sam... He had a sister called Anna... she died... in hospital...'

'I was in hospital with pneumonia when my brother went away...' Anna saw the look of realisation spread across Daisy's face and her cornflower blue eyes danced.

'You are Anna,' Daisy laughed, 'but you are not dead.'

'No, Dais,' Anna pinched her own arm, 'I am not dead. I don't intend to be either.'

Moments later, they were hugging each other, dancing around, laughing, crying, and jabbering like monkeys in their haste to share information What did he say? What did he feel? Anna wanted to know all about her Sam's departure.

'He only left because they said you died,' Daisy told her. 'They said he would have a better life...' Quiet for a moment, as if seeing the scene playing out like a film on the picture house, she did not say who *they* were. 'I got my legs slapped for calling out to him before... before...' Daisy could not say any more as huge tears rolled down her cheeks. This cheeky nurse with the voice of an angel could not get the words out now.

'Holy Mother,' Ellie was visibly shocked, 'I wish I had a huge revelation to share.' Refusing to be excluded, she hugged them both.

26

It didn't take them long to get into the swing of things and a few months later, the three of them were sent to the casualty clearing station at Passchendaele, all hands desperately needed there, and soon Anna and Ellie realised that genteel nursing was impossible as they viewed a crocodile line of incoming wounded and had to *get stuck in* as Daisy put it.

Giving immediate instructions to nurse anyone who needed it, Anna quickly learned how to haul ten-stone men onto stretchers between completing bedpan rounds, preparing food and drinks on leaking primus stoves, which reeked of paraffin, and in rare moments of quiet time, even helped shocked soldiers write letters home.

Separated from Ellie and Daisy, Anna was far too busy to notice how tired she was, and she soon fell into the rigorous routine. All romantic notions of propriety and meekness quickly dissipated after hours in the fields.

When she later flopped onto the bed recently vacated by another nurse, Anna was still wearing her uniform. Luckily, she did not have time to crease it, as a short while later another batch of wounded were brought in on stretchers, over shoulders, any way they could get to the clearing station. Having learned quickly to run in her sleep, she was heading towards the ambulances to go and collect the injured. By the end of the month, she knew for certain why she felt the need to be here.

'This kid needs a blood transfusion,' the medic said. 'Doc Robertson has brought in a new method of transfusion.' he continued as she worked with the medic who had been assisting Doctor Robertson set up the first blood transfusion equipment at the casualty clearing station on the Western Front in early spring. He worked as he talked, extremely fast. Teaching other medics the things he had learned on the battlefield. 'In the case of severe primary haemorrhage supplemented by shock, this transfusion of blood produces immediate and remarkable results.' His rapid effort was accompanied by equally speedy speech, which Anna could barely make out as the Canadian medic had his back to her, his voice almost drowned out by the thick mask, which she recognised as a female sanitary towel, covering his face to protect him from a poisonous gas attack.

'Hurry, nurse,' the medic asked, holding his hand out for a scalpel.

'I've only got one pair of bloody hands,' Anna called impatiently, accustomed to the salty language now, 'and it's *Sister* to you, not bloody nurse!' She found letting go of the odd expletive kept her sane.

'I would recognise that censorious tone anywhere in the world, but I didn't expect to hear it here on the battlefield and anyway I thought you were dead!'

Anna felt a hand on her shoulder and was being turned round. But nothing on God's green earth could have prepared her for the sight that met her eyes.

Anna's wide eyes filled with tears and she pressed her hand to her throat, coming face to face with the brother she had not seen for seven long years.

'Sam! When did you...? How did you...?' Words failed her as she threw her arms round his neck Laughing. Crying. 'Sam. Sam. Sam.' His name was a balm on her lips. 'I never thought I would ever see you again! But why did you think I was dead?'

'Me neither because I was told you were dead before I left the orphanage. That's why I didn't come to see you before I left for Canada,' Sam said, holding her at arm's-length now. But to see you again, alive, and here of all places ...

Anna could hardly see him for happy tears.

Suddenly another boom lifted her off her feet and she suspected the gunfire had pierced her eardrums. Nevertheless, in no time, Sam had dragged her out of the mud. She could hear again. The deafness, caused by an earful of mud, soon remedied.

'I see you for the first time in years and you saved my life,' Anna shouted over the noise of exploding shells.

'My work here is done.' Sam let out that familiar laugh the whole family shared... *Had* shared. However, Anna knew this was not the best time for reunions.

Sam had to move away to attend to another soldier who had been blown off his feet, and before she had a chance to speak further, her wonderful brother had the other young soldier hooked up to a bottle of blood.

'You're a doctor?' Her voice sounded incredulous, amazed at his swift expertise. Transfusions were unheard of at the beginning of the war but from the spring of this year, many lives had been saved by another man's claret, and it was hard to imagine a time when none was available.

'Let's just say I'm a gifted amateur,' Sam answered. 'I've been taught by the best.' They watched as the colour began to return to the soldier's ashen face, 'It's a long story, but we'll have plenty of time to go over it later.'

'Nurse! Over here, we have more coming in.'

'It's *Sister* to you,' Sam yelled, and Anna smiled, reluctantly leaving to tend new patients in the clearing station. She did not want to miss another moment with her beloved brother. She wanted to know everything that he had gone through, from the moment he left her at the hospital, until the fabulous moment she met him once again on the battlefields of Passchendaele.

Sam hurried forward to another casualty and, bending over the soldier, pumped his chest. 'We've got him back,' Sam said with a nod of thanks to his team, 'although he might need a pint of claret too, so keep the stocks up, and tell the troops they can have two biscuits with their cup of tea if they volunteer to give blood. If they do not offer,' he joked, 'tell them they're on a charge.'

'I think this guy will be all right now, doctor,' said an orderly, 'where shall I put him?'

'Put him here in the side ward,' Anna said, used to allocating beds to soldiers in most need back at Ashland Hall, 'he's ready to go to the hospital ship.'

'Well soldier, your war is over for now,' said Sam, 'that's a lovely Blighty wound you've got there, it's back home for you tomorrow. Take him over now,' he instructed a male orderly.

Life had changed so much for both of them after their family was killed that Christmas Eve... All she wanted to do now was find out what Sam had been through... However, there was no chance of that happening any time soon. In a moment, he was gone again, and she felt that familiar shock of panic run through her. What if he were injured. What if she never saw him again? What if that was their final goodbye?

* * *

Anna was on the go all through the night, collecting casualties, distributing them to the clearing station, field hospital, advanced operating theatres, or isolation. Anywhere they were going to get the best treatment. She and all the other nurses worked so hard, Anna sometimes wondered how body and soul stayed together.

When Anna returned to the billet to sleep, Ellie was already on a bed gently snoring, giving Anna no time to tell her of her discovery. Her brother, Sam, wonderful Sam, was alive and well and right here in Belgium.

Even though she was exhausted, Anna could not relax. She prowled the field hospitals and clearing stations, but she could not find him. In the end, she wondered if she had imagined it. In the theatre of war, anything was possible.

Returning to her billet, she began to write a letter to Ned. She would tell him of the strange happening. He would understand...

When the next call came, she was up and out before Ellie was even half-awake.

'Come on, slowcoach,' Anna beckoned Ellie. 'I've got some wonderful news to tell you.'

'I am coming,' Ellie said, hardly hurrying at all, and Anna knew that if Matron caught her dallying there would be hell to pay. However, grabbing her arm, they were soon on their way. Anna had hardly any time to wonder what was in store for them.

'What is it you have to tell me, Anna?' said Ellie as they got settled.

Anna, still buzzing with excitement could hardly get the words out. 'Sam's alive, Ellie. I saw him yesterday. He's a medic here at the hospital and a good one too. I am so relieved to find him. He thought I had died in the hospital before he left for

Canada so he was overjoyed to see me. Hopefully, I will be able to see more of him while we're here.'

* * *

Behind the wheel, Daisy looked both ways as they approached a crossroads. They had been travelling through the night, helping injured soldiers. She took the road to the right and suddenly all was quiet again. Anna heaved a sigh, but the silence unnerved her more than the shellfire did.

'Maybe the enemy have all gone home for a kip,' Daisy said and, relieved, they laughed as the weak morning sun broke through the clouds. Soon, they discovered a group of wounded French soldiers, who informed them that there were more injured troops further on. All three medics continued on foot and Anna found the casualties without difficulty, and after taking them to the clearing station, Daisy, Anna and Ellie quickly got back in the ambulance and were on their way again.

'Looks like we're here,' said Anna in a low voice, as a vibrant discharge of adrenaline shot through her, hitting her heart with such force it pumped fiercely in her chest. The gunfire was now deafening. It was obvious they were getting nearer to the Front. The action was uninterrupted as Daisy threw her ambulance round every corner.

'Just another fine day at the infirmary,' Daisy called from the front of her ambulance, emblazoned with the words; '*Presented by St. John's, Newfoundland. For service with the British Armies in the field.*'

* * *

'I am so tired I could sleep standing up,' Anna said, wanting to flop down on a comfortable bed. Anna now driving her own ambulance was fighting to stay awake. Her sleepless night had caught up with her so that the windscreen wipers which were fighting a losing battle against the torrential rain were having a hypnotising effect on her eyes.

'Not one dry day since the beginning of July,' Daisy said, having jumped into Anna's ambulance for a hasty sandwich. 'Bloody relentless it is.' Officially known as the third battle of Ypres, Passchendaele saw a huge scale of casualties, but a girl had to eat. 'It's the mud that gets you down,' Daisy said, 'bloody sticky and it stinks like shit.' Her colourful language went over Anna's head these days, it was the only respite from the dreadful conditions they worked in, and Daisy used it with enthusiasm. 'The German blockade could soon cripple the British war effort,' Daisy said knowingly. 'I heard some of the soldiers saying Haig wants to reach the Belgian coast, to destroy German submarine bases there.'

'I hope they do,' Anna said with feeling. 'Our boys seem encouraged by the success of the attack on Messines Ridge in June. It must have been some sight when nineteen mines exploded simultaneously,'

'They were placed at the end of long tunnels under the German front lines, that must have been a real confidence boost to our boys,' Ellie replied, not to be outdone in the knowledge stakes. 'As well as one hell of a firework display.'

'Although, unlike Verdun, Ypres is not a specially constructed fortress.'

'Yes, but it is a key point in the Flanders line of defence,' Anna countered, 'as it blocked German access to Calais and Boulogne.'

The girls, competitive now, trying to outdo each other in

giving information, had become very knowledgeable since they had come to nurse so close to the front line.

'The channel ports are essential to the British Expeditionary Force,' Ellie said, 'especially in keeping reinforcements and supplies and, like now, for evacuating the wounded.'

'You don't say,' Anna answered wryly, she had been out on every ambulance shout, and was well aware of the need to evacuate the wounded.

The continuous, relentless shelling churned the clay soil that actually smashed the drainage systems. After the hot and sultry July came the heaviest rain for thirty years, which turned the soil into a quagmire, producing thick mud that clogged up rifles and immobilised tanks.

Thousands of men fell. Drowning in mud was as much of a possibility as dying by bullets. The men were not just fighting the enemy, they were fighting the extreme torrential rain. The combination of massive bombardment of the battlefield and the relentless mud made conditions not just impossible but also horrific.

Troops had to fight across what had become a dark muddy honeycomb of deep cells, which, if fallen into, Anna was horrified to discover, men and horses were drowning in, unless pulled out immediately by their pals. When Anna and Ellie came to Passchendaele, they met the war head on. It was chaotic; there were bodies all over the place.

'It seems impossible,' Anna said, 'one minute we are travelling a beautiful country lane, then driving into the jaws of hell the next.' Scrambling from the ambulance now, they quickly headed out to the boggy morass.

'Do not leave your equipment there.' A voice barked behind them.

When Anna turned, she saw a nursing sister, efficiently

organising wounded men into lines. The most urgent cases placed at the side of the ambulance ready for dispatch.

'Send the walking wounded over there,' another nurse called to Anna, 'to the farmhouse.'

'Where shall I dump the grazed and terrified?' Ellie asked, checking a wounded soldier as she spoke.

'Anywhere you like but get straight back here.'

'Yes, Sister,' Anna said, 'there's a convoy of gassed soldiers coming down now.'

'We need all the hands we can get,' Sister shouted.

Anna assumed she had been on duty since the beginning of the war if her tired face was anything to go by.

'And put your gas masks on!'

'They don't give you much time for rehearsals,' Anna told an unconscious soldier.

'Bad news, I'm afraid,' Daisy offered, coming towards her, 'there are no gas masks.' Then reaching into the khaki knapsack she wore over her shoulder, Daisy brought out a package, 'Here, take these, I've got them from medical stores.' She passed Anna a packet of sanitary towels. 'They're better than nothing, and I'm sure they will do the job. You put the loops around your ears.'

'So I gathered,' Anna's face turned every shade of pink through to puce, as she put a pad across her own face and that of the soldier, who was now beginning to come round.

'Modesty aside,' Daisy told her, 'these could be the things that save your life.'

'Looks like it's straight on with the show then,' Anna took the pulse of the soldier, just as a body landed at her feet. She quelled the desire to scream as, quickly and efficiently, she bent down to estimate the seriousness of his wounds, all banter now forgotten. Deciding little could be done, she went on to the next one.

'You don't want to mind Sister Bronwyn,' Daisy said, helping to load another soldier onto a stretcher, 'she's a good sort really.'

'She doesn't frighten me,' said Anna, 'I was born in Liverpool docklands.' The conversation hid her fear as they ministered to the wounded.

* * *

Back at the hospital, Ellie stood by the canvas flap used as a door to the billet. 'I must go and see if there is anywhere more suitable for us to sleep. We can't be expected to do a full day's work if we do not get proper sleep.' With a sniff, she turned away.

'I wish you luck with that one,' Daisy said, 'and if you are successful ask if we can all have a comfy bed and a connecting bathroom, if you please.'

Anna, amused by the very nature of this young woman, who seemed to hurtle through life and rattle the status quo, enjoyed sharing the tent. Daisy's bed was festooned with feather boas and other artistic paraphernalia, a vanity case full of colourful theatre make-up, wigs and... daringly, a red silk dress. She wondered how on earth Daisy managed to bring all this kit with her.

'Does this place have to look like something resembling the stage of a low-grade music hall?' Ellie asked, when she realised, she was stuck with the situation.

'You really should practise your beautiful smile more,' Daisy told Ellie, 'it doesn't hurt a bit.'

Anna tried hard not to giggle, but it was impossible; Daisy was instantly likeable, as long as you were not Ellie.

'Tell me, Daisy,' Ellie said peevishly, 'what made you take up driving an ambulance instead of going onto the stage?'

Daisy looked quietly at Ellie for a long moment. Then her

eyes filled with a sadness neither Ellie nor Anna could contemplate and with no hint of joviality she said: 'I wanted to get back home... It seemed the quickest way to get out of Canada.'

27

Even though the work could be back-breaking sometimes, Anna noticed that Daisy never once complained. Nothing was any trouble.

'D'you think I'll get a chance to move from the ambulances, and work in the clearing station or the hospital?' Daisy said one night during a lull in shelling. 'I could work on male surgical.' Anna and Ellie had just finished mopping, sterilising, and emptying bedpans in the sluice room. Anna, heading towards her thin iron bed, grimaced; knowing the last thing she wanted to think about now was the operating room. Daisy was lying on her bed staring at the top of the white tent. 'I'm not complaining but I'm sure I would sleep much easier, if I had a few male bed-baths to look forward to in the morning.'

'Daisy, is that you not complaining?' Anna laughed as she changed out of her uniform for the first time in two days. Slipping into her winceyette nightdress and warm, woollen dressing gown, all she wanted to do was snuggle up in her bed, get out her pen and paper and write a letter.

She missed Ruby and Archie, but most of all she longed to see

Ned. He was out there somewhere. His letters still made her laugh in this godforsaken place, and if she could not talk to him, all she wanted to do was write this letter, snuggle down under her bedclothes and dream of their last hours together. However, Daisy seemed to have other ideas.

'Ah no,' Daisy giggled, 'I just want to see what a real live willy looks like.'

Anna and Ellie shrieked with laughter, unable to believe what they had just heard.

'You are incorrigible, Flynny,' Ellie laughed, 'you do not mean to tell me that you have never seen a...' she was unable to say the word.

'I only drive the poor buggers to the casualty station,' Daisy looked affronted, 'they never let me near the goods.' More shrieks ensued, and Daisy looked perplexed. 'Don't tell me you're not curious?' she said, obviously put out.

'It may have escaped your notice, Dais,' Anna laughed, 'but we are nurses, we see things like that all the time.'

'You have a great way with the Tommies, I must say,' Daisy answered, making Anna feel a few inches taller, 'but they won't do a thing I ask. Only the other day, I was driving at breakneck speed to get them to the first aid, dodging bullets, and bombs, picking up wounded soldiers at every turn. Then, one asked for a bottle. Then another one asked, then another until they all wanted one. It was stop, start, stop, start. I felt like a hiccup.' They all laughed now. Anything to take their minds from the carnage around them. 'Sister was only a whisker off putting me on a charge when I got back.'

Even though Anna knew respectable women did not smoke, she could not hide her fascination as she watched Daisy release a slow sophisticated stream of tobacco smoke that mixed with the smell of cordite in the air.

Daisy shook her head and ground out the discarded stump of the lit cheroot under the heel of her black-buttoned boot. 'I could have throttled them all. *P.B.I.*, my foot'

'You're better than a tonic, you are, Daisy,' Anna continued.

'You have a rare gift for calming the younger ones down,' said Ellie, 'even the older, more unruly soldiers can be calmed with a kind word.'

'I threaten to sing them a lullaby, that's why.' Daisy laughed now.

'Are you going to nurse until you get married?' Ellie was eager to find good-quality marriageable males.

'Married?' Daisy gave a huge shudder. 'Have you lost your mind.' She pounded her pillow to a pulp, and eventually settling down, she said: 'If we keep losing men at this rate, there'll be none left to marry.'

'Don't be too sure,' Ellie said, opening a copy of *Jane Eyre*.

'Who in their right mind wants to scrimp and scrape and pop babies out at a rate of knots anyway?' Daisy said. 'Not me, that's for sure. Life is for living, not for drudgery.'

'Methinks you doth protest too much,' Anna smiled, discarding her pen and paper, vowing to write her letter when these two comedians were asleep. She could not write beautiful prose in this music hall atmosphere. With blankets tucked under her arms, she picked up her stocking to darn a hole in the toe.

'Weren't you one of those suffragettes, who march round with banners, chaining themselves to railings, Ellie?' Daisy asked, combing one of her dark stage wigs. 'I never got the time for all that militant stuff.' Daisy did not go into detail. 'But I admired their gumption.'

'No,' said Ellie, 'I was a suffra*gist*, not a suffra*gette*. There is a difference.'

'You are a case, you, Daisy,' Anna said in local Liverpool vernacular.

'You sound like me mam, so I'll take that as a compliment, shall I?' Daisy scrambled into her little iron bed, pulling the blankets to her chin and sighed. Then she smiled mischievously, 'It doesn't mean I don't like men, though.'

'You would scare the pants off a docker,' Anna laughed. But beneath all the bluff and bluster, she got the distinct feeling that Daisy was not as happy as she made out.

'If I got the chance, I would, but I didn't know that was how you did it.' They all laughed, even Ellie, and Daisy's blue eyes opened wide. She sat up suddenly, put her hands on her heart, and said with a theatrical flourish, 'Will I ever get back to Blighty at this rate?'

28

'*Wipers* has got to be the arse-end of the world,' Daisy said, describing the third battle of Ypres, also known as the Battle of Passchendaele. One of the major battles of the war to date. Daisy, Anna, and Ellie had hardly slept for three days and nights, grabbing only a fleeting shuteye when there was a bit of a miraculous and all-too-rapid lull in the bombardment. 'Surely between the British, Australian, New Zealand, Canadian and South Africans, we can beat the shit out of the German army,' she said, thoroughly fed up now.

'We'll take control, Daisy, don't lose heart.' Anna was watching the Belgium part of West Flanders light up like a massive bonfire. The air choked with thick black smoke in an effort to drive a hole in the German lines. British troops, intending to advance to the Belgian coast and capture the German submarine bases there, were under heavy fire and they were expecting massive amounts of casualties. Another explosion close to the white hospital tents sent them scurrying to action stations. They had moved closer to the battle ground and were stationed at a field hospital nearby.

'It's getting pretty fierce down here,' Anna said, attending a soldier who was writhing in pain.

'Sister said no time for chatter.' Ellie, her nerves in shreds, threw her arms over her head as another horrendous bombardment broke out above them.

'I have to get these men in the *ambolance*.' Daisy, whose pronunciation of the word, ambulance, always raised a smile, could see there was no hope for the soldier she was tending. She went on to the next. Those who showed any sign of life went straight to the casualty clearing station. Anguish was not an option. There was no time.

'A bit of chatter gets you through, Ellie,' Anna gently admonished her friend, knowing if she wanted to survive in this rain-soaked country for longer than five minutes, she would have to have her wits about her. Passchendaele was a quagmire that did not suit Ellie's home-comfort nature. As most of this battle was taking place on reclaimed marshland, it was swampy even in dry weather.

Persistent heavy rain made life miserable for all of them, producing an impassable morass of deep liquid mud. They knew that already thousands of soldiers had drowned. Anna had never seen such devastation. Even the newly developed tanks silted up and had become almost impossible to use.

'Arse or elbow?' Daisy asked, bringing a stretcher. They had not stopped collecting casualties for the last twenty-seven hours, and it seemed there would be no let-up any time soon.

Anna took hold of the stretcher and helped carry the young infantryman to the tent at the other side of the boggy field. Putting him on the floor, she knew he would have to wait his turn, no matter how gravely injured he was.

Every operating table was full. The doctors were working flat out, and there was an endless stream of casualties coming in all the time. Anna wanted to scream at the futility of it. All this slaughter for a couple of inches of gained land. It had to be bloody well worth it

'Outa the way, Nurse.'

'Sorry,' Anna said, dazed, finding it difficult to string two thoughts together. 'I don't know if I'm upside down or inside out at the moment.'

Suddenly, someone took her arm and dragged her outside the huge tent that served as a makeshift hospital. The place where they tried desperately to save the dying or move the less seriously wounded to more secure establishments.

'Follow me.' The voice behind the thick dark beard was commanding. 'We need help over here.'

Anna followed at a run, flinching at the sound of shells bursting overhead, but continuing, nonetheless. The noise was terrific now as guns, bombs and missiles flew in every direction. The sky was crimson with shellfire, bodies everywhere.

'Here, catch hold of his leg, I think this one is still alive.'

Anna helped the doctor pull a young half-drowned soldier from a water-filled crater. The orderlies, blown to smithereens, had previously done the same job.

Anna did not have time to feel revulsion, or fear. Instead, the adrenaline that should have made her want to run accumulated to a rage of invincibility as they got the soldier who had already lost his fight and put him on the wayside. And she was not at all surprised when somewhere over her shoulder she heard a weary wag singing, '*Oh, oh, oh, what a lovely war...*'

Nevertheless, her interest was short-lived when she saw another man lying unconscious in the mud. Her first thought was that he was dead. However, her instincts told her he was not.

'Move it, nurse,' the doctor roared, but Anna was transfixed by the warrior clad in a Canadian uniform, his face unrecognisable and caked in mud, lying unconscious only feet from the ambulance. She could have sworn she saw his chest move.

'We have to save that soldier, sir. He's alive.' Anna could not leave him lying there.

'He's clearly dead,' the doctor shouted, 'and we will be too if we don't get a move on.'

'No, sir, I don't think he is.' Anna could not put into words what was drawing her to the young soldier, but she knew she had to save him. She had seen signs of life. Surely. It was only a tiny movement but... Crawling on her stomach, Anna edged closer, knowing she would not be able to live with herself if she did not try to save his life.

'Come back here this instant, nurse.'

Anna, ducking bullets and ricocheting shrapnel, could hear the fury in the senior medic's voice. Nevertheless, she did not intend to leave this man. When she reached his apparently lifeless body, she felt for a pulse at the side of his throat. It was weak. Still, there was a pulse.

'Over here,' Anna screamed, relieved she had not left him to die. His pulse, almost too faint, told her this soldier might not see out the night, but it would be through no fault of hers. Praying now, she knew she would never give up. She *must* save his life.

'If you do not move, nurse, you are looking at a court martial for disobeying an order'.

'I don't care,' she called, looking down at the young soldier. She put her hand behind his head and, pulling down his lower jaw, she coiled her fingers right into his mouth, scooping out the thick, choking sludge from his throat and she listened... Nothing. Pulling him closer to her, his head resting in her lap as she knelt in the mud wiping the filth from his face with her apron, Anna was met with the unmistakable face of her brother.

'Sam,' she cried. 'I let you go one time before,' she told her unconscious brother, 'but I am not going to do it again.' Picking up his dog tag, Anna's suspicions were confirmed: Captain Samuel Cassidy, C.A.M.C. 'Hold on, Sam... My darling boy, hold on.' Looking up to the heavens, the rain mingled with her tears. 'Please God, don't let him die, too,' she said, stroking the unconscious face of her younger brother. 'Doctor, over here, hurry. He's alive.'

The doctor came hurtling back. Bending close now, he listened for the faintest of breath. Anna could not imagine a God so cruel as to give her back the most precious thing she had in the whole world, and then immediately take him from her. Sam must live. She would do everything in her power to help him. A vivid snowy picture of bygone times entered her head. She was cradling a small, lifeless body that night too.

'No, please Lord. No.' She grabbed the lapel of Sam's khaki jacket, and instinctively shaking him with such force, it dislodged what mud was still in his throat, and Sam coughed out a huge plug. Suddenly his body gave a shudder and she stopped.

Still, for a moment, Anna listened. Then, her brother took in a huge gasp of damp, summer air, and although his eyelids remained closed, he began to draw in small breaths. But when she felt his pulse, it was racing.

'Stretcher over here,' the doctor yelled, all the while checking for other injuries, applying pressure when he found a huge gaping wound in Sam's stomach. 'Quickly We've got to get this kid on the table now.'

Two orderlies hurried forward.

'Good work there, nurse,' the Canadian doctor said. 'Your keen observation may have saved this kid's life...'

'He's my brother.' A dry shuddering sob rocked her body, but no tears came, she would save them for later. 'I swore I would never let him down.'

It seemed like an eternity before they managed to get Sam to the clearing station just a few yards up the road.

'You are English...?' the doctor called over his shoulder, with Anna following at a run.

'And so is he,' Anna replied, 'until he was taken from us.' Orderlies, all around, were busy heaving dead bodies out of the way so that the doctors could concentrate on the wounded still alive.

'You are not assisting in this procedure, nurse,' said the doctor with a fierce determination, then he ordered another medic: 'Take her to the nurses' station where she can get cleaned up.'

'But I want to stay – I need to stay,' Anna cried above the noise of the guns.

'We do not care what you want or what you need, nurse,' he barked, 'you just take yourself out of here and I'll come see you when I've finished.'

'Come on, sweetie,' Ellie who had appeared at her side, gently took her arm. 'Let the doctors do their job.'

'Take cover,' shouted the orderly over his shoulder. Suddenly there was a loud bang, and Ellie landed at the bottom of a greasy pit. Almost instantly, Anna was on her feet, dragging her out of the crater. She did not intend to lose a friend.

'You have a quick recovery time,' said the orderly.

'It comes with plenty of practice,' Anna said, looking round to make sure Ellie was in one piece. She had never lost the survival instincts honed on the dockside streets of Liverpool. And Anna smiled for the first time that day when she saw Ellie, who was obviously enjoying the attention of another doctor, was having her ankle checked for broken bones and whooped with delight when they put her on a stretcher.

'We think it's just a sprain, but I'm going to have it X-rayed to make sure.' Ellie waved as she was taken to the casualty clearing station, 'Toodle-oo for now.'

* * *

'How are you supposed to get any rest in this godforsaken place?' Anna prowled the farmhouse that doubled as staff accommodation. 'And how can a compassionate God ever let this happen, to men who have no argument with anyone?' She was angry. There was no respite from the fear gripping her heart.

Not allowed in the operating room, as she insisted, she should be, and ordered to take some time off, Anna was invited to sit with a group of nurses at the table drinking much-appreciated cocoa. They welcomed her even though she was filthy in mud-caked clothing.

'Here, nurse, have my seat,' one of the orderlies said, rising from the long form. 'I'm going back now.'

Anna, grateful, slumped onto the wooden bench, and a cup of something steaming was put before her. She drank the hot sweet cocoa without even tasting it.

'How much longer is this awful war going to last?' she asked, staring into the smoke-filled kitchen where medics of every shape and rank took a much-needed, seldom sufficient rest. 'How many more lives will be taken before those back in the safety and comfort of their Whitehall offices decide that enough is enough?'

* * *

'They are doing everything they possibly can for Sam,' a kindly nurse said when she came to find Anna later. 'He was lucky that medical treatment was started almost on the front line.'

'I wonder if it was quick enough, though,' Anna said, unable to rid herself of the fear he might not see the night out. He was holding on by a thread when they rushed him towards the hospital. Sam was so close. Yet now, Anna felt they could not be further from each other.

'He's copped a Blighty one,' the nurse said, her eyes filled with compassion. 'If he survives the night, he will be on the next hospital ship home.'

Anna's lips pressed together to stop herself from saying something trite, knowing these were the words they used when there was little hope. The nurse was trying to help, but that was impossible.

'Where is his home now?' Anna asked eventually, hoping that Sam, still a British citizen, would be sent back to Blighty, knowing he was far too ill to fight any more. Nevertheless, fight he must. His battle now was to stay alive.

'He may be sent back to Canada.'

The thought sent terror shards shooting through her heart. Anna could not bear the thought of seeing Sam go away again. She had spent too many years pining for the brother she thought she had lost for good.

'Leave it with me,' Ellie said, her ankle miraculously pain-free, and with not a limp in sight. 'I know someone who knows someone who can help.'

'Do you really?' Anna knew if Ellie could not pull the rabbit out of the hat, then nobody could. She was a genius at being able to *persuade* the commanders to see things her way. Anna could only marvel at her successes. The other day she managed to procure the bandages they had been begging weeks for. Although Ellie did not say where she got them from, and Anna did not ask. As long as they had supplies for their men, it was good enough for her.

'I will see you later,' Ellie said as she headed towards the exit. 'I have a few egos to massage.'

Anna gasped at her audacity. Ellie was as bold as Aunt Ruby.

* * *

Later that day, Anna went to see the commander in charge, whose office was situated midway between the front line and base camp, about five hundred yards from the river, and saw the injured men being transported via horse-drawn or motor ambulance.

She wanted Sam away from the battlefield and on a hospital ship as soon as was humanly possible. The company commander told her that the only way to do that, given his wounds, was via the hospital boat, which meant being sailed down the river with a full-time nurse. In addition, the next boat was not leaving for Canada until next Friday.

'We could get him back to the First Western at Fazakerley, it's the hospital for Canadian soldiers and it is leaving tomorrow!' Anna told the Commander. 'And I would like to take him home.'

'I don't give a monkeys cuss what you would like to do, Sister,' said the tough-talking commander. 'We cannot spare you, Sister,' He had to be firm and fair to all nurses, Anna understood that, but surely, he could see she was desperate to take her brother back home after all these years. 'Your brother will be in good hands, whomever is assigned to take care of him.'

'Yes, Sir.' Anna was devastated that she could not accompany Sam, although she had to be glad her brother was still alive and she must rejoice in the fact that his war was over. However she was determined that he would be going back to Liverpool where he belonged.

* * *

Ellie had managed to pull some strings so Anna was able to tell Sam the good news.

'I have made arrangements for you to be taken to Ashland Hall once you are well enough to leave the hospital in Fazakerley. I will be home in a few weeks, time,' Anna told him when she went to see him later that day. Still very weak, he squeezed her hand and smiled when she told him that Aunt Ruby and Archie would spoil him something rotten, which was no more than he deserved.

'Who is Uncle Archie and Aunt Ruby?' Sam asked. 'The people who took you in after the fire?'

Anna nodded, there was so much catching up to do.

'I sent a telegram...' Anna explained, 'although I imagine Ruby will have kittens when the Post Office turn up, and will expect the worst kind of news, but she will forgive me, I'm sure.' She noticed Sam's eyelids close, and she decided it was time to let him rest. 'As long as we are still alive, and get back in one piece, that is all that matters.' She could see he was losing the battle to stay awake. 'I will come back tomorrow, get some rest...' Even before she left his bedside, she knew Sam was sleeping.

The farmhouse door opened and Ellie, her face covered with a scarf in case of a gas attack, blew in on a gust of howling wind.

'Put the wood in the hole,' a collective cry went up, and Ellie closed the door quickly and headed for the stove.

'Those doctors are performing operations that are nothing short of a miracle,' Anna said before the fierce wind drowned out the rest of her words as the door opened again. Turning, Anna was pleased when she saw Daisy in all her finery.

'Daisy,' Anna rose quickly from the table, 'where the bloody hell have you been? You were there one minute and gone the next.'

'I've been a bit busy,' Daisy let out her customary hoot of laughter that caused Ellie to scowl, 'I'm getting ready for the concert.'

'What concert?' Anna and Ellie chorused.

'The one I am doing tonight, for the troops, to boost morale.'

'Right,' Anna said a little perplexed and vaguely wondering where they were going to hold a concert, but no matter now. 'There is something I want to talk to you about.' Anna beckoned her over to the table. Pouring tea from the huge pot on the stove, Daisy looked from Anna to Ellie who shrugged. When all three girls settled, Anna took a deep breath and said without ceremony, 'How would you like to go home?'

'Home?' Daisy's fine brows pleated. 'Where's home?'

'To England...' Anna could feel the thrill of excitement rise, knowing that she was about to offer Daisy something which she had longed for every one of the last seven years. 'To Aunt Ruby's place on the shores of the River Mersey.'

Daisy's eyes widened until they formed tears as she said: 'Does that mean I have to tell your Aunt Ruby I've come back in your place? She will batter me.' All of a sudden, they were laughing, and crying, and hugging each other. Humour, Anna knew, was their way of coping, staying sane in this mad war.

'I want you to take someone home for me,' Anna said when she could be heard over Daisy's excitement.

'Who?' Daisy's eyes looked almost fearful with anticipation.

'Come on, I will show you.' Anna looked to Ellie and winked her eye. It was only right that Sam and Daisy should return to their homeland together, after all these years.

'You have found my Sam!' Daisy did not wait for an answer. She was off. Quicker than a bullet from a gun. When she came back after getting short shrift from Sister, she danced. 'I managed to see him for a moment, but I hardly think he realised it was me.'

'He will remember, Daisy,' Anna said, smiling. She was glad Sam was going home with the girl who escorted him from England.

'I will put on the performance of a lifetime tonight, girls, you see if I don't.'

29

Tallulah Starr applied a slick of ruby lipstick to her pouting lips. Any moment now, she would be out there on the stage, doing her best Marie Lloyd, singing her heart out for the troops, knowing she would finish with a song that would break their hearts and have them baying for more. However, tonight would be different. Tonight, she would sing with hope in her heart, imagining her Sam could hear her from his hospital bed. Every song was for him.

Some of the injured lads were recovering in the annex over the road, on the mend and almost ready to go back to the trenches somewhere. They would make the most of the concerts. Tallulah was going to make it one of the best nights of their lives. After all, she had much to be glad about now.

During the day, she was Daisy Flynn, the VAD who ragged the ambulance through the mud-spattered fields, collecting wounded soldiers. By night, she sang rousing, risqué songs, raising the spirits of the brave Tommies, at the Front.

Back in Canada, her life had been one of work and drudgery. Not many Home Children were welcomed with open arms as far as she knew, tolerated at best, and unloved, except when she sang. The only male who had ever shown her any consideration was Sam Cassidy. Her Sam, as she thought of him. Now they were going home, where they belonged.

'You're on next, Miss Starr.' Out of her khaki uniform, Daisy heard the call that came from the corridor outside. Her dressing room was the medical storeroom, while the 'concert hall' was the oblong first aid hut, erected by the soldiers.

She took one last look in the rust mottled mirror and sighed.

'On with the show' she whispered, 'this one is for you, Sam.'

Tallulah Starr sashayed onto the stage, arms wide open waving to her *boys*. Accompanied by a military brass band, who doubled as stretcher-bearers on the battlefield, she could hardly hear the music for the thunderous clapping and the stamping of heavy, newly polished boots.

Almost deafened by the appreciative applause, Tallulah laughed, raising her hands in pleasure. Lapping up the adoration, which, she was sure, had little to do with the silk dress in pillar-box red, and edged in black swansdown, which provocatively showed off her silken shoulders. The dress had belonged to her last employer.

When Daisy became Tallulah, she felt, for the first time, as if she mattered.

Looking out at the eager crowd showing their enthusiasm with whoops and whistles, her eyes were drawn to the skylight, above the audience's heads. She could not fail to notice a vivid orange glow in the vermilion sky.

Tallulah sang louder, beckoning the audience to join in, to drown out the occasional cannon boom a mile or two further down the line. For she and the approving audience were trying their best to ignore the offensive, which was now at its height.

A couple of hours later, exhausted, and exhilarated, Daisy

knew that tomorrow she would be taking some of these men to the casualty clearing station, or to the hospital ship. It was only right she should give them a good time tonight. She finished her repartee as she always did, with a rousing rendition of 'Keep the Home Fires Burning'. When she finished there was not a dry eye in the house.

* * *

The following day, Anna, Daisy and Ellie were chattering like magpies, reliving the wonderful concert, laughing as they left the farmhouse.

'You dark horse, Daisy,' Ellie said, 'you did not tell us you had such a sublime voice, absolutely wonderful.'

Daisy basked in Ellie's rare praise.

'The concert was wonderful, Daisy, you had those soldiers eating out of your hand,' Anna agreed.

'And the officers too,' Ellie shrieked delightedly. Daisy and Ellie had now become best friends.

'For as much as I would love to sit here chatting,' Anna, always the sensible one, said, 'Sister will organise a firing squad for us going absent without leave, if we do not move ourselves.'

'Oh, hark at her, Daisy,' Ellie laughed, 'she's missing her Ned, so we have to excuse her.'

'I forgive everybody anything.' Daisy's eyes were alight with joyful elation. 'Because I am the one who is taking my Sam back to where we both belong.'

As they left, the farmhouse door, dragged from Anna's hand by the strong wind, blew against the wall of the farmhouse. They had to hold on to their wimpled headdress, as any further conversation was impossible through the lashing rain, accompanied by the noise of the bombardment. Daisy jumped into her ambulance out of the rain, and it juddered and shook. Suddenly, Anna felt her bag whip from her hand by the swirling wind. She bent down to pick it up.

'I'm a right giddy kipper, lately.' She laughed; thrilled Daisy was taking her brother back home to England. 'Butter fingers, that's me,' she said trying to grip the mud-soaked handles as the lashing rain saturated her right through in no time.

Standing up, she triumphantly held up her bag. A few steps further on and she would be on her way to pick up casualties but then noticed Ellie's wide-eyed expression of horror, her mouth open as if in a silent scream. Anna did not turn her head to the place where Ellie's finger pointed. Instead, she hurried over and hugged her. Too afraid of what she might see.

'The ambulance was right there behind you,' Ellie gasped, shaking her head in denial. Anna turned her head, as if in slow motion, her petrified eyes taking in the acres of mud, the skeletal trees, and the melancholy sky, and the tank that had pushed the ambulance against the wall of the building they had just left and crushed it like a piece of paper into a mangled wreck no human being could possibly survive.

Gazing in disbelief, Anna initially refused to take in the sight of the place where Daisy had been only moments before. She felt the blood drain from her face and a small cry escaped her lips. Her body rigid. She could not move.

Daisy's eyes were wide open when the medics dragged her from behind the crumpled wheel of her beloved *Bessie* and looking as if she had been given the worst kind of news. Stunned, Anna saw there was not a mark on Daisy, but the crush had killed her instantly. Her wonderful friend, who brought such joy to so many, was dead!

A stinging slap across her cheek caught Anna by surprise. Nevertheless, it terminated the strident, high-pitched scream emanating from her mouth, as whizz-bangs, with devastating accuracy, whistled loudly overhead, cutting off further communication as Ellie dragged her to the floor.

'Jesus, Mary and Joseph pray for her.' Tears streamed down Anna's cheeks, and she made the sign of the cross in the thick, slimy mud.

'Let's get her to the clearing station,' Ellie said, quickly coming to her senses and taking control.

'There's nothing they can do for her in the clearing station now. There is nothing any of us can do.' Anna kneeled beside Daisy's lifeless body and she gently stroked her cheek. Closing Daisy's eyes for the last time, it didn't seem possible that not five minutes ago she was her usual effervescent, cheerful self.

Anna's heart stuttered, everything was moving in slow motion, and she was watching the battle raging from the side-line of her worst nightmare, remembering this same feeling the night their house in Queen Street was deliberately set alight by Jerky Woods, and nearly her whole family were taken from her. 'I'm not leaving her here to be trampled into the mud by another passing tank.'

'Too right,' Ellie said as tears streamed down her face and Anna went to fetch an unaccompanied stretcher, closing her mind down to the possibilities of where its handler would be. It was something Ellie had learned to do quite quickly. If she could stop herself from thinking. Wondering. Imagining. She could do her job. Men were dying all round them. They could not relinquish their duties. They had to carry on no matter how mechanically.

The long battle of Passchendaele had now ended with a victory for the allies but Sam had taken a turn for the worse and had been unable to travel to the ship which would take him back to Liverpool. Knowing that the depths of the night were the worst time for dying, Anna spent many nights sitting beside her brother's bed, watching his every breath, willing him to survive as his breathing became more laboured. If Sam were going to survive, he would need round-the-clock care and if, God forbid, he was going to die, she was going to be right here at his side.

Through the long slim window, she watched a new day dawn and noticed Sam's eyelids flicker. He murmured something. Anna could not understand what he was saying. Leaning forward, she listened carefully, trying to make out his words.

Sam, with some effort, lifted his hand. His fingers curling round the locket she wore always under her stiff white collar and which had now worked its way out of her pale blue uniform dress. The locket was the one Sam had bought for their mother on that fateful Christmas Eve and Ruby had passed it on to Anna, after she retrieved it from the priest who had taken it from Sam before he was sent to the orphanage.

'Hello Sam, it's me Anna,' she whispered as tears filled her eyes, 'you're going to be fine. Ellie... you haven't met her yet, but she knows all the high-up officers who make the decisions... she had a word and guess what? I can take you home after all.' Her brother was going to make it. She would make sure of that and for a fleeting moment, Sam's eyes flickered open and registered the eyes of the sister he had been separated from for seven long years. Then, a faint smile lifted his lips and as his eyelids closed, a single stray tear rolled down his face.

He seemed to be sleeping more soundly now, comfortable due to the heavy sedation he had been given. She knew the medical team had done a terrific job, but he was still in a bad way. Her eyelids grew heavy in the silence of the long bed-lined ward. The beds were crammed so closely together, there was just enough room either side of each bed for a nurse to administer the care these heroic men needed. A small rustle at the bottom of the bed caused her eyelids to open quickly and she looked round in the direction of the hushed whisper.

'He is going to be fine, Anna, trust me.'

Anna was surprised, but not alarmed when she saw Daisy standing there at the bottom of Sam's bed. She was hallucinating through lack of sleep. She must be. Daisy had died and had been buried here, a final resting place for the madcap ambulance driver with the exquisite voice and the raucous laugh who paid no heed to titles and was one gifted medic.

'Daisy?' Anna reached out, but Daisy's image evaporated like smoke from a cigarette into the air. 'Oh, Daisy I will miss you. We would have been the best of friends.' Anna wondered a few minutes later, if she had been dreaming, until, somewhere in the distance she received the proof that Daisy had come back to say goodbye when she heard the familiar golden voice along the corridor...

'*What's the use of worrying. It never was worthwhile. So...*'

And, not questioning how or why she knew, she just did. Daisy was in a better place.

'Come along, Sister,' Matron said, putting a gentle hand on Anna's shoulder, 'you could both do with some rest now.'

Her body aching, Anna stood up and began to pace the ward in an effort to get some feeling back in her stiff limbs. This place, in sharp contrast to the battlefield, was an oasis of calm efficiency, and gazing through eyes half-hypnotised through fatigue, she blinked at the men whose shattered limbs were bound together with splints. Bandages covered faces with no eyes. They were all asleep now, most were knocked out with morphia to begin the long job of healing.

Their bodies may mend, she thought, but their minds would need a bit more work. Anna wondered who could recover from such unbearable injuries and be the same as they were before? Some of these men had young families, only joining the war for the pay it brought. What price a life? she wondered. These soldiers had no axe to grind, no personal argument with the enemy. All they did was follow orders.

'Nurse? Nurse!' The voice belonged to an officer at the end of the ward.

'He is having electric shock treatment in the morning, poor soul,' Matron told Anna, who knew the treatment terrified most patients. 'He lost the use of his legs,' Matron explained, carrying a treatment tray containing bandages and the obligatory syringe of morphia.

'Shot or infection?' Anna asked, admiring the calm efficiency of her fellow nurse, silently admitting that these men were in the best possible hands.

'Shellshock,' answered Sister. 'He came in screaming in pain after going over the top. Most of his men were killed.'

'I've heard many similar tales of officers who felt impotent and scared but were not allowed to show it,' Anna said, knowing that natural emotions were forbidden on the battlefield and the officers developed symptoms that doctors could not yet explain. 'Will he be sent home?'

'He is being sent to Moss Side Military Hospital in Maghull,' Matron informed her, and Anna's eyes widened in surprise.

'That's not far from Ashland Hall,' she said. 'I've heard good things about the treatment the officers and men are receiving.'

'It's one of the first institutions in the world to recognise shellshock as a medical condition, not a weakness of character,' Sister said with authority. 'This fellow made a bit of a name for himself as a daredevil, and the powers-that-be considered his actions reckless, maybe even downright dangerous.'

'And his legs?' Anna asked.

'Some say his lameness is a ploy to avoid being shot for putting the lives of his battalion at risk,' Sister continued. 'The doctors cannot find anything physically wrong with his legs.'

'I feel so sorry for them all,' Anna said. She knew she could not sit here and do nothing when nurses looked to be rushed off their feet at any moment and she did what she was trained to do in these circumstances. She made herself useful.

31

Sam's condition was beginning to stabilise so Anna was hoping that arrangements could soon be made for him to be taken down river to the port when she was called to see sister.

'I think, under the circumstances, you and Nurse Harrington have both done your duty out here, Anna,' Sister said, 'now you must *both* take your brother home.'

Too full to speak, Anna could only nod. She needed time with her family. And Sam would need her now.

Her nerves in shreds, Anna did not think she could take many more shocks. But this was one of the better ones to be leaving this place with both her best friend and her beloved brother. She knew, if it had not been for the wind, or losing her grip on her bag, or stooping to pick it up, she would have been the one being buried, instead of poor Daisy. Her funny, irreverent, courageous friend who was buried with full military honours in a tranquil spot near the sea she so loved.

Daisy, fun-loving and full of life, had plans for the future. She loved her work and paid no heed to pompous bureaucracy if the situation was uncalled for. Nevertheless, she was the kindest, most generous person Anna had come to know. Daisy did not judge anybody, not even Ellie, with whom she had become good friends. She did not whinge and whine. Daisy was a heroine and Anna was proud to call her a close friend. She would be the one to tell Sam, as gently as she knew how, what happened to her.

Just before Christmas, Anna and Ellie accompanied Sam on the barge, a very gentle journey, where the seriously injured moved slowly down the river towards the hospital ship. Throughout all of the five-hour journey along the river, Anna prayed while she and Ellie held Sam's hand.

'I won't let *you* die, Sam,' she cried, 'I'll look after you now.' As she gazed down at his fair lashes resting on alabaster cheeks, she wondered how many more lives would be sacrificed before this damned senseless war was over. The sooner she got him out of here, the better.

As they neared the port the sound of anti-artillery fire became louder and when they arrived at the berth of the hospital ship that would carry Sam back home all lights were out on board.

'Not tonight,' Anna heard a male voice when she asked permission to board the ship, 'what with the heavy raid and no moonlight.' The voice seemed to come from a sky filled with searchlights and fragments from the bursting anti-aircraft artillery. This place of death was a live, seething mass of noise and activity. 'You have to take him over to the hospital,' said an orderly from the ship, 'we can't take patients until the raid is over, or 'til morning when it's light.' It was a bitter blow, but Anna had to admit that they knew what they were doing.

She and Ellie went back to the barge and proceeded a short way down the river to the small cottage hospital, where Sam was taken onto a ward. Once Sam was settled, they would go in search of something to eat.

'I am starving,' said Ellie as they headed to the only place where they suspected there might be some food. The field kitchen was not particularly busy. By the look of things, the cook was not having the best of times.

'Bloody bombs put my fire out, so dinner may be a little late tonight,' a burly cook thundered as he grabbed a heavy pan and headed for safety in the stables across the field. 'I suggest you take cover.'

'Cook hates being disturbed when creating a culinary master-piece,' quipped the orderly and Anna was sorely disappointed, she could not remember when she'd last ate.

'I could eat a horse between two mattresses,' Ellie grumbled, shaking her fist to the frenetic sky. 'Bloody Hun stop firing 'til I get some food.'

'I bet you two nurses could sleep on a clothesline?' The order-ly's conversation had to be shouted over the noise of the bombardment and Anna surmised he was going to talk until the shelling ended, or until he was, whichever came first.

'I will concentrate on staying perpendicular for the moment.' Anna gingerly picked her way through the chaos of war, not in the mood for a chat.

'Righto,' called the orderly, 'mind that crater.'

'Pardon?' asked Anna, but it was too late, before she knew it, her feet were cart- wheeling down a slimy embankment as her body tried desperately to stay upright. Just in time, she was gripped by a strong hand that prevented her landing in a heap at the bottom of a gigantic muddy shell hole. Anna felt herself steadied.

'You nurses never listen,' said the orderly as he plonked her back on her feet and fixed the tin helmet back on her head.

'Are you all right?' Ellie asked. 'One minute you were there and the next you were hurtling.'

'I'm fine,' said Anna, the only thing that was hurt was her pride.

* * *

Later, when she returned to the hospital where Sam was sleeping, she heard a man call painfully from further down the ward.

'What can I get you, soldier?' Anna said. Ignoring his horrendous injuries, she tried to remain cheerful. 'Can't you sleep? Would you like me to wet your whistle?'

'What are you doing Saturday night?' He tried to pull himself up on the pillow.

'Lie down this minute.' Anna's voice was immediately professional, and the soldier did as he was told. *Just like little boys, some of them*, she thought. 'You don't want to do yourself a mischief.'

'Ahh, those domineering tones, Nurse. You sound just like my missus. How I have missed them.' His face was badly swollen and a deep plum purple, almost black from lip to eyebrow, but he managed a half-smile. 'You haven't seen my eye rolling around anywhere, have you, Nurse? I lost it at Marne.' He sounded almost cheerful in the dimness of the ward and Anna decided it was best to play along.

'How careless can you get?' she said, automatically straightening his covers, 'but I have to say, you will look rather fetching with an eyepatch, and your wound has earned you a back-to-Blighty ticket.'

'Do you think so, nurse? Do you really.' His voice sounded like a young boy, eager to be reassured, and her heart went out to him. Then he said brightly, 'You wouldn't mind hopping in and giving me a little cuddle, just to keep me going 'til I get back to see the wife?'

'I'll give you a king-sized enema in a minute.' Anna could not help but smile. She did not mind their impudent banter. It proved they were still alive.

'Nurse, you do say the nicest things.' He chuckled as Anna wet his lips with a little gauze soaked in water, knowing he was still not to have anything to eat or drink. Giving her hand a little squeeze, he was so pathetically grateful that she almost cried when she watched him grow weary, all bravado swept away on the morning breeze through the open window. She left him only when he was quietly sleeping.

'Will you go and get some sleep, nurse, you are no good to us if we have to step over your unconscious body on the floor,' Sister said sternly. 'You have been awake for nearly two days, and we can't have you collapsing with exhaustion.' Anna had to admit that sleep was a luxury she could barely afford so far, but she knew, if she did not rest soon, she would be fit for nothing.

'Sam Cassidy...?'

'I'll let you know if anything happens. Now sleep.'

Anna, giving Sister a weary smile, nodded agreement.

32

FEBRUARY 1918

The hospital ship which Sam should have been on had long since sailed without him, Christmas and the new year had come and gone with not much reason to celebrate.

Anna had been on duty the previous twenty-four hours and it seemed only minutes since she closed her eyes and drifted into a deep sleep, but it must have been quite a while, as the sun was beginning to go down and an orange dusk descended.

'Nurse! Nurse. Anna.'

She felt the urgent shaking of her shoulder and, groggily, Anna looked up. Her screwed-up eyes refused to focus.

'Sister is asking for you,' the young Australian nurse gave her a cup of water and Anna drank it greedily. Groaning, she would have loved another couple of hours.

'Sam? Is he all right?'

'He had a restful day. The doctors are doing a good job.'

Unable to find a comb, Anna raked her fingers through her hair, before loosely tying it into a chignon at the nape of her slim neck. 'You said Sister wanted to see me.'

'She is with Lady Ashland.' The nurse said no more as, quickly and efficiently, she led the way.

Anna scampered behind the hurrying nurse, about to tell her Lady Ashland was back home. However, intuition told her to stay silent.

When she reached the little kitchen that doubled as Matron's office, Anna found Ellie in tears and her brows pleated. Lady Ashland? She did not comment as she had never seen her so distraught. Ellie was as tough as old boots. However, the reason for her tears soon became clear to Anna when Sister asked her to sit down.

'I'm afraid Captain Sloan died a couple of hours ago, Lady Ashland was with him.'

'Captain Sloan?' Anna tried not to show the confusion she now experienced. She had not heard Ellie talk of a Captain Sloan.

'Rupert,' Ellie sniffed, 'we met him at a fundraising dinner at Ashland Hall.'

'You should have woken me.' Anna put her arms round Ellie's shoulder, surmising that her friend's tears were a culmination of many things. Daisy's death. Exhaustion. The men who would never see loved one's again...

'We cannot cry over them all,' Sister said, 'no matter how much we care.'

'It is so futile,' Ellie cried, 'to die for a couple of inches of gained ground. It is madness.' She put her head on Anna's shoulder, and cried as if her heart would break. Patriotic fervour had all but diminished now. So many lives had been lost. So many young men on all sides sacrificed.

'He will be buried in a small plot at the other side of the field tomorrow morning.' Sister's manner was more compassionate now. She bent her head and gently cleared her throat; allowing tears in her office was a rarity. 'Excuse me,' she said a moment later, lifting a large stack of hospital reports. 'I must get on.' There was no mistaking the now-move-along intonation in her voice as Anna turned to Ellie, her eyes wide.

'Since when did you become Lady Ashland?' Anna asked as they made their way to the food hall. The shelling had subsided, and they were ready for something to eat.

'I had to say something,' Ellie replied, 'the dragon would not let me on the ward.'

Anna smiled, knowing Ellie would use any means possible to get what she wanted.

'Nurse Cassidy, will you come with me please,' a nurse said in a hushed tone as Anna finished her beef soup and her blood ran cold. Sam! She felt the fizz of terror sear right up to the roots of her hair. But even though the look of supreme professionalism etched on the other nurse's face, gave nothing away, Anna feared the worst. 'There is somebody here to see you.'

'Ned,' Anna's voice was barely a whisper when she saw her darling fiancé sitting at Sister's desk. He turned as she entered and quickly stood up, his navy-blue cap in his hand. Moving forward, she longed for him to take her in his arms. However, Sister's beady eyes were upon both of them.

'Sister, Doctor Evans wants to see you on ward two,' the Australian nurse gave Anna a sly wink as she followed Sister from the office leaving Ned and Anna alone.

'Oh Ned,' Anna could hardly believe her good fortune. 'I have missed you so much.'

'I've missed you too, my darling.' Ned searched every inch of her beautiful face, her small tip-tilted nose. He gazed into her trusting marine-coloured eyes that now burned with love, silently daring her to respond in a way not dictated by her virtuous position. 'Sister tells me you have leave due.' Ned could have kicked himself. He did not intend to blurt his intentions so quickly. However, seeing her now, he realised he had developed only a gossamer memory of her loveliness. How quickly the mind's delicate retention protects the longing of the heart, for, if he recalled in sharp detail her exquisite beauty, he would have risked being absent without leave just to be near her, to protect her, to hold her.

Ned deftly caught Anna round her slim waist. Over the heady scent of Lysol disinfectant and carbolic soap, he detected a hint of the *Fleur de France* perfume, which he had once bought her, and felt a surge of overwhelming adoration wash over him. He loved her. He needed her. He wanted her with every beat of his heart.

His fevered imagination could not fail to envision the men she had tended. However, that mattered not one iota now, Ned thought, banishing septic considerations, knowing war did funny things to a man's mind, especially when he was engaged to the most beautiful nurse in the world. However, now she was here, in his arms, and her attention was his and his alone.

Her eyes were silently imploring him to kiss her. Unable to resist, Ned bent his head, and their lips met for the first time in what seemed like eternity. Anna was the only girl he had ever loved, and he knew that she felt the same way about him.

He took her hand, and folding it in his own, Ned held it to the thick navy-blue serge of his greatcoat, aware she could feel the thundering beat of his heart. Her head resting against his shoulder, Ned could see the rosy flush of her cheeks. Looking up to him now, the brilliant sparkle of happiness in her eyes showed no hint of sights a woman should not see.

'Ned,' Anna whispered, a little self-consciously, 'what's wrong?'

Pulling her close, feeling her slim curves form into the hardness of his body, he had intended to greet her with the courteous reserve their positions called for. However, as soon as Anna had walked into the room, all Ned's good intentions had flown out of the window. He wanted her so damn bad it hurt. Without answering, his passionate lips explored hers. Fervent kisses resonating the thundering beat of his heart.

'Oh Ned,' Anna gasped when, finally, she could find her voice, 'can't we get away from here.'

'Come with me,' Ned smiled, breathlessly taking her hand in his, knowing they both needed exactly the same thing. Each other.

* * *

'Ellie will keep an eye on Sam for me,' Anna said, carrying a picnic basket for their day in the woods as far away from the bombardment as possible, her eyes dancing with delight. 'I have an unexpected twenty-four hours' leave.' A surge of pleasure and excitement shot through her. Ned was here. Now. This minute... She could hardly believe it. This was more than she ever dared dream. Proudly, she linked his arm. The brave nursing sister walking tall with her courageous naval officer. Suddenly, even the war did not matter, as long as she was with Ned. When his eyes met hers, they glistened like the most precious of diamonds.

'The break will give us a chance to catch up and...' Ned was hesitant now.

'What is it?' He seemed a little restrained, something Ned had never been. Something was troubling him, she could tell, it unnerved her. The war had changed all of them. They would not be human if it did not. However, Ned was quiet now, even politely formal. Usually, he took life by the scruff of the neck and got the most out of it.

'I have a surprise for you.' He smiled and reached for her hand, 'Well, hardly a surprise, more like a hotel room.'

Anna's jaw fell open. She knew what he was suggesting, and it was not his revelation that shocked her now, but her own reaction to it.

'Will you come with me?' Ned's hands, encasing hers, were trembling ever so slightly. His eyes were bright, expectant. 'I have not slept for days knowing I was going to see you again, then, when they told me you had gone to the hospital ship, I was frantic, especially when they said it had already sailed.'

'Sam was not ready to travel, the doctors did not want him moved at that point,' Anna sighed. 'They said he could join the next one instead.'

'I know that now, my darling,' Ned let out a relieved sigh. 'I saw Ellie, she told me everything... About Daisy and Sam and...'

Anna put her finger to his lips. 'We are wasting time...'

33

'Ned seems troubled,' Anna told Ellie while throwing clean drawers and a chemise into a small vanity case. 'He seemed nervous... with me'

'You should have asked him,' Ellie said, holding up a pale silk nightdress. Ellie shook her head, her colour rising. 'Not that one,' she said, 'that is for my wedding night, if I ever have one.' Without Anna noticing, Ellie slipped it into her valise.

'I could not ask him something so personal.' Because if she was honest, Anna had a feeling he was going to tell her something she did not want to know.

'Maybe he's just tired,' said Ellie. Removing the pins that secured her headdress, and shaking her hair free, she unfastened the deep white collar and stiff uniform sleeves.

'I hope that's all it is,' said Anna, 'at least that can be easily fixed.'

'Don't worry,' Ellie said, 'everything is going to be fine.'

'How do you know that?' Anna thought Ellie was being flippant, taking her situation lightly. She even looked a little smug and that was most unlike Ellie who hurried along to the staff dining room ahead of her. Ned was already waiting for her, gently drumming his fingers on the table and watching other people come and go. At this time of day, after a long and sometimes difficult night shift, Anna would usually be ravenous. Now though, she had completely lost her appetite.

Ned stood up and pulled out the chair nearest his own. Quietly she sat down and looked at the cups.

'Shall I pour?' Anna asked. This was all so civilised. Very stiff and polite, he nodded.

He said nothing as she poured, making her feel even more nervous. Handing him the cup, her hands shook. He looked at the watch she had bought him for his birthday.

'Am I keeping you from something?' she asked him, but Ned did not answer. He seemed preoccupied. Then, he looked at her for a long while before speaking.

'Anna, do you remember when I asked you to marry me?' he said quietly.

'Of course I do.' Anna was shocked that he would ask such a question as he gently took her hand. Had he changed his mind? Had he found somebody else? Her heart was pounding as he lifted her chin, so that her eyes were looking directly into his.

'Do you still want to marry me?' he asked in a voice barely a whisper.

'Of course I do,' she answered again, her voice full of trepidation.

'Will you marry me today?' Ned asked. Anna looked round her before answering, to see if anybody was listening. Today how could she marry him today? It was impossible at such short notice.

'You know I would, if I could, but....' Anna rose as Ned gently pulled her to her feet.

His smile was as wide as ever now, he picked her up and

spun her round. 'I've got a special licence, had a word with the chaplain. It's all done. The only thing you have to do is turn up.'

'Matron will have my scalp.'

'She will develop a blind eye. Anna, it's all fixed, can you be at the chapel in half an hour?'

'Wild horses won't keep me away.' Anna knew she was going back to England with the hospital ship soon. She did not think she would be going back as Mrs Ned Kincaid.

Ned, relieved, let out a long, low whistle, 'I was afraid you would say no.'

'No fear.' Anna's eyes shone with happiness and she longed to kiss him but not here.

'I thought you would want to wait until the war was over,' Ned told her, 'and have the big ceremony at Ashland Hall, with Archie giving you away...'

Anna shook her head and as the news sank in, unable to resist any longer, she kissed him. She did not care who was looking.

His rank of Chief Petty Officer meant he led many hundreds of men. Training brave young matelots in the way of the sea at war. His keen logistic abilities meant he was an expert in planning and decision-making. Now he had organised her wedding day. The man was a genius.

'Although,' Ned said hesitantly, causing Anna's excitement to dim just a little when she saw the solemn pleat of his brow, 'I have to leave tomorrow. The Lieutenant has come down with something nasty.'

'What kind of nasty?' She looked up at him now.

'Shrapnel,' Ned answered, 'we were picking up wounded men whose ship had been sunk.' Ned looked sheepish, 'I'm sorry.'

'Are you asking me to marry you because you are being shipped out, or because of our day in the woods when we almost...?' Anna could not finish her question knowing they had come so dangerously close to making love.

'Not at all,' Ned said, quickly allaying her fears. 'I'm asking you for much more selfish reasons.' He could not tell her he was going on another mission, so dangerous even he did not have the details. There was a chance he might not come back. All Ned knew was that this would be his last mission one way or another. If he was successful, he would be given a free pass to leave the Navy if he so wished, and if he wasn't successful, he did not want to die without being united with his one and only true love. His darling Anna who noted that familiar, wicked twinkle in his eyes, 'But you have to admit, my love, I have waited so very long.'

'We have both waited, Ned,' then she said, with an equally wicked twinkle, 'much too long.'

* * *

Arriving at the church in a Red Cross Rolls-Royce ambulance, Anna's fingertips fluttered at the circle of pearls at her throat, which Ned had given her, to compliment her creamy complexion, he had said.

Nervously, she entered the village chapel, to see Ned standing at the altar, his body half-turned towards her as she walked slowly up the aisle on the arm of a French farmer she had only just met.

Looking up into his handsome face, his eyes upon her, loving her, consuming her with his adoration, she felt every inch a loving bride, simply dressed – thanks to Ellie's help in securing the clothes from who knows where – in a straight-cut, dove-grey chemise dress belted under the bust, to enhance her neat curves. Anna's matching silk hat, she was told, brought out the true beauty of her eyes, sparkling as she and Ned became man and wife.

The ceremony, held in the small village chapel, was three miles west of the battlefield. The weather was glorious, the rain had stopped, it was beautiful. It seemed to Anna, there was no war. It was so peaceful. The sun shone, the birds sang, and lavender filled the air with its sweet fragrance, a gift to them all.

Under the circumstances, the ceremony was not long, but the bride and groom were thrilled when a war photographer took a single photograph, to commemorate their happy day. Anna was surprised when she left the chapel on Ned's arm, to see some of the remaining villagers form a guard of honour outside. Tilting her head up, she lovingly accepted Ned's kiss, her face beaming with happiness.

'The farmer's wife has put on a small celebratory buffet,' Ellie was all smiles, 'but we do not expect you to stay.'

'Ellie,' Anna cried, thrilled at her wedding day arrangements, 'I'm sure you've played a big hand in all this. But I can't understand how you've kept it all so quiet.'

'It was easy for me,' said Ellie. 'I only found out about it from matron half an hour before you did.'

'Matron was in on it?' Anna could not have been more shocked. 'How strange.'

'She said you have been through such a lot of late, you deserved to have your day.'

'We both had our share of heartbreak in this war,' Anna said as a shard of pain pierced her heart. She would have loved her darling brother to be here to see her married, or better still, to give her away, but it was not to be and Daisy...poor Daisy would have loved all this.

'But nobody has asked me to marry them, have they?' Ellie said, childishly rolling her bottom lip, raising Anna's spirits again, but still, something niggled. She tried to dismiss it as they raised a toast. However, she could not. Everybody had been so obliging... Even Matron...?

'Just make the most of today,' Ellie said, 'let tomorrow take care of itself.'

'I will,' Anna smiled brightly hugging her friend as Ned came over, putting his arm round her waist. Was his mission as benign, as he had led her to believe?

Five minutes later they were heading towards the small unscathed hotel, which Ned had found, before he came looking for her. Their time was so short and precious. It was not the time for doubts and questions.

34

'I don't want you to go.' Anna's voice held a note of desperation, as Ned inched closer.

'I will be back before you know it,' he whispered, stroking her arm, kissing her bare shoulder, Anna was glad that he could not see her fear. His body spooned into hers after consummating their love. With Ned's tender care, Anna enjoyed his powerful body with an abandonment she did not know she possessed. His skilful lovemaking ensured she did not suffer the cautious inhibitions of many new brides. 'What will we do when the war is over?' Ned nuzzled the words into her hair, and she writhed comfortably into him, dreaming of the future.

'Aunt Ruby is talking of permanently turning the house into a country hospital,' Anna said, stretching luxuriantly under Ned's tactile caress.

'A hospital for rich clients, I suppose.' He gave a low throaty laugh and Anna turned to face him.

'She wouldn't, would she?' Anna could think of nothing worse than having that beautiful house turned into some kind of institution where veterans went to waste away.

'Of course not,' he said, gazing into her eyes, watching her dark pupils swell with desire. 'Although, there will be many men who have seen the business end of trench mortar bombs, and gas attacks, who will need a place like Ashland Hall, with its clean air.'

Anna nodded, having seen first-hand the devastating effect of bombs and poisonous gas.

'They will still need skilled nurses,' Anna reminded him, and Ned hugged her even closer. 'Although as a married woman I might not be able to continue working.'

He smiled, loving the way she was so single-minded about things she believed in. He also loved the way she was so set on doing things right. That was why he was determined to marry her as soon as possible. Ned knew he might be dead this time tomorrow. 'I don't want to sleep,' he said in that husky drawl that made Anna's insides turn to jelly. 'I want you awake, loving me.'

She giggled when he turned her over, kissing her eyes, nibbling her ears, and nuzzling her throat, making her squeal with delight. She looked up into his love filled eyes.

'I feel rejuvenated already,' Ned laughed. 'I need as much loving as possible before I go.'

'What time are you leaving?' Anna gasped, silently berating herself for asking. She did not want to think of war or of Ned leaving. She wanted to pretend they were on honeymoon, free to do as they pleased. However, she did not want to start her married life living a lie.

'I won't be gone long, darling,' he said, wrapping his legs round her body.

'Don't put yourself in front of any shells, will you?' Anna was well aware of his maverick reputation.

Ned laughed softly, cupping her face in the palm of his hands. 'I'll try not to.' He placed a finger on her lips, to still any further words, and when he looked deeply into her eyes, he knew he had managed to allay her fears.

* * *

Anna was enjoying the nearness of him as they lay quietly spent, lulled by the gentle breeze coming through the window.

'Do you mind terribly being Mrs Ned Kincaid?' Ned asked, hardly recognisable to the boy he once was. His face serious now.

'Terribly!' Anna declared, visibly delighted, whilst gently mocking his seriousness. 'Terribly, terribly, awfully.' They were both laughing now, clinging to each other as if they would never let go.

'So that's a yes, then?' Ned laughed, while Anna assumed a solemn expression, but not for long, when he pulled her to him, gently nipping her shoulder, her throat, her breasts... Anna squealed with unbridled delight. This was the most perfect day of her life.

'I love you so much, Ned, it is almost unbearable.' Her voice was full of wonder as, with his head resting on the palm of his hand, he gazed down into her face. 'Somebody had to catch that unruly charm and I reckoned it should be me.' Anna had never been this happy in all her life. So blissful, she wanted to fling her arms wide and shout it from the veranda, just beyond the French windows.

Ned pinned her, laughing, to the bed. He could not resist her beauty and her courage, something he had enjoyed from a young age. 'I'll give you unruly,' he said.

'Oh. Yes please,' Anna purred, and the giggling squeal was impossible to hide when she wriggled from his grasp.

'You minx, come here.' Ned caught her, kissing her until she was helpless. Then, shuffling down the bed, the sheets tangled round their legs, Anna lay in the crook of his shoulder listening to his heartbeat, sleepy with delight and satisfaction.

'This is perfect,' she said lazily, 'but there is just one thing that might put the fly in the ointment.'

'What's that, my precious darling?' Ned asked, loosely curling her hair round his fingers.

'Someone has got to tell Aunt Ruby she missed the wedding. She'll be livid.'

'I'll let you deal with Ruby.' Ned laughed. 'I'd rather fight the Hun.'

As Anna draped her body across her new husband, she wished she could dissolve into his skin and be with him forever. His leaving did not bear thinking about. As she listened to the regular pattern of his breathing, she knew he had fallen asleep. Gently disentangling herself from his protective embrace, she slipped from the bed.

Gazing at him now, sleeping in the half-light, she could not think of a better time. He looked so handsome, so serene. Bittersweet tears rolled down her cheeks. She wanted to beg Ned not to go. If they had to die, she would rather they died together. She had already lost him once before. She could not bear the thought of living another single day without him. Ned turned, his hand subconsciously searching for her, and quickly Anna wiped away the indulgent tears with the pad of her hand.

She was being slightly hysterical, she knew. Of course he would not die. Ned was invincible. They had managed to survive Liverpool's dockside streets. This awful war was a doddle. All they had to do was duck the bombs and bullets. Besides, there were rumours that it would be over soon. She would not allow him to go feeling guilty for leaving her. Thousands of men left their cherished women, every day.

Anna tried to push the awful belief to the back of her mind, when a niggling voice warned her that many men would never return to their loving wives. Nevertheless, she had to bury the notion. She must not let Ned see her distress, which some women wore like a badge of honour. However, try as she might, she could not stem the silent tears.

'Don't cry, my darling.' Ned now awake slid from the bed. Draping the bed sheet round both of them, he stood behind her, wrapping his arms round her waist and brushing his warm lips across her bare silken shoulders. 'I'll be back quicker than you think.'

She sniffed, and turning to meet his gaze, Anna gave Ned a watery smile.

'I'm sorry, I didn't mean to wake you,' she turned, pressing her face against his muscular chest.

'Well, you shouldn't go howling at the moon,' he laughed, trying to lighten the mood. It worked.

'I'll have so much to keep me busy; I'll hardly notice you've gone.' Her heart ached just saying it. But Anna, now closely wrapped in Ned's arms, felt that nothing could part them. However, all too soon their perfect world was shattered when there was a knock on the door. They knew what it meant.

Anna held Ned tight, as if, in doing so, she could prevent him from going, or she could make time stand still. 'It's too soon' she whimpered. The promise she had made to herself, not to beg, went right out of the sash window.

'I can't breathe.' His voice was a teasing rasp, and Anna self-consciously let him go.

Nonetheless, Ned pulled her back. Kissing her repeatedly, and then he kissed her some more.

'The boat leaves in an hour,' called the hotelier, through the locked door.

'I'm ready,' Ned called back. Anna noticed there were tears in his eyes too. 'Grit,' he said, wiping them away with his thumb.

'I am going back to England and Ashland Hall with Sam soon.'

'Which ship?' Ned asked, hardly able to bear to take his eyes from Anna.

'I join the Gigantic when it's ready to sail later this month.'

'I'll keep an eye out for you.' Ned told her unhooking his uniform trousers from behind the door.

'Ships that pass...' Anna said unable to finish her sentence as her throat tightened.

Ned, taking her in his arms, kissed her so desperately, it stilled any further words. He did not tell his new wife he was serving in a Q ship, a Special Operations vessel, and a major warship, considered a high-value target. All too soon, it was time to go.

'When you come home again...' Anna whispered, locked in Ned's arms until he gently eased her from him, his gentle kisses, like butterfly wings, preventing further words.

'I have arranged a car to come and collect you,' he said, turning away quickly. A gruff clearing of his throat told Anna that he, too, was so full of emotion to say any more.

'Aye aye, Captain,' Anna whispered, tears now spilling down her cheeks unable to stem their flow.

'No, my darling,' Ned gave her a crooked smile. He was trying to keep the mood light, Anna knew, but it was impossible. 'I am merely a Royal Navy Chief.'

'You are perfect to me. No matter what they call you.' They gazed at one another for a long moment, drinking in the beauty and courage of each other. 'Please don't die.'

'This is not goodbye, sweetheart,' Ned reassured her. 'True love never dies; it makes the heart stronger.' He gave her one last lingering kiss, before her fingertips reluctantly broke from his.

She could hear his footsteps now as they quickly descended the stairs.

Ned was gone.

Anna closed the door and, emotionally spent, she rested her head on her uplifted arms. She remained like that for many minutes, unable to move. Not wanting to continue without him. Her hand automatically went to her lips. She could still feel the imprint of his lips, the musky, manly scent of his skin on hers. Anna closed her eyes, imagining he was still here, in this room, quietly sleeping...

The full beam of the sun on her face should have evoked happy thoughts. Paradoxically it brought on that awful feeling of dread, which poured into her body, heart and soul like molten lead. The black cloud descended so quickly, and now cloaked her in its intensity, bringing back painful memories of those dreadful trips through Olden Passage. The harbinger, Anna thought, of everything bad that had ever happened to her.

Still, this was not Olden Passage. Those days were long gone. Lifting her hand to move a stray curl from her face, damp now from her tears, the brilliant glint of her new wedding ring in the rays of a breaking morn caught her eye. With every beat of her heart, she prayed he would be safe.

35

MARCH 1918

Tenderly, Anna picked up her brother's hand, checking the nailbed, her trained eyes examining the cuticles around his fingernails for any discolouration, which would tell her his body was starved of oxygen and he was dying. However, to her utter joy, they were a healthy pink.

'He is recovering better than we expected,' Sister said brightly. 'He will be transferred to the hospital ship *Gigantic* this afternoon, and you will escort him.' Then she turned to Ellie and said with more than a hint of eloquence, 'Lady Eleanor will also accompany you.'

* * *

As she gathered the things, she would need for the journey, Anna placed Ned's letters in her suitcase. There had been no word since he left, but she did not expect any. This was a war zone, and it was highly unlikely there would be any mail drops. All the ships and aircraft were busy elsewhere. She knew that. Maybe when things calmed down a bit, she hoped, the powers-that-be would get the letters through to them.

* * *

During the weeks at sea, Sam had been making steady progress and the doctors were hopeful he would make a full recovery.

'He is going to need all the strength he can muster,' Ellie said, 'and there is something I have to tell you.' She continued, 'He is being well cared for by a very attentive nurse.'

'That's interesting,' Anna said, Tell me more.'

'She is Canadian,' Ellie explained. 'And she knows Sam very well. Her name is Millie.'

'Millie?' Anna asked, 'I remember Daisy telling me that Sam is very fond of a girl called Millie. She is a Canadian nurse.' Anna's brows pleated. Surely, she could not be the same Millie?

'By the way she is tending to his every need, I would say she might be the one.'

'Really?' Anna was relieved and perplexed at the same time. Obviously, she was glad that her brother was being so well looked after, but what if this nurse was Millie – his sweetheart? And what if he decided to go back to Canada to be with her?'

* * *

Anna liked the Canadian girl who had left her homeland to serve on the hospital ship. The daughter of a Canadian doctor, Millie told Anna, in their quiet moments, when neither of them could sleep, how Sam had come to be their *house guest*. Not the Home Child he had set out to be. She told Anna the tale of how he came to live with her doctor father and her family. Then, shyly, she told Anna that it was because of Sam, she decided to join the war.

'My dad knows some powerful people,' she said with a half-laugh. 'I was astounded when they let me come on board, after being told Sam had been transferred on here.'

'Thank you for taking care of him,' Anna said with tears in her eyes. 'If it wasn't for your family, I dread to think what might have happened to him.'

'He's a fighter,' Millie's voice, laced with pride, was full of love for Sam, Anna could tell. 'You must eat', she urged, nodding towards the plate of food next to Anna.

'You're right,' Anna said, knowing she was no good to Sam if she, too, became ill. She lifted the dome and grimaced: mashed potatoes, braised liver, watery cabbage, and soggy carrots, all covered in thick lumpy gravy. Her stomach lurched higher than the stormy waves. 'I can't,' she said, retching, 'maybe tomorrow.'

'How about a piece of dry toast,' Millie smiled, 'or an arrowroot biscuit?' They both looked at each other.

No. Surely not? Realisation dawned. Not so soon?

'I can't be pregnant!' Anna exclaimed, spreading her hands across her abdomen.

'You are a nurse,' Millie smiled, 'you, above all people, should know about these things.'

'Perhaps a small sandwich,' Anna said, stunned.

36

Back in Ashland Hall, Nipper was considered well enough to be sent home to be cared for by his mother, who brought Lottie with her to fetch him. He had trained himself to write with his left hand and gave Ruby a letter for Anna.

'For when she comes home,' he said, 'she looked after me real good before she went to Flanders, and I never did tell her properly how sorry I am for the hurt caused all those years ago.'

'You look after yourself, Nipper,' said Ruby, 'and when you are feeling up to it, there will always be a place for you here if you need a bit of work.'

'Much obliged, Miss Ruby,' said Nipper, eager to get back to normality. Whatever that was.

'Anna will know you had nothing to do with what happened to her family.' Ruby said, knowing Nipper would not have stood a chance trying to persuade his older brother to do some good. Jerky Woods only thought about himself.

'You haven't seen the last of me, Archie,' Nipper told him and Archie was glad the young man had something to look forward to.

* * *

Lottie Woods does live here, yes?' Archie said, he liked to call into the shops and have a chinwag with Lottie and Izzie over a cup of tea and he wanted to see how Nipper was faring now he was home. The two women would be up in the flat for their midday meal any minute and Nipper had the cups prepared. He looked at the young woman, from the General Post Office knowing her arrival at the door was usually cause for alarm.

`I'll get her for you.'

`Why'd I be gettin' a telegram?' Lottie's eyebrows knitted together. She had not seen Jerry since that night when her baby died. A few of her cousins were at the Front, but surely, any word about them would go to their Pa. She wiped her hands nervously, heading to the door and prayed the news was not bad.

'Telegrams never bring good news do they, Archie?' Lottie said, looking defeated.

`I'll stay with you, Lass.' Archie's voice did not betray the uneasiness he felt for the young woman, whom he had known since she was a nipper.

Lottie took the envelope; her hands were shaking as she opened it. `Jerry's dead.' Lottie said, her voice laden with shock. 'He was buried at sea.'

`Hey, Lass, I'm so sorry for you, I'll go and fetch Izzy,' Archie said quietly.

Izzy and Lottie had known that Jerky had secured a job as an orderly on board a Royal Navy ship. Failing to dodge war work, the police convinced him it either was a life at sea or prison.

Lottie pushed the telegram into Izzy's hand, then hurried to the scullery. They'll all be glad, she thought, sitting at the well-scrubbed table picking up a potato peeler. *Keep going*. 'Our separation don't alter the fact he was my husband, I s'pose.' She had loved him once, and she was sad that he was dead. Although not as sad as she might have been, if he had not put her through so much heartache, she suspected.

* * *

'Lottie's better off without him,' Ellie said when she read Aunt Ruby's letter telling how Lottie was coping.

'He was still her husband. But you're right, he was a bad lot.' Anna's voice drifted as if talking to herself. She had received news the week before that Ned was missing. However, she refused to believe he was dead. Not her Ned, he was too canny to die.

'I wish I could take away your pain,' Ellie said, holding her friend.

'Aunt Ruby has offered Ned and me a cottage on the estate,' Anna said with feigned cheer. 'Ned loves the outdoor life, and he will work with Archie at Ashland Hall when the war is finally over.' She refused to talk about him in the past tense.

'I'm sorry you are going through all this.' said Millie, taking a rare break from tending Sam. 'It must be awful for you with your brother injured and your husband missing.' Her voice lowered as if she were talking to a child. 'But, Anna, there is something you must hold on to...' her voice trailed.

A heave of nausea spurred Anna to jump from her bed. Throwing her head over a white basin on the dresser, she retched until her ribs ached.

'You have to face facts. Ned has left you a legacy.' Millie and Ellie smiled to each other as Anna's face lost all its colour.

'I will have to tell Matron,' Anna said. 'I wanted to wait, until I was sure.'

'It only takes a heartbeat for new life to form, you should know that.'

* * *

'We get back to Liverpool soon,' Anna sighed wearily, telling Ellie, 'I'm being sent home on medical grounds.'

'If you're not careful, you will be in danger of keeling over before then.' Ellie's concern made her overprotective and annoyed Anna. She was miserable. Everything she ate ended up over the side of the ship. She needed to keep busy. Sam was on the mend and being fussed over by Millie. She felt redundant.

Anna lifted her head but said nothing as another sea swell threatened to upend her stomach. Being at sea was not the best place to be when she was suffering like this.

'Oh Anna, it sounds harsh, I know, but you really have to pull yourself together for the sake of the child if nothing else.'

Without warning, Anna was on her feet, her eyes full of rage and indignation.

'How dare you tell me how to behave, Ellie. My husband, the man I loved with every fibre of my being, is missing, believed dead. I will never be able to replace him.'

'And I lost two good friends, Daisy and Rupert,' Ellie's words were steel tipped, as if she was doing her best to keep her temper in check. 'Don't you think it counts for something that you have hope. You will have something to show for your love.' She got up, covered the deckchair and quietly walked away.

Suddenly contrite, Anna slumped. She had been so wrapped up in her own misery, she did not worry about what Ellie had gone through and she felt thoroughly ashamed of her outburst. She had never spoken to anybody like that before, let alone her best friend. It was not in her nature to be cruel. Ellie was like a sister, whom she loved dearly.

'Oh Ellie,' Anna cried as she followed her to the galley. 'I'm really sorry, forgive me?' Anna could see by Ellie's red-rimmed eyes she had made her cry and she threw her arms round her best friend's shoulders.

'Don't be daft.' Ellie sniffed 'It's the strain of this awful, bloody war; ignore me.' She also gave Anna a much-needed hug. 'There. All better. Forgotten.'

When, finally, Anna blew her nose and took a deep breath, she realised she had to take Ellie's advice and pull herself together. She could not possibly make everybody else as miserable as she was.

'If you fancy a cry, you have one,' Ellie said, 'but don't cry over the patients, it gives the wrong impression. And it wets their bandages.'

They both giggled and sniffed into their hankies. Before long they were almost hysterical with laughter, and no matter how hard Anna tried, she could not stop.

'Come on, Nurse, let us all in on the joke,' called an injured serviceman, looking over the top of his paper from his bunk, as they took hot cocoa down the ward.

Anna and Ellie sobered slightly.

'Now you can begin to heal,' Ellie said with a smile.

'I imagine the process is going to be a bit slow,' said Anna. A whole lifetime maybe. Straightening, she smoothed down her apron.

'That's the ticket,' Ellie said. 'Now go and swill your face, you look far too shiny. Oh, and Matron wants to see you.'

* * *

'We dock at Liverpool tomorrow. Do you have any plans?' Matron said, while Anna stood in front of her desk. Her hands fluttering to the stiff collar and cuffs, nervously smoothing her pristine apron.

'I will go home and see my family, Matron.' Anna said knowing she could not serve any longer. Being a married woman and especially now she was expecting.

'Very good, Sister. I am so sorry to lose you, but your discharge papers are ready.'

Then, to her surprise, Matron came round the desk, her face wreathed in smiles. She took something from a box. It was a medal, Anna realised.

'With recognition from the war office for the sterling work you have done in the service of your country,' Matron said as she pinned it to her apron.

Anna's eyes filled with tears again. This was all too much to bear.

'I didn't do anything, really.'

'You have given more than you could ever know, Sister Kincaid, and we are all enormously proud of you.' Matron called her by Ned's name, and it sounded right. Anna wondered, would she ever be able to share this honour with him? 'There is something else,' Matron went to the other side of her desk and took out another box from her desk drawer, handing it to Anna to open.

'It is certainly a day for surprises,' Anna said, opening the box. And her heart jumped. when she drew out a beautiful silver filigree picture frame containing the only photograph of herself and Ned on their wedding day. She had forgotten they had even had it taken. 'Oh Matron, it is perfect.' In the photograph she was looking up at Ned and he had such adoration in his eyes. The love shone from both of them, his arms wrapping round her. So obviously in love. Anna could hardly see it for the blinding tears and Matron offered her a clean handkerchief. 'Even the medal can't beat this,' Anna said with such heartfelt gratitude. This was the best present she had ever been given. 'Thank you so very, very much,' Anna's watery smile could not dim the light in her eyes. 'I couldn't wish for anything better. I will treasure it always.'

Dazed, but happy, Anna decided she would not send a wire to Aunt Ruby, letting her know she was arriving home. She would only fuss and bring half of Ashland Hall with her.

* * *

'Anna are you busy?' Sam was sitting in a wheelchair getting some much longed-for fresh air when Anna left Matron's office. He looked to his older sister who had spent long hours by his bed filling him in on all those years he had been away.

'Never too busy for you, Sam,' Anna beamed, proud of her younger brother who had bravely fought for weeks to regain his strength. When he left Liverpool, he was a fresh-faced boy, now he was a grown man with a full beard and moustache. 'Is something the matter?'

'Not at all, just the opposite in fact,' Sam answered, his smile showing perfect straight white teeth, a sign he had been well cared for in Canada. 'I wanted to tell you first.' He wheeled the chair forward, and put his hand on her arm, something he never would have done years ago. 'I'm on the mend thanks to the expert care I've received on board,' he said lightly, 'and Matron said I could have a job at The First Western if I want it.'

'What about Millie?' Anna asked, knowing the Canadian nurse was besotted with her brother.

'That's the other thing I wanted to talk to you about.' He lowered his eyes to the floor and Anna had an inkling of what he was about to say. If Millie's love for him was so obvious, it cut both ways, because the young nurse could not walk along the corridor without his eyes following her every move. She doubted Sam was going to let Millie go back to Canada alone.

'You want to marry Millie?' Anna said, and Sam gave her that bashful grin she remembered so well. She flung her arms round her brother, and she gave a small squeal of delight.

'Well,' said Sam, 'I have to ask her first, but I'm sure she will say yes.'

'Big head,' Anna teased, knowing any girl would be lucky to get her handsome brother. Then she was quiet for a moment. 'But you must be sure, you must be...'

'Strong enough to offer a girl a good future?' Sam asked, then he nodded. 'Believe me, I am strong enough for both of us.'

'I do believe you are, my boy,' Anna laughed. When she found him drowning in the mud-filled shell-hole at Passchendaele, she would not have bet on his chances of surviving the night. But he was growing stronger by the day with the loving care of a Canadian nurse.

'There is just one other thing,' Sam said, his voice hesitant. He was on the mend, but he would need months of recuperation. Somewhere that was clean and wholesome, not full of smoke and smog.

'I was just thinking,' Anna interrupted, 'I would love to see the place where you grew up, do you think you and Millie would invite me over to Canada one day?'

'You mean...' Sam's eyes were wide with surprise, 'you wouldn't mind if I lived in Canada?'

'Of course, I'll mind.' Anna smiled; she would be sorry to see her brother go again. But this time it was his choice, and they would be in regular contact. He had already told her he wanted to become a doctor, and with Millie's father's help he would do that. If he stayed in Liverpool what chance would he have? He would end up working on the docks. 'However, I would mind it even more if you did not follow your heart – and there is always that invitation I was unashamedly hinting at.'

'Anna, you truly are an angel.' Sam could not be happier.

* * *

'I've snapped the button off this skirt and we dock soon.' Anna cried, distressed that her button had come off at the worst possible moment. Anna was trying to keep her feelings of excitement in check. She hated 'goodbyes' and wished she could have left the ship during the night when everybody was asleep.

'Here, try this one,' said Ellie, holding out a slightly larger, ankle-length khaki skirt.

'I can't wear your skirt!'

'It's either that or sew the button back on.'

'There isn't time,' Anna said. We have to get the stretchers and the wheelchairs ready to disembark.'

'Well,' Anna continued, taking her dove grey dress from her locker, 'they say that exchange is no robbery, so you can have this, I know you've always liked it.'

'But, Anna, it's your wedding dress,' Ellie was already holding it up to her slim frame and admiring her image in the long mirror.

'I've got my picture and I have grown a little thicker round the waist. You have it.'

'Thank you very much,' said Ellie. 'It goes lovely with that beautiful pink silk scarf.'

'And you can have the scarf, too,' Anna laughed, knowing their banter delayed the time when the ship's company would say goodbye.

* * *

'It's a grand sight,' Anna whispered as the ship sailed past Formby Point and along The River Mersey heading towards Princes Dock. Her eyes wide with unshed tears when she saw The Liver birds coming into view, and her heart swelled. Since its completion and crowned by a pair of clock towers mariners could tell the time as their ships passed along the river. Legend had it that while one giant Liver bird looked out over the city to protect its people, the other bird looked out to sea watching the sailors coming safely into port.

Now that the time had come, Anna felt nervous. She did not want to leave the ship. The questions. The explanations. She had it all to come from Aunt Ruby. 'I should escort Sam,' Anna felt guilty she had not been with him when he left England.

'You have brought him back home, now you must rest,' Ellie said. 'Anyway, once he's had a thorough check-up at The First Western, he will be coming back to Ashland Hall to recuperate.'

'Then he will be off to Canada for a new life with his beloved Millie.' Anna smiled, and Ellie gave her a reassuring hug. She would be due some leave soon and would join Anna at Ashland Hall. Life would never be quite the same again, for any of them.

Later Anna was trying her best not to get tears all over her brother's shoulder, but it was hopeless. She was not particularly good at saying goodbye.

'We'll be home before you know it.' Sam said as Millie guided the wheelchair down the gangplank and into the waiting ambulance heading for The First Western, the Canadian hospital at Fazakerley.

'You'd better be,' said Anna before turning to leave.

'And don't do anything daft, like going straight back to work when you get back to Ashland Hall,' Ellie told Anna. 'You've got other things to think about now.' She looked pointedly at Anna's abdomen and they both gave a false laugh.

And No matter how much she told herself she would not look back; she could not resist.

* * *

Her heart in pieces, Anna disembarked from *Gigantic* as a vicious wind whipped up the River Mersey and took her breath away. Shivering, her khaki jacket gave little protection, as she touched terra-firma at Princes Dock. The jetty was crammed with jostling crowds, eager to catch sight of the great liner, bringing England's heroes home. Decked out in the neutral colours of mercy, white against the silver-grey sky, the red cross of Geneva was proudly vivid in the middle of her hull. But as the *Gigantic's* tumultuous arrival signalled the end to her own hostilities Anna struggled to push the terrible images of war from her mind. She wiped away a tear, before turning to walk away.

Edging past the slow disembarkation of stretcher cases, hampered by huge crowds desperately waiting for the sight of injured loved ones, her tired eyes caught sight of a boy no older than Sam had been when he was taken from her.

'Carry yer bag to the taxi rank, Miss?' Anna recognised the keenness of a young lad, whose cap was far too big for his head but almost hid the lean look of hunger, and she decided not to take the overhead railway today.

'I'll take a hansom.' She handed him her valise that contained her one precious photograph. Nodding to his naked feet, slapping the cobbled sets, Anna said: 'It can't be easy lugging cases in your bare smacks,' using the local vernacular, 'haven't you got boots?'

'Family ter feed, Miss,' he panted whilst keeping up with her brisk strides. 'Boots don't come cheap, empty bellies and plates need filling.'

Anna suspected she had embarrassed the boy. This little chap had seen many a clean plate, and she had known men, not much older, who would not see another. She was glad of the life in him.

Anna slipped a florin into his grubby hand, watching his eyes light up. He knocked back his cap.

'Strike me,' he said, flicking the precious coin into the cold November air. 'It's not every day you meet a real angel.' Then solemnly he lowered his voice and whispered: 'This is much 'preciated, Miss...' He hesitated before continuing. 'My ould fella caught the business end of a toffee-apple at the Somme... I'm the bread-winner now.'

'Good on yer, lad,' Anna said proudly, watching him swipe his dripping nose with the cuff of a threadbare sleeve. Sadly, she had seen the devastation trench mortar bombs caused a body.

Managing a sympathetic smile, knowing a proud little fellow like him would not welcome her pity, she did not ask any more questions.

He tugged the peak of the cap that had probably belonged to his father, before disappearing into the crowd, to earn another bob. His eagerness to fend for his family brought back memories, long-buried recollections of her brother and her beloved husband, stories that she would pass on to her own child one day.

Her hands rested on her lap as the carriage pulled away, and Anna got herself into a comfortable position for the journey ahead, whilst the rhythmic sway lulled her.

Looking out of the small window, gazing up to the stone-coloured sky, where a light mist mingled with the smoke from many chimneys, Anna took in familiar landscapes. To the right, the back-to-back soot-covered terraced homes, with alehouses on every street corner, ribbed the backbone of the dock road. To her left, the docks: Canada, Brocklebank, Langton, Alexandra... The bleak, colossal warehouses and timber yards; forbidden playgrounds of her brothers... Her poor brothers... Maybe it was a blessing they did not grow to see the carnage she and Sam had witnessed.

Anna shivered, as the freezing smoke-filled air, heavy with the tang of lumber from distant lands enveloped her. And her thoughts drifted to another time... Another place. Thinking of the little chap, she wondered where life would take him, knowing there were heroes at home, too...

'Germany is crushed,' Sam said, having stayed on to help at the First Western hospital until the cessation of hostilities, and a hearty cheer went up in the long ward where three rows of iron beds held recovering servicemen. 'Rumour has it, morale is so low their soldiers are giving themselves up.'

'Has it been worth it?' A groggy voice came out of a completely bandaged head.

'It's not my place to say, soldier,' Sam answered. All he and his colleagues could do was patch the heroes up and hope for the best. Not that any of them saw themselves as heroes, himself included.

'It was such a pointless war,' said the man with the bandaged head and Sam nodded. He supposed it was to some people. Yet, to his way of thinking, that view was a slur on the memory of the brave men – and women – who had fought and died in the name of victory. Like hundreds of thousands, he had not come out of the war unscathed either.

In the quiet hours, doing his rounds, Sam tried not to dwell on the young girl in a jaunty tam-o'-shanter hat, wearing a coat that was too big for her slight frame. A girl who sang like a nightingale and had the world at her feet. Daisy Flynn might not have had much, but she had a heart as big as Canada. A heart that was crushed. His throat tightened, and he gave a small, throat-clearing cough.

'Not long now,' he said, 'we'll have you all back at Ashland Hall this afternoon.'

* * *

'Anna, are you ready?' Ruby asked, holding the telegram.

'Of course, I am,' Anna said even though the twinges she felt in her stomach were driving her mad. She would not miss this particular homecoming. Even if it meant she was to give birth at the station, she would be there. It had been her dream for so long, she could hardly bear it.

'We'll miss the arrival,' Ruby cried.

'Oh, don't fuss, Aunt Ruby,' Anna said as a twinge of pain shot through her side.

Doctor Bea who had recently arrived back to Ashland Hall advised Anna to lie down and take things easy and Anna had told the over-protective doctor that she, too, had dealt with lion-hearted casualties abroad under the hailstorm of bombs and bullets and a few twinges were not going to slow her down.

Anna knew Doctor Bea was not an easy woman to ignore, but between her and Aunt Ruby it was hard to know which one was the most formidable. But she was in no mood for those pair of dreadnoughts who were battling for supremacy. Anna wanted to be there when Sam arrived at Ashland Hall and nothing was going to stop her.

* * *

All the people in the village turned out to welcome English and Canadian soldiers, to show their appreciation and respect for the sacrifice they had made. The troops arrived in ambulances and were greeted with loud cheers from children at the local school who waved Union Jack flags. The Boys' Brigade banged their drums and blew their bugles. The Deputy-Mayor, in a short but passionate speech, said how glad they were to see the heroic champions.

He thanked them most sincerely for their services and wished them a speedy recovery, only for a wag in a wheelchair to call out: 'I hope it's not too speedy, I quite fancy a little holiday by the seaside.' The quip caused no end of happy cheers. All in all, everyone agreed it was a lovely welcome.

'She looks a bit flushed, Bea.' Ruby said, worried. 'Do you think it's all been too much for her?'

'What can you expect? Coming home from the battlefields after seeing things that no young lady should and having to do things that girls her age would never imagine before the war.'

'I think Anna may need to sit down,' May said when she saw the next fleet of ambulances arrive and the crowd dispersed to let them though.

Anna whipped her head round to see what everybody was looking at and her eyebrows shot to her hairline, craning her neck to get a better view when suddenly she slapped her hand to her mouth to stop herself from crying out.

It was impossible to say who saw whom first. But lightning couldn't move faster when Anna caught sight of Ned. And her shriek of delight and disbelief was momentarily mistaken as one of pain when Anna headed towards the ambulance Ned had just got out of.

'He is home!' Anna cried. 'He is alive!' Anna did not care that she shouted her news, vaguely aware everybody was looking at them both. In seconds she was in his arms and Ned rained so many kisses, she was breathless.

'You're alive.' They repeated the words over and over to each other. Ned folded her in his arms, and he was crying, and he was laughing, and he was talking nonstop. She looked up into his handsome face, afraid to blink in case he disappeared. This was all so much to take in.

Sam and Millie brought stretchers from the ambulance, and handed them over to orderlies, and Millie who was softly spoken was caught up in the euphoria to let everybody know she would take care of her husband-to-be.

And Anna who could not have been happier, called to Sam. 'Sam, this is Ned, my husband. He's come back to me.'

Sam rushed over and shook his hand. 'Ned, it is so wonderful to see you home. We've all been so worried.' Turning towards Millie he continued: 'And this is Millie, my fiancée. We'll be getting married soon and you and Anna you must come over to Canada for the wedding.' Sam looked so happy he might burst, and Anna knew she had not lost him this time, because from now on she would know exactly where he was, and although the miles may separate them, they would never be truly apart again.

'We won't be going anywhere for a long time.' Ned laughed, holding Anna at arm's-length, and taking in the miraculous, impending birth of his first-born child. Then he was quiet for a moment, holding on to her as they watched the throng disperse, afraid to let her go. 'Let's not go back yet,' said Ned, hardly able to take his eyes off his beautiful wife. 'Let's go for a little walk, we need time together, with no interruptions or distractions.'

Anna followed him gladly. She was never going to let him out of her sight ever again.

As they walked along the shore, the water lapping at the sand, she took his hand and placed it on the gentle mound of her stomach. 'Can you feel him kicking. He knows his daddy's home.'

'How did this happen?' Ned laughed, thrilled beyond reason and Anna's cares were nothing but a distant memory now. She had everything she ever wanted right here.

'Well, if you don't know, my love, I don't know who does.' They clung to each other.

'I may need some practice.' Ned laughed into her hair, pouring loving words, which echoed in her heart. They were laughing and crying and best of all they were free, with a new life ahead of them. Ned felt a huge kick. 'He's saying hello,' he laughed, knowing their worst fears were a distant memory. 'I can't believe it.' Ned nuzzled her hair. 'I am the luckiest man in the whole world.'

When Ned drew her into his arms. She clung desperately to him.

'I've ached for this moment,' Ned whispered in her hair.

'Me too, my love, but we have to go now.'

As they reached the house, they heard a commotion coming from inside. A huge cheer went up and Archie hurried out.

'The welcoming committee?' Anna asked, breathless now as another pain gripped her.

'Ruby and May have put on a lovely homecoming spread, but I can't see anybody eating,' Archie said, barely taking his eyes from Anna who gasped, her eyes wide as she hugged her abdomen.

'I think this little one wants to join in the celebrations,' Anna gasped and was helped into a wheelchair by Ned who hurried her up the pathway towards Ashland Hall.

'Can we have some help, here, please.'

* * *

Ned and Archie were prowling the kitchen, while VADs boiled plenty of water, and scolded the two men for getting in the way. The air buzzed with excitement and even the patients, fresh from Flanders Fields, waited for news from Doctor Bea. Ruby and May had stayed upstairs, behind closed doors. And it seemed like a lifetime before Ruby came out of the room, which had once been Anna's bedroom, her sleeves rolled up to the elbow and her face beaming.

'Forget the armistice!' she called over the bannister. 'Anna has brought a perfect, seven-pound six-ounce baby into this now-peaceful world.'

Ned took the stairs two at a time. Nothing was going to stop him seeing his son.

'*She* wanted to greet her daddy,' Anna gave a tired but happy smile when she saw the look of pride and wonder on Ned's face as he took his newborn baby daughter from her hands and gave Anna a loving lingering kiss.

'Let's leave them to it,' Doctor Bea whispered, and Ruby reluctantly agreed. There was plenty of time now. Ned and Anna didn't even hear them leave the room. Their joy was complete as they gazed into the adorable navy-blue eyes of their daughter.

'We are free, my darling.' Ned kissed Anna and her eyes glistened with happy tears watching her Ned tenderly cradle his precious daughter. 'And we have a new life to cherish.'

'What shall we call her?' Anna's eyes were already half-closed.

'Let's call her, Hope,' Ned whispered, watching Anna's beautiful eyes slowly close.

'Perfect,' Anna murmured through smiling lips, 'and her middle name is Daisy.'

ACKNOWLEDGMENTS

Thank you so much to the wonderful Boldwood team of editors: Caroline, Jade, and Sue who pull it all together.

MORE FROM SHEILA RILEY

We hope you enjoyed reading *The Mersey Angels*. If you did, please leave a review.

If you'd like to gift a copy, this book is also available as an ebook, digital audio download and audiobook CD.

Sign up to Sheila Riley's mailing list for news, competitions and updates on future books.

http://bit.ly/SheilaRileyNewsletter

Why not explore the *Reckoner's Row* series, another bestselling series from Sheila Riley!

 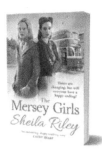

ABOUT THE AUTHOR

Sheila Riley wrote four #1 bestselling novels under the pseudonym Annie Groves and is now writing a saga trilogy under her own name. She has set it around the River Mersey and its docklands near to where she spent her early years. She still lives in Liverpool.

Visit Sheila's website: http://my-writing-ladder.blogspot.com/

Follow Sheila on social media:

facebook.com/SheilaRileyAuthor

twitter.com/1sheilariley

instagram.com/sheilarileynovelist

bookbub.com/authors/sheila-riley

ABOUT BOLDWOOD BOOKS

Boldwood Books is a fiction publishing company seeking out the best stories from around the world.

Find out more at www.boldwoodbooks.com

Sign up to the Book and Tonic newsletter for news, offers and competitions from Boldwood Books!

http://www.bit.ly/bookandtonic

We'd love to hear from you, follow us on social media:

[f] facebook.com/BookandTonic

[t] twitter.com/BoldwoodBooks

[i] instagram.com/BookandTonic

Made in United States
Orlando, FL
28 February 2023

30539980R00173